BREATHE

By Tania Trozzo

Ellen,
I hope you enjoy
Gabe + Clara's
Story!

ISBN 978-1-54398-815-4 (print)
ISBN 978-1-54398-816-1 (eBook)

Dedicated to you, Papa',
for your unwavering faith in me.
I didn't always know what I was doing,
but you sure thought I did.
Thank you for that.

PROLOGUE

The phone rings. Groggy from sleep, Nina picks up the phone grumbling, "Hello?"

"Ms. Salvino?"

"Yes, this is she." She glanced at the time, worry in the pit of her stomach. Her hand gripped the phone tightly.

"Nina who is it?" her husband Frank asked, sitting up and turning on the light.

"Mrs. Salvino, this is Detective Constanza, Detective Blanchard told me to call you. I am so sorry to bother you at this hour but he wanted me to let you know as soon as we received news. The police department in Chicago just contacted us. They found her Mrs. Salvino, they found your niece and she's alive!"

Nina gasped and tears sprang to her eyes to actually hear those words. She wondered if she was dreaming.

"Ms. Salvino – are you still there? I can imagine you are in shock."

"Yes, yes I'm here..I just...oh my goodness...where is she? Is she ok? Is she hurt? Does she remember us?"

"Detective Blanchard is getting all the details, he didn't want to wait to tell you knowing you needed to make arrangements to get here..."

"Who is it?" Frank asked again.

"It's the police, Frank. They found her! They found Clara!"

With tears streaming down her face, she handed the phone to her husband while she sprang from bed waiting to hear the rest. "This is Mr. Salvino, my wife just told me they found Clara. Tell us where we need to be and everything you know."

Nina ran from the room to wake her oldest daughter while her husband got all the details. It had been a little over 2 years but she never gave up hope that they would find Clara. Someone up there had heard their prayers.

1

CLARA

The bell rang. Clara slammed her locker. *Deep breath. You can do this. Another deep breath.* Although Clara was nervous she also felt that this year would be different. She looked down at her schedule. She had studied the layout of this school but her nerves were getting the best of her today. She wanted this school, it was bigger than the other local high school. Some would see it as a way to get lost in the shuffle, but not for her. She figured it was her chance to decide where she fit in since there were so many students, so many different groups, and therefore, opportunities.

"Are you sure?" Her aunt had asked her the night before, more than once. "Josie and Stephanie go to Harriston, you would know someone."

"I'm sure." She wanted to start fresh, especially after leaving the catholic high school she began 2 years ago. She hadn't fit in there and although Harriston High would probably have been nice, especially since she knew some people there, she still pushed for East Cynwood surprising everyone. She wanted to make her own friends and find her own group. She wanted to decide where she wanted to fit in. Surprisingly, it seemed her uncle understood this need for her to make her own way.

Everyone knows Sal there, they would look out for you," Aunt Nina continued.

"I know. And I know you're worried. But I need to do this. Plus this school has an amazing soccer team, and newspaper, more so than Harriston. I may actually have a chance to make the team even though I am late. All of you are close by, it's not like I'm going away. I am still home every afternoon."

Her uncle spoke up. "Nina, leave her be, she isn't moving to a foreign country for God's sake. She'll be fine. But if you change your mind, Clara, at any time we will figure it out."

"Clara, you're lucky. If that were me, he would have said, suck it up Laura, you chose to go there, now you are going to finish there," her cousin Laura said.

Everyone at the dinner table laughed. Yes, he probably would say that to his oldest daughter. Clara looked down and as she glanced up, Uncle Frank was observing her. He whispered, "I'm proud of you" as he patted her hand.

She looked at her schedule again. First period was Math followed by Spanish. Then third period made her smile: English. She could have probably taken Honors English, but she had heard about this teacher. He was on the younger side, loved by most students. He was known to be tough and not take crap, but he pushed his students to think outside of the box and most of all he pushed for creativity. Many times, he got students to talk about things that they normally wouldn't with other teachers, but maybe that is why so many liked him. He was real and he was the teacher in charge of the school paper, so she knew this would be her best bet to make a good impression. So here she was. Looking down at her schedule, she tried to remember how to get to her math class, but as she turned the corner, she had nearly collided with another girl "OMG, I'm so sorry!"

"Don't worry about it! Lost, huh? It happened to me my first day here last year too. The school is huge. Where are you going?" It took Clara a few seconds to gather her bearings. She almost narrowed her eyes trying to decide if the girl was being sincere or not but stopped herself. *Calm down.*

"I have math, in room 119." Clara replied.

"Oh, follow me, I'm going that way anyway. I'm Rosanna, by the way, but most people call me Rosie. What's your name?"

"Clara, nice meeting you. Thanks for helping me out." *You can look people in the eye Clara, they won't bite.*

Rosie turned towards her and shrugged. "No worries. Nice to meet you too. We newbies got to help each other out, right? You'll get used to the school. It's pretty big but once you get the layout, you will be rocking these hallways in no time. Are you a junior?"

"Yes," she said almost whispering. *Why was she so nervous?* She cleared her throat. "Are you a junior too?"

"Yep, where did you transfer from?" Rosie asked.

"Mount Saint Peter's."

"That's the all girls school, right? Ugh, you said that with such dread in your voice, I take it you don't miss it too much," Rosie laughed.

Clara nodded and smiled. "Yeah, I guess you couldn't call it exciting."

"Well, I can guarantee this school is much more fun. First and foremost, we have guys and that already makes it better, right? But we have some cute ones to top that off. And tons of activities. To meet those guys at, of course!" Rosie smiled. They continued to chat as they walked. Clara had to admit, she seemed nice. With long black hair, brown eyes and long lashes, Rosie had a petite body with curves all in the right places and a gorgeous smile. But as usual Clara was always skeptical. Girls were not that nice at her old school but Clara promised herself she would give people a chance and she promised Sal that she would open up a bit more. And her therapist. And her aunt. Ok, so maybe she promised she would open up a bit more to a few too many people. In a way she did it so someone would actually hold her to it. She wanted to be more than she was, if that wording made any sense. She wanted to live but it was just so frightening at the same time. She took another deep breath.

As they walked to her next class, she continued speaking to Rosie and answered various questions while asking questions in return. Hell, she was super nervous but she felt bold, she felt strong and she hadn't felt this way in a long time. She definitely didn't talk this much at her old school. She also kept looking around as they walked, cognizant not only of the direction they were heading in but of various other things along the way. She also noticed some of the looks people gave her, but she wasn't surprised since she was new.

"Here we are, room 119. I have to rush to my class but what is your next class?"

"Um...Spanish with Mr. Aguirra? That's in the other building, right?"

"Yep, I have Spanish with him too. It's a sign, we were supposed to meet! I just realized I totally distracted you so you probably didn't realize where we walked. Sorry!"

"No worries, I'm usually pretty good at remembering my surroundings, typically you don't have to show me twice," Clara replied. That was something that she learned quick and something she would probably never lose. *Be aware of your surroundings. Pinpoint where you are, remember specific details that will help you find your way back. Always find your way back.*

"So, you're one of those, huh?"

"One of what?" Clara tensed.

"Gorgeous and smart! Great. Thank goodness I got on your good side."

Clara stiffened and then Rosie burst out laughing. "You should have seen your face. I was kidding! Well, not really. I just meant it in a nice way. You seem like you're the whole package." Clara rolled her eyes and smiled. *If she only knew.* But, this girl had spunk. She admired that. "Ok, well, see you later then."

Rosie replied, "Absolutely, see you right here. And Clara?"

"Yes?"

"Breathe. I know you're nervous, but you've got this."

Clara was shocked that Rosie had read her so easily. Maybe she was already being more open or maybe Rosie was just perceptive. For some reason, that comment reminded her of what one of her aunts always said "Clara, some believe angels live in heaven but I believe they live on earth. They are that every day person we meet that helps us or says something to us to remind us to continue along that particular path. It's that right person at that right time. The one that makes us smile or feel hope. You just have to be open to it and to them." Either way Clara was going to find out. She took a deep breath, squared her shoulders and walked into first class. She was going to be just fine. New school. New Year. New life.

2

GABE

"Dude, you missed a kickass party this weekend. Where were you? It was epic!"

"Hey Bobby, I was busy. I do other things you know, other than party. You should try it sometime. And besides, you say that about every party."

Alex laughed. "Yeah, you do."

Bobby chuckled, "Ok, maybe I do, but it was really a great party. You guys were missed."

"I am sure that there will be plenty more and I am sure we didn't miss anything spectacular," Gabe replied. "Let me guess, Joey was probably trashed since he slacked at practice this morning. Mave got together with Gracie again. If Leo was there, he hooked up with Claudia. Jamie and Sarah were being their usual bitchy selves etc."

Bobby grinned, "Yeah, pretty much but it was the last one before school so I guess it seemed different. Not to change the subject, but there are not only some cute freshmen, but some pretty cute upperclassmen roaming these halls this morning."

Alex replied "I have to admit, I saw a hottie this morning coming out of the office, she definitely was new and not a freshman. No way I would have missed that last year."

"Hi guys!"

"Hey, Rosie." Gabe replied as she was walking down the hall. He tilted his head, she wasn't walking with her usual friends.

"See you in math, Bobby!" Rosie smiled.

Who was that? Gabe thought.

"Gotta go guys, I'll see you later. I have history and then creative writing."

"Creative writing? Why are you taking that class?" Alex said.

"I like Mr. Brooks, he's cool. Challenging as he is, he's real and not like most of the douches here, that's why," Gabe replied.

"Hmmm...I guess. I still wouldn't be able to take that class. I hear he makes you share personal shit and write about experiences. You're not going to start getting all sentimental on me, are you?" Alex said.

Gabe laughed. "Whatever, I'll try not to get all mushy and sentimental around you, ok, cuz? See you later." Even though he did. Alex knew him better than anyone. Hell, he was more than his cousin, he was a brother especially since Alex spent most of his time as his house. Not that he could blame him with his mom and all. She was a very difficult woman focused solely on her friends and never around, failing to show support at any time for either Alex or his sister Sonia. They had grown up together and they were extremely tight. Everyone knew not to get between them. Sonia would soon join them. She was starting a week later than expected, transferring from boarding school thanks to his dad putting his two cents in and getting her out of there. This year would be interesting. He felt it. There was a buzz in the air and he was looking forward to it.

3
CLARA

Finally it was time for Creative writing. Spanish wasn't too bad. She sat next to Rosie who seemed really nice. Clara would have preferred to wait until after class to introduce herself formally, but she knew she had to approach the teacher with the sheet that the office gave her. She walked in and approached his desk. Mr. Brooks was standing there, dressed in light blue dress shirt with gray pants and vest to match. He wore a leather cuff on one hand which gave him a certain edge.

"Mr. Brooks?"

"Yes." He responded, not lifting his gaze.

Clara cleared her throat. "Hi, I'm Clara Salvino. I'm a new student and the office told me to give this to you since I probably would not be on your original roster."

"Welcome, Clara." Mr. Brooks looked up at that moment and looked straight at her. He tilted his head just a tad as if ready to question her but then he smiled. "Take a seat wherever you like, I'll make sure your name is added."

"Thank you."

"Wait. I believe Ms. Mancini spoke to me about you. You want to join the newspaper, right?" Mr. Brooks asked her.

"Yes." Oh boy. Ms. Mancini, the school counselor/psychologist probably told him about her. But how much did she tell? "Yep, that's me. I wanted to talk to you about that if possible. If I could have a few minutes of your time later?"

"Of course. Stop by on your way out and we can discuss," he said reassuringly.

"Ok, thanks Mr. Brooks," Clara replied. *Breathe.* Right at that moment, she glanced up and saw these startling blue eyes staring right at her. And it was at the moment that she felt the world stopped. *Breathe.*

4

GABE

Gabe walked into his English class. As he glanced up he noticed Kristin and Sarah. He groaned inwardly. He was definitely not sitting next to them, Kristin already couldn't take a hint. He had regretted paying her attention this summer and he was trying to let her down easy but she wasn't giving up. He chose a seat a few spots away and stretched. This morning seemed to be going by very slowly. This morning, he was glad school started, but at some point he became irritated. Everyone wanted something from him, in particular his time or his attention and he didn't give those two things freely. He couldn't wait for practice later. Out on that soccer field, he could leave it all behind. Gabe didn't mind the pressure from coach and the school to win, he thrived under that pressure and loved it.

Connor sat next to him on the right offering a buffer between Gabe and the girls. He nodded to Gabe and smirked. "What's up, man?"

"Nothing much, you? Ready for practice today?" Gabe asked.

"Yeah, coach is going to kill us but I'm ready for it," Conner said.

"Hi Gabe! How are you?" Kristin asked.

"Fine, thanks," Gabe answered.

"We missed you at the party during the weekend. It wasn't the same without you," Kristin pouted. *Here we go*, Gabe thought to himself.

"Yeah, where were you, Gabe?" Sarah asked.

Connor raised his eyebrows and turned around before Gabe could answer ready with a comeback. "Since when did any of us, especially Gabe, have to answer to you?"

"We didn't realize that we couldn't make conversation," Kristin replied as she continued to pout thinking it was cute.

"No need to be mean about it either. So defensive. Is Gabe hiding something?" Sarah chided.

"Drop it," Gabe said sternly looking straight at Kristin.

At that moment Mr. Brooks walked in. "Hello, everyone. Give me a minute to get everything together and do a roll call."

Gabe, Connor and everyone else looked straight ahead. Sarah was shooting daggers at the boys, while Kristin couldn't decide between glaring and looking hopeful. *Whatever, get over it.* Gabe opened his notebook and glanced at Connor who was facing the door. He raised his chin at Gabe telling him to take a look. Gabe turned his head and looked towards the door. This must be the new girl Alex and Bobby were talking about. Tall and thin yet with a hint of curves in the right places, and killer legs coming out of a short jean skirt. She had long straight brown hair and smooth skin. She spoke when she approached Mr. Brooks' desk but he wasn't really paying attention to what she was saying. As he tuned in to the conversation, Mr. Brooks was telling her to stop by at the end of the class to discuss the newspaper. She finally turned towards him and her gorgeous green eyes looked straight through him.

"Clara, I'm Connor and you can come sit right in front of me. I promise I won't bite," Connor teased. Gabe tensed instantly, glancing at Connor and clenched his fists. *Calm down. Wtf was wrong with him?*

Mr. Brooks sighed, "Clara, don't pay any attention to Connor. Go sit right next to Gabe over there, he's not as disruptive." Mr. Brooks looked at Gabe intently.

"What? Mr. Brooks, I was just trying to be a gentleman and welcome a new student to class," Connor remarked.

Mr. Brooks smiled and shook his head. "Connor, I am sure you welcome every girl whether they are new or not. But, if you really want to be a gentleman then you can welcome her after class." He continued, "Now, let's get started. Welcome to creative writing. I am going to cut to the chase right now and let you all know that if you think this is going to be an easy class, you can leave now."

Mr. Brooks went over his expectations for the year regarding his class. He began speaking of the first paper that he assigned to his students. It was probably the most difficult one, where everyone had to write about something that happened to them that changed them or their view of the world. As soon as he mentioned it, Gabe noticed out of the corner of his eye that Clara's face paled for a second.

Curious, Gabe looked over at Clara to his left. She was paying attention to what Mr. Brooks was saying and had briefly closed her eyes as if she was taking a deep breath. Then she must have felt Gabe staring at her, so she turned her head, and locked eyes with him. Those eyes seemed so guarded, perhaps a bit hesitant and there was something sad there too, but he also saw a fire in them, he saw strength. She looked straight through his walls. She didn't just look at him, she looked in him and to be honest, he wasn't sure how he felt about that. She looked back towards Mr. Brooks and so he decided to do the same.

Although the day had been dragging by slowly, this class, of course, passed by quickly. Before he knew it, the bell rang. As he was getting up, his body automatically turned toward Clara to introduce himself. He opened his mouth to say hello, when all of a sudden, he felt a hand smooth down his back, he whipped his head to the right and there stood Kristin trying to act all seductive. "Gabe, babe, what's your next class? I thought we could walk together. I missed you this past weekend."

Gabe hesitated for a fraction of a second. He didn't want to be rude and have Clara think he was an asshole but also didn't want Kristin to get her hopes up. She was not taking the hint.

Right at that moment, Mr. Brooks called for the green-eyed beauty to his left. "Clara, before your next class let's discuss the newspaper, shall we?"

"Of course," Clara replied.

Connor quickly glanced at Gabe and smirked. "Mr. Brooks, I thought I was supposed to be a gentleman after class, remember?"

Mr. Brooks shook his head "Connor, go to your next class ".

Gabe intentionally stepped away from Kristin, ignoring her and shook his head. He turned to look at Connor and made a motion with his head, "Come on Connor, let's go," and they both exited the classroom. Right before he exited he took one last look back at Clara who was now by Mr. Brooks desk. Mr. Brooks looked up and noticed him looking a Clara, he gave him a questionable look but quickly turned his full attention back to Clara.

Gabe headed out of class to his next one. He would look for her later, maybe at lunch. She was new, so he was curious, like half of the student body probably is. He didn't like the way she managed to look right into him. Just like he didn't like those legs of hers, or that long hair. Or her smooth skin. He had yet to see her smile but he was sure he wouldn't like that either. Nope. Not at all. In fact, during his next class he couldn't seem to get the image of those green eyes out of his head. He understood the hesitancy there. She was probably nervous, but something else was there behind her shield.

He looked for her as he walked the halls throughout the day but they didn't cross paths until lunch where he saw her briefly from afar. She was sitting with Rosie. He noticed how all the guys were checking her out, some even had the guts to stop at her table and so tactfully ask Rosie to introduce them to her. She however, seemed oblivious to all of it. Rosie's table wasn't far so he was able to pick up a few words here or there. He didn't want to be like the other guys and go over so he just observed. But halfway through lunch she got up and left. He thought he was really good at hiding the fact he was watching her until then, when he basically with his gaze, he followed her on her way out. Alex, who was sitting in front of him, tilted his head and followed his gaze and then looked at Gabe with a question mark. He didn't say anything, but he knew something was up.

5
CLARA
___

Her first day went by rather quickly. Before she knew it, she was home and had already gone to her karate class for the day. She was in her bedroom when a knock sounded on the door. Figuring it was one of her cousins, she yelled, "come in!" She turned, surprised to find 4 curious sets of eyes.

Looking at them quizzically she asked, "Why are you guys hovering in the doorway? And why do you guys seem nervous?" she looked straight at Julia with a quizzical look. They all walked in.

Vincent sat on her bed and kicked his feet up, Sal turned her desk chair around and sat down, Laura sat down next to Vincent and Julia just leaned against the wall. "We wanted to hear all about today, we've been waiting, but you went straight to karate instead. Was that to escape or just a normal class?" Vincent asked. Sal tilted his head and observed, probably trying to gauge her reaction and if she was hiding anything.

Laura on the other hand stated, "I have a feeling it went ok, am I right?"

Clara smiled slightly. Laura could read her moods easily enough and if not, she bulldozed through with her questions wanting to know the answer because although Laura often believed in openly sharing, Clara didn't always confide in her. Julia, on the other hand, was the youngest out of all of them, quiet but extremely wise for her age. She always seemed to know when Clara needed someone to just be there. Vincent, on the other hand, was sometimes nervous around her. He had once told her that the reason he acted like that was because he just always wanted to make sure she was ok and didn't know how to do that. The three of them, Vincent, Laura and Julia became her siblings the moment she returned home. She knew she could count on them, and they treated her like she was the 4th child in the family. Even though technically they were cousins, for all intents and purposes they were more like brothers and sisters.

Sal, on the other hand, was a cousin to all 4 of them. Clara couldn't pinpoint the exact moment, but somewhere along the way he became super supportive of her karate lessons, helping her practice, and wanting her to be confident so that she could protect herself. He observed her more, usually quietly, and didn't question her like Laura. In recent years, he and Clara became close, almost like another brother. He was also the one that introduced her to soccer and practically trained her.

"Yes, it went well. Actually, I also kind of made a friend. She seems ...nice."

"Give people a chance, Clara," Sal said. "I'm not saying not to be careful. But don't be so closed off."

"No lectures, guys, we wanted to make sure she was ok. I'm getting good vibes here. I am going to refrain from asking you a bunch of questions, even though it is practically killing me to do so, but 2 things are of mighty importance," Laura claimed.

"What would those things be?" Clara asked. "Wait let me guess, Aunt Nina is dying to know?"

Vincent responded, "Yes, that is one of them, the second is that we are starving and want to eat but we were waiting for you. Mom wanted us to wait since it was your first day and all, so before I faint from malnutrition, can we please go downstairs?"

Julia laughed, so did Sal.

"Of course, you didn't have to wait for me. But I am kind of surprised that you are not assaulting me with questions, Laura." Clara said putting emphasis on Laura's name.

"I thought I would be nice and wait a week. That, and I thought we'd wait where we didn't have an audience so I could ask you about the guys," Laura laughed.

"That, and Dad told her not to." Julia laughed.

Clara smiled but gave nothing away. *Don't think about those blue eyes she told herself.* "Ok, well give me two minutes to get changed and I will be right down."

"2 minutes, Clara. Or I am coming up to get you," Vincent told her.

They filed out of her room, but Sal waited behind. "You're sure that everything went ok? You can tell me the truth you know, I'll always have your back. We will always figure something out."

Tears welled in her eyes. Damn emotions. She looked at him, "I know you do. But it went ok today. I was super nervous and yes, maybe a bit closed off but not like I usually am. In the end I still spoke to someone, right? I also got a spot on the school paper, which is great. I need some time to settle in, but I think I will be ok."

"Ok, and try out for soccer. I can still try to put in a good word for you. I don't understand why you won't let me," Sal said.

"Because, I have to do it on my own, Sal. I know all of you mean well. But if it's meant to be that I will be on the team then I will. I'll figure it out and see if I can do it on my own. If they won't even give me a chance, then I promise I will come to you JUST to see if you can get me a tryout. Nothing more. But only then. Promise me you won't interfere. Please. I just need to do this." Clara said quietly, looking down at her hands.

Sal blew out a breath and tilted her chin up, "Ok. And I do think you'll be fine, I just wanted to make sure. I get it. We are all protective of you. But can you blame us?

"No, I can't." Clara responded.

"We are all proud of you, but it took you a long time to come out of your shell and you still aren't fully out of it. Sometimes like when you are doing karate, I see that confident girl that can light the world on fire, or there are moments when you play soccer that your face lights up like you feel free. But even with us, you still have your guard up, like you're afraid it's going to all be taken away. You're stronger than that Clara, stop doubting yourself. There are bad people out there, but there are some good ones too. I have a really strong feeling, that people at East Cynwood are going to be awed by you," Sal sighed. "I realize that a part of what I just said is really contradictory. One minute I'm worried, the next I'm trying to motivate you. We are all protective of you but that is because we see you hesitate, we see your doubt. But we also know what you are capable of. We want nothing more than to see you shine, ok?"

"Guys, gets your asses down here, I'm hungry!!!" Vincent yelled.

Sal rolled his eyes, "He acts like he hasn't eaten in 3 days. Get changed, and hurry, I'll meet you downstairs".

As he walked out and closed the door, Clara sat on her bed. *Deep breath. New School. New Year. New Life.* And as she said that an image of those blue gray eyes appeared in her mind.

6

CLARA

It had been a busy week, and it was already Friday. Clara was able to spend a lot of time with the team at the newspaper getting to know them. Mr. Brooks was a force of nature and helped Clara get settled in. He was extremely supportive, offering guidance when needed but allowing the team to be independent as well. Clara had a feeling that he knew more about her situation then he let on, but, what she liked about him was that if he did know about it, he didn't show it. The last thing Clara wanted was pity.

Clara had tried the entire week to speak to the soccer coach but it seemed impossible due to some changes. For years the girl's coach was Mr. Donovan but he was promoted recently to the boy's team and looking to replace his position. Every time she went to speak to him, he was busy or on the phone. Rosie's friends recommended speaking to the girl's assistant gym teacher Ms. Lawson. She was extremely nice and they were sure she would put in a good word. When she got to gym class on Friday she went in a few minutes early to speak to Ms. Lawson. She explained her situation, and why she wasn't present at tryouts. Just as Rosie and her friends predicted, Ms. Lawson was very compassionate and she quickly thought of a way to make it happen.

"Ok, then Clara, let's do this. Let's give them something to talk about, you ready?" Ms. Lawson said. "We'll play soccer today during class. Show me what you got. But, take note that there are a few girls in this class that are on the team. They may like the competition, and they may not. So, if you want to get noticed, give me all you've got. We're clear, yes?"

Clara nodded. "Yep, got it. I'll go get changed quickly. Thank you, Ms. Lawson."

"Don't thank me just yet," she responded and winked.

Clara quickly got changed. She hated locker rooms. She always felt out of place. It was also the perfect place to be taunted. She went out to the gym to wait for everyone else. Ms. Lawson arrived as almost everyone was there and she was discussing something quietly with Mrs. Chiaro, the gym teacher. Mrs. Chiaro raised her eyes and looked at Clara. She nodded briefly and Clara heard her say to make it happen.

"Ok, class, today I'm running the show. If everyone is changed and ready, we are going outside to play soccer. Let's get organized quickly as we all know how time flies. Hustle outside in line as usual and I will separate you in two teams," Ms. Lawson ordered.

The girls quickly went outside and lined up. Ms. Lawson quickly put everyone in two teams and after a very short lesson in which she explained the major rules of the game, they began to play. As they played she would guide them or stop the game briefly to explain why or why not they should do a certain play. As Clara played she quickly realized how unfair the teams were split. The other team had the captain of the girls' soccer team as well as 2 strong players. Clara quickly whipped her head to Ms. Lawson and narrowed her eyes. Right at that moment the other team scored. Clara felt as though she had been set up. Ms. Lawson was supposed to be nice and helpful. Clara asked for a time out and Ms. Lawson tilted her head and smiled, "of course, team, 2 minutes." Clara quickly took charge and called her team over.

"Ok, I know this is gym class and so most of you probably don't care about winning or making a goal but I do. You aren't even trying," Clara told them.

One of the girls responded, "I'm on the soccer team, we are up against 3 of the strongest girls from the soccer team. We don't stand a chance. I don't even know why they split us up this way. It's totally unfair."

"Agreed," Clara answered. "What position do you play?"

"I play defense, and I'm Moira, by the way," the girl replied.

"Perfect, Moira! I'm Clara. I usually play forward or striker. You're right, they are probably showing off and underestimating us. They know all of you, but they don't know you may have a secret weapon."

"Secret weapon? What would that be?" answered another girl.

"Me. They don't know me but I assure you I can play. I know it is unfair as to how we were split in teams. We are the underdog but we don't have to stay the underdog. Let's work together and try to get that ball to me if you can. The worst that can happen is that we lose which we already are. But I think we can do more than that," Clara looked at each girl in their eyes.

Suddenly one of the girls smiled. "Ok. I would love to wipe that smug look off Jamie's face. She thinks she is all that. You've got spunk. I'm in. Come on Gracie and Emma, let's do this." Gracie, Emma and the other girls murmured their agreement.

Clara smiled and nodded. She grouped them explaining who to mark on the field. "Gracie, you have the girl in the plain white t-shirt. You don't let her out of your sight. Moira, you have the girl with the red t-shirt. You are out for blood. Try your best to NOT allow her to pass you and if she does, just make it as difficult as possible without fouling. Block her. Whatever you must do. I have Jamie.

Agreed? I will tell the rest of you who you have to shadow, got it? You don't lose them. You do everything you have to do without fouling to get the ball, to make it harder for them to keep the ball. You girls that are midfield, just get that ball to me and I'll prove to you what I'm capable of. And of course, if you think you can make the shot, take it." After Clara relayed everyone's task as quickly as she could all the girls separated. As she looked at her makeshift team, they look determined. Gracie looked at her and nodded. Clara knew she needed only one goal to have the team fully buy in and she was going to show Ms. Lawson not only what she was capable of but that she had truly underestimated her. They began to play and during the time, Clara made sure to encourage them and to yell out instructions. She noticed a few of the girls from the opposing team had quizzical looks on their faces as though they were curious if she really knew how to play, or she was just trying her best. But Jamie, totally just smirked at her, and Clara was not one to let her get away with that. She had been the underdog for far too long and she was done.

After the defense had blocked a play, they managed to get it to Gracie in midfield. She was pretty decent at moving the ball, and after blocking a steal she pushed forward and passed the ball to Clara. Clara still had a way to go before she could make a decent shot but this is where she thrived. Sal had mentioned that there were few times when she seemed free, one of them was occasionally on the soccer field and she felt it now. That freedom, that anger inside her morphed and pushed her, she dribbled the ball, faking it to the left and moved right. At that point, someone tried to foul her but she was able to predict it and she saved herself. She had always played with boys and because of this she learned how to play soccer a bit rougher. When she played with the boys, they always thought she was easy to beat, she always proved she wasn't. This was one of those times. She heard yelling around her "What the hell, who is this? Get the ball, Jamie, what are you waiting for?"

At that exact moment Clara went for the goal. It was a tough shot a little bit farther to the right then she would have liked, but she hit it with everything she had, all that anger focused on that ball. It lifted in the air and in the net, it went. Everyone screamed around her, Moira ran up and hugged her. She looked straight at Ms. Lawson, who was smiling and nodding and speaking to someone on her left. She high-fived a bunch of girls and then looked at them and said, "so, are you ready to do that again?"

All the girls smiled. "Hell, yes!" a few of them said.

"Good, no stopping now. Let's prove that wasn't a fluke," Clara remarked.

They started their formation again. Clara made 2 changes that she felt were better suited, also to keep the other team on its toes. While a few girls glared at her, a few had a look of respect in their eyes. One girl who Clara knew was on the soccer team, seemed stunned but her look was full of admiration. In fact, she was smiling. She high fived Moira and encouraged her. They continued to play. Where her team lacked in technique they made up in effort and determination. They lost the ball a few times but Moira could defend pretty well. At a certain point however, Jamie, the captain of the soccer team scored again. Clara's team managed in the next play to get the ball back to the other side of the field. Another girl managed to get the ball away from Emma right when she was about to pass to Clara. Clara knew she would turn right to take the ball away and towards Jamie or to get the ball out. That is exactly where Clara raced, and she came up on her left, turned and took the ball. It all happened so quickly, she briefly saw the surprise but didn't have time to focus on it, she pushed through, dodging around someone with only one focus in mind. Get the ball in that goal. She was taught that is your primary and only concern. Always. Those words rang through her mind as she pushed up, saw where the goalie was, faked left and kicked the ball right. Score! Two more inches to the right and it would have most likely hit the poll but Clara got it right in. Clara slowed down, and took a deep breath. That play took a bit out of her. As she recouped, her team members came over and were all jumping up and down and hugging her. Ms. Lawson blew the whistle, telling everyone that class was over in a few minutes and to get their butts in the locker room to change. Clara's team had tied with the other team and they would rematch it next time. It was in that moment that Clara looked clearly to where Ms. Lawson was and for the first time she noticed Mr. Donovan, Mr.Rossi, Mrs. Chiaro and the entire boys gym class was there. She felt someone's gaze on her, and as she turned her head and lifted her eyes, there they were, those blue gray eyes staring right at her. There was admiration there and something else. He smiled at her. It wasn't a full-blown smile, but a small smile, as if it were only the two of them sharing some kind of secret. She heard someone calling her name and jerked her head towards the voice.

"Clara, come here please." Mrs. Chiaro said. Clara took a deep breath and jogged over. "This is Coach Donovan, Coach Rossi and of course, you know Ms. Lawson."

Clara shook their hands. "I hear you have been trying to get a hold of me, sorry about that. I have time now so how about we discuss the girls' soccer team? Do you have class next?" asked Mr. Donovan.

Clara widened her eyes. "Um, no I have lunch but I can skip that," she answered quickly.

Coach nodded, "Great, let's walk on over to my office. Boys, class is over, head back to the gym and the locker rooms and I'll see you either this afternoon or next week. Ms. Lawson, please join us."

"Good job Clara. I've got to get the next class started." Ms. Chiaro said.

They all walked to his office. When they got there, he closed the door and they all sat down. "Where did you learn to play like that?" coach asked.

"From my cousins," Clara answered.

"How long?" asked Coach Rossi.

"Um, roughly 4 years. Maybe 3 and a half."

Clara looked at all of them. She looked directly at Ms. Lawson and refrained from narrowing her eyes. Ms. Lawson began to speak about how Clara rallied her team, motivated the other girls and yet used technique. "You didn't just play well, you had them all believe in you without even knowing you," concluded Ms. Lawson. Suddenly it all clicked to Clara, that maybe Ms. Lawson had done it on purpose.

"So, does that mean I get to try out?" asked Clara looking at Coach Donovan and Coach Rossi for the answer.

"Unfortunately, the training for the season has already started, so no official try out," Coach Donovan began to say, "but I think we can consider gym class today to be your try out. You are a bit behind though. We have practice right after school Monday through Friday. I would like you to start Monday. This weekend you will start on your own and you may have to train a bit in the mornings. You have to catch up. Coach Rossi is officially taking over the soccer team with Ms. Lawson as Assistant Coach. Are you willing to do that?" said Coach Donovan.

Clara let out a breath of relief. Hearing the beginning of his answer, she had held her breath, ready for a rebuttal but she hadn't needed it. Looking at the coaches now, they were all smiling. *Are they for real? she thought to herself.*

Coach Rossi looked at her and said "Clara, we need an answer. This isn't going to be easy but you have talent. First and foremost, you are going to have to prove and earn your right on the team with your team mates. You have quite a bit of catching up to do and we are not going to take it easy on you." Clara realized out of shock she hadn't responded to the previous question which was why Coach Rossi felt the need to clarify.

"I'm sorry. Of course, I am willing to do what it takes. I'll make you proud." They talked for another few minutes, set a schedule for the following week and a few exercises for her to do during the weekend. She quickly walked out of the office to make it to the locker room to get changed and hopefully grab a bite to eat before her next class.

On her way out, she saw Ms. Lawson. "Thank you for helping me out," Clara told her. Clara wasn't sure if she should say more. She wasn't positive if Ms. Lawson had done it on purpose to help her or not.

"You're welcome. I had a feeling you could do it and I was surprised that even making it difficult you were able to do what you did. Make sure you do your workout this weekend. Get your cousin to help you if you need it. And come in at 6.30 to run drills with me before school starts. And Clara? It's Coach Lawson to you now," as she winked.

Clara rushed to grab a bite to eat before her next class. She smiled on her way to the cafeteria. As soon as she walked in, Rosie saw her and jumped up and came over to hug her.

"I knew you would do it! Woo hoo!"

They chatted a few minutes and as Clara got something to eat she realized that she hadn't smiled this much in a while. On her way out, she glanced to her left. And sure enough, even though he was looking down, as she looked at him, he jerked his head up. Gabe looked right at her, like he always had since the first day at school.

7

GABE

"So, are you going to talk or what?" Alex asked Gabe.

"About?" answered Gabe.

"Dude. I've been waiting all week. Do you think I haven't noticed how you look around all the time or the fact that you don't let the new girl leave your line of sight when you do see her in the cafeteria? Or on that soccer field? You also walked by coach's office twice, while she was in there. It's me. Deny it to anyone else, but not me. I think we are well beyond that."

Gabe sighed, "There is nothing to tell. She caught my eye, that's all. She's new."

Alex raised his eyebrow. "And....?"

"And, yes, she is gorgeous," Gabe replied.

"Of course, sooner or later you are going to talk to this girl, right? Have you even said 2 words to her?" Alex asked.

"No, I haven't. I haven't had the chance and when I do have the chance like in creative writing class, Kristin and Sarah are there and it's like I want to protect her." Gabe continued, "but seriously, there is nothing to tell. There is something about her. Her eyes are sharp and focused but there is so much uneasiness there too. I can't explain it."

"I've noticed. She is on guard, always watching, not totally carefree, kind of like us. She seems like she's lived a different life than most teenagers," Alex said thoughtfully.

"Who are you talking about?" Gabe's father asked walking into the room.

Gabe hesitated for a second but realized there was no reason not to talk to him about it. "There's a new girl at school. We've just noticed there is something about her. She seems uneasy and anxious sometimes. I'm not sure if that's even the right word to describe her. I've seen her play soccer so I know she has confidence and I've heard she's on the newspaper but...".

"Well, you said she is new so that isn't easy to begin with especially in a school your size. It's high school. What's her name?"

"Clara Salvino. Rumor has it she lives with her aunt and uncle. Gabe failed to mention that she's gorgeous, but in a way that she doesn't realize it. She is totally oblivious to it. She's got a lot of guys with their panties in a bunch," Alex answered and had to hold in his laugh when he noticed Gabe's glare.

"Salvino. That name sounds familiar," his father looked pensive. "Alex, did you just say aunt and uncle? So, her true last name may not be Salvino?"

Alex responded, "not sure if that is her real last name or not but I heard from her friend Rosie that her parents passed away and she lives with her aunt, uncle and cousins."

"Hmmm. Remember always what I say that you don't know what someone has been through. I have heard enough to know that if someone is uneasy or guarded there's a reason so she may need support at some point. I have to go now but we can talk about this another time. I did want to ask about Sonia and make sure she was back?"

"Yes, Uncle Ralph, she's back," Alex answered.

"Good. Everything should be set at school for her. Let me know if you need anything. Liz and I have a dinner function tonight. We shouldn't be back too late."

Gabe nodded. His father was a hotshot lawyer, the top in the city. He took quite a few pro bono cases defending the undefended as he called them. Abused victims, many times children. And he never lost, especially those cases. He had heard quite a few horror stories and often told Gabe and Alex to always do the right thing. It's probably one of the many reasons there weren't many bullies in their grade. Alex and Gabe would never tolerate it. Gabe's mom loved kids and after she passed, his father took on more of these cases in a way as if to honor her. He often attended a lot of events, when he had to with Liz, his girlfriend.

Gabe and Alex nodded. "What do you think?" Alex asked him.

Gabe thought about what his father had said. He shook his head, "Not sure, but whatever, let's go out. Is Sonia coming with us?"

"Yeah, I told her we would go pick her up. Let me text her," Alex responded as he continued looking quizzically at Gabe. He smiled and shook his head. "Shit, be careful."

Gabe raised his eyebrow but who was he kidding, this was Alex. "Care to elaborate?"

"This girl. I have a feeling that she is going to get under your skin."

Gabe laughed. "Really? Just because I have been checking her out?"

Alex shook his head. "No. Because she has you thinking. And because you are lying to yourself." He laughed, "This year is going to be very interesting."

Gabe sighed, "Let's go get your sister. And not a word."

"Dude, I don't have to say anything. Sonia will pick it up on the first day or hell, she will probably pick up on it tonight at the party if this girl is there. Nothing gets past Sonia."

"True, but there is nothing to tell so stop harassing me. Let's go." They went to get Sonia and decided to go get something to eat before heading to the party at Connor's house. Sonia was Alex's sister, who had been away to boarding school for some time thanks to their mom but Gabe's father stepped in and demanded from his brother that he put in his two cents and get her out of there. Sonia was a wild child, constantly getting in trouble at that school. The only ones that were able to reel her in were her brother, Alex and her cousin, Gabe. She was finally able to leave that awful boarding school and come to school with them which is where she belonged. As they headed to the party, laughing in the car and joking around, Gabe's phone was going off like crazy. As he hung up his last phone call, he got a text from Kristin.

Gabe sighed, "Who was that?" Sonia asked.

"Henry on the phone, and the last text was Kristin."

"Still not giving up on you, is she?" Sonia asked.

"Nope. Want to take care of her for me?"

Alex laughed, "Make sure you get something out of the deal little sis, this one is a tough one."

"Don't worry, I've got her," Sonia said.

They got out of the car and walked into Connor's house. The place was packed, there were even kids from Harriston, but Connor knew a lot of people. He was super friendly, had been on a few travel teams throughout the area, had an older brother in college who was popular and a younger sister in middle school. As they got out of the car, everyone parted to let them by, even some of the seniors. People were swarming everywhere, beers were handed out. They headed out to the back deck where they knew Connor was hanging out. They found him on the sofa talking to Bobby, with a girl in his lap. Bobby noticed them, smiled and got up to grab a few more chairs. People shifted and room was made for all three of them.

"A lot of people came out tonight, Con" Alex said.

"Yeah, I know, more than I expected. Help me keep things in check guys. There are people from other schools too," Connor answered.

"You got it. Don't worry," Gabe responded, and Alex murmured his agreement.

Connor was a mid-fielder on the soccer team with Gabe. Many often referred to them as the dynamic duo. They had been friends since elementary school and he was probably one of the few that both he and Alex respected and trusted. He always had Gabe's and Alex's back without expecting anything in return. He was a good guy, a bit of a ladies man with a different girl on his lap every week, but a good guy none the less. He noticed Connor kept glancing at Sonia and knew if Alex noticed he would go apeshit.

They all took a round of shots and Gabe sat and nursed his beer, looking around when he heard Bobby say, "Sal Capalbo and David Rade are here."

"Really? I'm surprised they are here. They don't usually show up to our parties," Alex said, "and we're juniors so that is really weird. Are they looking for someone?"

"Nah, they walked in with that new chick, Clara," Bobby answered.

Alex and Gabe shared a look. Connor immediately told Bobby and Henry to make sure they had drinks. He patted the girl on his lap to get up and stood up.

"I'll go say hi. They are both friends with my brother. He would kill me if he knew they were here and didn't make sure they were taken care of."

The girl went to follow him, "No, stay here," Connor said. The girl started to pout.

"Why don't you bring them over here?" Alex asked. Gabe tried to act all nonchalant but his eyes kept darting around. Was she dating one of them? He shook his head. *Snap out of it. You don't even know the girl, so why should you care?*

But sure enough, a few minutes later, Connor came over with them. Sal and Connor were joking around and David was adding comments here and there but he kept glancing at Clara. He leaned in to her and whispered something to her ear. While she was nodding, she looked around and spotted him. Her eyes widened. David went to put his arm around her shoulder but she stepped away. Gabe was relieved to see that but he kept noticing Sal glancing at Clara as if to check if she was still there.

"Guys, this is Sal. He went to school with my brother. Both of them were on the soccer team. And that is David Rade, quarterback for UPenn." Everyone murmured their hellos in some form. Some of them were in awe that two guys from college were at their party.

Connor then turned to Clara, "Hi Clara. Thanks for coming. Personally, since Mr. Brooks didn't allow me to be a gentleman that first day, I was worried you wouldn't come."

Clara slightly smiled "Thanks for inviting me. I hope it's ok, I brought these two," motioning her thumb toward David and Sal.

"You have an outstanding invitation anytime there's a party here and you can bring whoever you want," Connor stated, winking at her.

Gabe tensed for a second reminding himself this was Connor and this is what he did. He was a constant flirt. The girl previously sitting on his lap, was easily forgotten and glared at Clara. But Clara, seemed oblivious to that fact or just ignored her.

"Back off Con, I told you she's my cousin," Sal said. Gabe's tension eased. *Cousin?* She then turned to Sal, and shook her head.

"Thank you, Connor, don't mind him, he likes to overreact."

"Hey, Gabe. Finally, you're here." Gabe tensed as Kristin walked up behind him and smoothed her hand down his back.

"I've been waiting. I was worried you weren't going to show."

She batted her eyes and pretended to do a pout. Of course she said it loud enough for everyone to hear so it seemed they had agreed meeting here. Gabe looked at Kristin to his left, stood back and removed her hand.

"I didn't realize you would be here. Do you know my cousin Sonia? I'm going to grab a drink."

He motioned Sonia towards Kristin and walked away from the group, dismissing her. Heading towards the keg, he hoped Sonia would get rid of her. As he turned he looked behind his shoulder and he noticed Clara looking at him. He smiled slightly and turned to head inside. He needed some liquid courage. He didn't know what is was about this girl. Any other girl, cousin or no cousin, he would have walked up to her. He wasn't a flirt like Connor but he had no problems getting a girl when he wanted. But with her it was different. He continued to hesitate. While Gabe had noticed her, he wanted Clara to notice him. Tonight, was the night to do that. He just needed some help.

He went inside and noticed quite a few of his other friends and team members. He grabbed a beer from the keg, joked around a bit and came back out. He headed back towards the group. Sal had his arm around some girl while talking to Connor and Alex. Sonia was nowhere to be seen, as well as Kristin. His eyes darted around looking for Clara but she was no longer there. Alex just sat there smirking at him and nudged his head to the back. Sure enough there she was, playing beer pong in the backyard with David Rade and two others. He nodded to Alex and turned to Sal and Connor.

"Hey," Gabe said as he approached them and Connor immediately took the cue.

"Sal, this is Gabe, co-captain on the soccer team. He's Alex's cousin."

"Hey, so you're co-captain of the soccer team and your cousin is captain of the lacrosse team, huh? I've heard about both of you," Sal commented, "your rep precedes you both on the field."

Sonia decided to rejoin the group and walked up to Gabe and Sal, "And I'm Sonia, Alex's sister. I'm not captain of anything. Yet." Everyone laughed but Sonia decided to ask Sal a question, "So your cousin over there, she's new?"

Sal tilted his head and looked at Sonia, trying to figure something out. "Yeah, she's new this year, why?" He was noticeably tense while responding.

"Just wondering. I'm new too. I went to a boarding school up until last week so I'll be starting on Monday. Since there are a bunch of catty princesses and stuck up snobs at this school, I figured I'd introduce myself."

Sal instantly seemed to relax some but looked at Connor and Alex for confirmation. "Well, Clara certainly doesn't do catty. She had enough of that at her old school. If you are looking for someone who is real, that's her. You girls should talk."

"Cool. I'll go introduce myself to her and her boyfriend," Sonia stated with just a bit of hesitation as if asking it as a question.

Sal smiled. "Boyfriend? Not her boyfriend or I'd have to beat the shit out of him. Too womanizing. But you are more than welcome to try with David although, your brother seems protective of you as I am of Clara so you may want to reconsider. But I warned you, total womanizer."

"You got that right," Alex laughed. He narrowed his eyes at Sonia trying to figure out what she was doing. Connor also was looking at Sonia.

Sonia looked at Gabe and winked. "Nope, not interested, I just presumed. I'm going to say hello now."

As Sonia spoke he turned to the backyard and noticed a lot of people were paying attention to the game or most likely to Clara. It was the first time he noticed her laughing and obviously so did everyone else. David Rade certainly did, as he was laughing and pulled Clara to him and kissed her head. Gabe's hands automatically balled up in fists.

Sonia noticing the entire exchange turned to Gabe, "Come on cuz, let's go introduce ourselves and challenge them." She pulled him by his arm and smiled.

"You can thank me later," she whispered.

Alex shook his head and laughed, "I have a feeling the real party is going to start now."

They went down the steps towards the table. Sonia, leading the way, stepped right up to them. "Hey Clara, David. I was just talking to Sal over there. I'm Sonia, this bozo is my cousin, Gabe."

"Hey guys!" answered David presenting his hand but he stepped forward as to shield Clara. This pissed Gabe off. He shook their hands and then Clara stepped forward.

"Hi guys," Clara glanced down, took a breath and looked up. She looked at Sonia and smiled and then turned her attention to Gabe. As their hands touched, their gazes locked.

"Hi," Clara said quietly, almost timidly.

"Hey," Gabe responded.

Her smile took on a different look and her striking green eyes broke down his walls. *Was he the only one feeling that she could look right to his soul? He wracked his brain thinking of something to say.*

Sonia cleared her throat as Gabe and Clara broke away. "I thought we could have a friendly competition, what do you say? How about girls vs. guys?" Sonia said. Everyone looked at her. It was totally not what Gabe had in mind and obviously not what Clara and David thought she would say by their expressions. But then again, Sonia always managed to keep everyone on their toes.

"Um, sure," responded Clara hesitantly, "David are you ok with that?" Clara asked. Gabe clenched his fists. Why was she asking him for permission?

"Sure."

"Cool. We are on this side, you boys on that side. Are you guys ready for us ladies to kick your ass?" Sonia declared, smiling at Clara.

As the boys walked to the other side of the table she said, "I start school on Monday, I heard you were new too so I figured we should meet. Plus, I wanted to see what all the commotion was about."

Gabe couldn't hear Clara's entire response but initially she looked a bit confused. He smiled. She really had no clue. Guys were wondering if they had a chance, but she had walked in with Sal and David so they were scared. Didn't get them to stop leering at her though. The girls on the other hand were mixed. Some looked at her with curiosity while others glared at her with jealousy. There was a group of them to the corner that he noticed had just taken court and were observing both Clara and Sonia. The fact that Sonia and Clara had paired up, put them on alert. He smiled and glanced at Alex. Alex flicked his gaze past Gabe to where Kristin and Sarah were openly observing the two girls. Sarah especially seemed concerned and looked at Jamie who walked up to her and they spoke in low voices. Sonia didn't give her attention freely to other girls, or openly be nice to them as she had with Clara. Hell, she usually stuck with Gabe and Alex. Of course, the vultures would notice that. Gabe shook his head and looked at Alex for a brief moment. Alex nodded.

"Game on," Gabe responded and made sure to glance in the direction of Sarah, Jamie and Kristin.

As they began to play Gabe thought about his earlier conversation with Alex and realized he was right. This year was going to be interesting. He just didn't know how much.

8

CLARA

Clara was a bit confused. "Commotion? I am going to admit that you caught me a bit off guard." She looked at Sonia while putting her hands on her hips. "Just to warn you, I am not great at this, but I am highly competitive. Not sure about your motives yet but I can decide on that later." She was not sure where her moment of confidence came from but Clara decided to roll with it.

"Good, but with me what you see is what you get. Now, let's play. Maybe, we'll even like each other by the end of the game." Sonia told her.

"Deal. Game on." They looked at each other and both faced forward. Clara knew everyone was looking at them. Gabe was at the top of the social chain at school and David, well he was a big deal period and he came with her. Everyone thought she didn't notice them whispering or their questionable looks, but she had. She wasn't sure about why Sonia had chosen her. She obviously came from high social status and everyone must be practically wanting to kiss her ass. But unlike some of the girls she noticed at school this week, Sonia seemed real, not fake. She was listening to her gut.

After they had been playing beer pong for some time, Clara slowly began to relax. Although she was still a bit hesitant towards Sonia, she had to admit the girl seemed cool. A lot of people were observing the game making her feel a bit in the spotlight, but it was

Gabe's gaze that made her nervous the most. Every time she looked up, their gazes locked. Most of the time Clara was the one to look away because it seemed as if he was trying to see past her walls and it bothered, yet excited her.

They had gotten to a point where they were pretty much tied. It was Clara against Gabe, she concentrated holding the ball in her hand, lifted her head, and she looked straight in his gorgeous blue eyes. She had tried to avoid looking at them for too long so she never noticed just how blue they actually were until that moment. She saw him take a shaky breath, as though he was just as affected as she was. *Could that be possible?* She noticed him observing her here and there but to be honest, everyone did that. She was new so many were curious, but she knew sooner or later it would die down. She was hoping for sooner. He nodded at her ready to take the shot, she pulled her lip between her teeth and took the shot. Both of them missed the shot. Sonia groaned as did David and they all burst out laughing. Gabe tilted his head and smiled at her as though thinking of something, but then shook his head and turned his attention to David.

"What the hell? You guys both suck. Don't you both play soccer? This is like a missed goal right in front of the net," David laughed.

In that moment Alex walked up to Gabe and whispered in his ear. Gabe tensed up. He nodded and looked behind him. "Great game, I'm considering requesting a rematch. But I have to help Alex take care of something first," Gabe said. Alex looked at Sonia and told her he would be right back. She nodded and then looked at Clara and rolled her eyes. The three of them headed to where Sal and a few others were sitting.

Clara excused herself to go grab a bottle of water inside and she needed to go to the bathroom. Sal looked over at her and opened his mouth to say something but she patted his shoulder bending down and quietly said to him, "I'll be right back. If anyone bothers me I'll just use my ninja skills. Relax." Sal nodded. Connor told her to use one of the bathrooms upstairs and not to worry.

She headed inside and noticed Gabe talking to Alex and another guy that she believed was on the soccer team. They were huddled together whispering. Gabe looked upset as he was speaking. She went upstairs to the first bathroom and after waiting outside of it she realized that there were 2 people inside and that they would probably take a while. *They could probably use a room and no one would notice instead of the freaking bathroom, she laughed to herself.* She continued down the hall, where Connor said there was another one. After she used the bathroom, she glanced at herself in the mirror and studied herself for a minute before shaking her head. She presumed she looked fine or at least she hoped so. She began to open the door when she heard a bunch of voices outside.

"What the hell? You told me that he was ok. Did you look at him? Not only is he wasted he's high."

They paused as another voice approached laughing, "Chill out, he'll be fine. It's just some weed."

"Just some weed? It may be just some weed to you, Bruno, but he's on the soccer team. They drug test regularly and typically by surprise. Henry and I can't help him if it shows up and you know this! Are you trying to ruin his season?" Clara knew instantly this was Gabe talking and he seemed really mad.

"Dude, chill out. It's none of your freaking business what he does or what I do so back off." She did not recognize this voice.

"You're right it's not my business what you do, but it is my business what he does since he is on my team and you are bringing him down a dangerous road. This is his future, man. He has a chance to get out of that hell hole and make something of himself and help his mom. You're the one who should mind his own business and back off. If you want to ruin your life go ahead but leave him out of it," Gabe exclaimed.

"Have you ever heard of free will? He can do whatever he wants. We grew up together so don't tell me that he isn't my business. I just gave him a few hits. I didn't realize that it would affect him like this. The stuff I have is good stuff not laced with crap."

"You mean the stuff you sell, don't you? Are you selling here in Connor's house? He will kick your ass here to God knows where, that is if I don't do it first." This sounded like Alex.

Clara could almost hear the other guy grit his teeth. "I only have a bit on me. I did not sell in Connor's home, alright?" For some reason, the way he emphasized the words in Connor's home, it didn't sound very truthful. Rather, it sounded like he made sure to sell outside of the house. Clara started to get nervous. She needed to get out of the bathroom.

Gabe immediately challenged him, "I don't trust you so if you only have a few hits, then you have no problem handing what you have over. Give it to me."

"No problem, Caruso. If you wanted to smoke it up, you just had to ask. Consider these on the house."

"I swear, I am two beats away from..."

"Enough, guys. Both of you are raising your voices and everyone is going to hear. Right now, we have to help Leo. Let's move him to a guest bedroom and get him some coffee or a soda and lots of water. You guys can argue about this later."

The voices moved away and Clara slowly opened the door and peaked out to the hallway. Connor had explained to her that if she continued down the hallway, she would end up at the back staircase to go downstairs. As she began walking she heard female voices giggling. She knew instantly that one of them was Sarah. She was in a few of her classes and she could pinpoint her giggle anywhere and usually it was at someone's expense. She turned around quickly. If she ran into the guys again, then hopefully they would think she came from the other staircase. As she turned the corner she ran into someone's chest.

"Well, who the hell do we have here?" Two strong hands grabbed her upper arms to steady her. "What sky did you fall from, angel? Although," and he made sure to look at her from head to toe, "I'm pretty sure you got the body of a sexy devil."

Next to him were Alex and Henry and they were carrying one of their teammates. Leo, she believed was his name. Gabe was on the other side. Clara cringed, it was obvious the guy was a total douche. She tilted her head, "I don't think you want to know what a devil I can be. Sorry I walked into you, but hands off." She stepped back and pulled her arms out of his reach and crossed them in front of her chest.

He laughed, "Oh, I wouldn't mind finding out how naughty you can be, trust me."

As he started to continue to say something, Alex came to her rescue and interrupted, "Dude, back the fuck off. I don't think you want to know who she came here with and I'm pretty sure there are others here willing to back her up. Let's help Leo, before I lose my patience with you."

"I'm just having some fun, or starting to at least. Did you see this beauty or what?"

At that moment, Clara stepped back again and turned away from him and she turned toward Alex and Gabe. "There are a few others coming up that way, so if you're trying to hide him, I would duck in a bedroom now."

Gabe nodded and thanked her. He looked tense, his hands were fisted. He moved in front of Leo in a way that she would have to go around Gabe and avoid the other guy with the big mouth. She was thankful. She headed downstairs but had to calm down a minute, or Sal would notice instantly that something was wrong. She walked into the kitchen to grab a bottle of water, even though she could probably use a shot right now. She was on her way out when David walked up to her.

"Hey, where did you disappear to gorgeous?"

"Just went to the bathroom. Where's Sal?"

"He's outside. Let me grab a drink and we'll head back out."

He grabbed her hand and pulled her back into the kitchen, not really giving her the opportunity to reply. He was always trying to touch her. He was a natural flirt but occasionally he tried to get a little too close. Thankfully she didn't see him often enough and he never really crossed the line. But she was sure that if she did give him the ok, he would. He grabbed a beer and went to grab her hand again to head outside when Alex and Gabe walked in. David was saying something and he looked at her with a question mark. He had obviously asked her a question and she had totally missed it.

"I'm sorry, David. What did you say?"

"I asked, if you wanted to go to the back yard for a few minutes or go straight back to the deck. Maybe one of your new friends is here."

"No, Rosie texted me earlier that she wouldn't be coming tonight and I'm really not in the mood to mingle. Let's just go back to where we were, please."

If David was disappointed, he didn't show it. He nodded but started to speak again. "Clara, you know that you can count on me too, right? If you need anything and Sal isn't there, just call me."

"Thanks David. I appreciate it," Clara answered.

She put her hand on his arm and he took the opportunity to try to pull her in for a hug. She laughed, ducking under his other arm and headed outside. She took a deep breath, put a smile on her face and headed toward Sal and the others that had now congregated around him. She looked at him and smirked, he immediately laughed, a silent conversation going on between them.

Sal's phone rang and he looked at the screen and immediately answered. He asked the girl on his lap to move, stood up and took a few steps away from the group. He was nodding and looked at Connor and called him over. They spoke a few minutes. "Shit. Now? Why?" Connor groaned.

"Some neighbor called the police due to the noise. You just have to make sure no one is out front loitering on the sidewalks and shit," Sal told him.

"If it's just Officer Clarke with his partner then it should be ok. He usually comes to check in. Let me ask Alex and Gabe to help me."

Connor took off inside. Sal turned to Clara. "Maybe we should head out. The cops are on their way and I'm not sure I want you here. Aunt Nina and Uncle Frank would kill me if something happened to you. Even though I am pretty sure that the cops are here only for a warning. But let's go, ok?"

Relieved to go, but yet disappointed to leave, if that made any sense at all, Clara agreed. They headed in the kitchen to head out the front door and to say their goodbyes. As Connor was saying that he would see her Monday, she caught a glimpse of Alex and Gabe talking to Bobby. Bobby headed upstairs after she heard him say "I'll check on him," probably to go check on Leo. Gabe and Alex headed outside. They ushered a few people inside, while a few other guys were throwing away cups and ensuring there were no beer bottles outside. Sal, David and Clara walked out the front door and towards their car. A cop car had already pulled up to the driveway and two officers were looking around. Connor stepped outside.

"Hi Officer Clarke. I haven't seen you in a while. I was wondering when you would come say hi," Connor joked. Clara knew he was instantly trying to lighten the mood.

Officer Clarke shook Connor's hand and said, "Hello Connor. The station got a call about a lot of noise coming from this address. Now, I'm here and I don't hear a lot of noise but I need to make sure it stays that way."

As he was speaking his partner looked at everyone and walked a bit to the side, where he picked up a little baggie with a few dots of weed. "Maybe we need to check a little further here," as he showed Officer Clarke the baggie.

"Now, Connor, please tell me there are no drugs on your property because then this is a totally different kind of visit then."

"Officer Clarke, sir, you know that I don't do that shit and I don't condone that behavior either." Clara had always noticed that Connor was a jokester and a flirt, but his tone completely changed. He wore a serious expression on his face. "My friends also know that crap doesn't fly here with me. I have no idea where that baggie came from but if I were to find out it was someone at my party, putting my rep and the soccer team on the line, I would be seriously pissed. You know that much about me. You can even search my friends if you have to, but I am more than sure you won't find anything."

Clara looked at Gabe from where she was. His hand instantly went to his front left pocket. *Crap.* She remembered the conversation she overheard upstairs while she was in the bathroom. He must have taken the leftover weed from the guy. What would happen if the officer really did search everyone? *Shit. She knew she had to do something.* He was located behind Connor and a bit to the side. The side that was towards another entrance to get to the deck and the back yard. She turned to Sal and told him that she forgot to say bye to Sonia. He looked at her like she was crazy and insisted that she would just see her Monday. As the officer and Connor kept talking, she turned to Sal, took a deep breath and looked at him with what she hoped were her puppy dog eyes.

"But, Sal, she starts school on Monday. You told me to make friends and from what I could tell she seemed cool. Plus, maybe we should take her home. The boys seem a bit busy here. Let me at least offer."

When Sal sighed, she knew she had won. "Fine, go get her or ask her if she wants a ride home. But hurry." He turned to the other officer, who he happened to know.

"Officer Bland, she is just going to get a friend, is that ok?"

"Yeah, Sal, you guys should be fine. This is probably just a misunderstanding and hopefully we will be leaving soon enough."

Clara smiled the best she could at the officer. As she walked, she turned around at a certain point to look behind her and she happened to slam right into Gabe. "I'm so sorry! I keep running into people tonight. Sorry."

"It's fine. Are you ok?" Gabe had grabbed her arms to steady her. Clara couldn't help but shiver from his touch.

"Yeah, I'm fine. Sorry. Total klutz." But she didn't look up at him. She couldn't. She continued rambling as she pulled away and walked to find Sonia, who just so happened to appear right at the entrance to the back yard.

"Hey, we were leaving, need a ride home?" Sonia looked at her and then at Alex. "Umm, I'm not sure. Let me talk to my brother." She spoke a few words to Alex and then went back to Clara. "I'm going to stay. He wants me to leave with you, but I refuse. I have to make sure everything is ok. Thanks for offering though. I guess playing on my team worked, huh?"

Clara laughed slightly. "Yeah, I guess so. See you Monday then." She turned around, nodded to both officers and walked toward Sal and David. She quickly got in the back seat. Sal said his goodbyes and got in the car and drove off. Clara sat in silence in the back.

9
GABE

As Connor told him a cop was on the way over to check things out, he didn't worry. This wasn't the first time someone had called the cops on them or a party they were at. Plus it was a cop Connor's family knew. The cops didn't tend to come inside because then they would see the booze and they would have to do something about it. But this way what they didn't see they couldn't report. Everyone knew they had parties, everyone knew they drank but as long as they kept it under control and didn't cause havoc, then it was ignored. They would get a warning but the moment someone stepped out of line then the cops did what they had to do. It was a bit hypocritical, yes, but when you have money and payed a lot in taxes, then the law tends to be a bit more lenient, especially when they weren't really hurting anyone. They also knew that Connor was a good guy from a good family and they wouldn't mess that up. At least he hoped. But the moment Officer Bland found that baggie, Gabe remembered what he had in his front left pocket. *Shit.* He was going to punch Bruno's face in. He already couldn't stand the guy.

Bruno was bad news. Leo was loyal to him because they had grown up together but he refused to see what Bruno was up to. Leo was a good guy and lived with his mom and 4 other brothers and sisters. Leo also worked to help out at home. His mom, however, kept telling him that she wanted him to focus on school and soccer so he could have a better future. But it seemed that Bruno was ready to ruin it for him. Gabe and Connor spoke to Leo about Bruno briefly, trying to get a feel for how much they could say. But Leo's mom worked with Bruno's mom and had known each other for years. She had been there through Leo's father's death so he felt that he couldn't turn his back on Bruno. Plus, Leo believed that what they thought about Bruno was a bit exaggerated. Hopefully by Monday Gabe could speak to him about it again. Bruno had always rubbed Gabe the wrong way but add the nonchalant way he acted about Leo possibly getting drug tested and then the way he had his hands on Clara, he really couldn't stand the guy. It took all his control to not pull her out of his grasp. Luckily, Alex intervened and Clara seemed to handle herself just as well.

As he stood on that lawn and heard Connor offer up the chance for the officers to check his friends for drugs, his hand automatically went to his front pocket but before he reached it and drew attention there he pulled his hand back to the side and kept his hands down. He was panicking inside but didn't show it. He knew his father would believe him in the end, or at least he hoped so, but he didn't want Connor to get in trouble or the hassle of having to explain everything. There were too many people caught in the middle. Just as he was listening to what Sal was saying to the officer, Clara started walking. He glanced at Alex and just as he did, she slammed into him. His hands shot out to steady her. She was extremely close. He inhaled her scent and looked at her. *Fuck, she smelled good. Seriously? Of all the times and the places, this was not the moment to focus on how good she smelled.*

She quickly apologized and kept doing so but just as he was about to say to not worry about it, she walked away. He looked to where she was going and noticed Sonia had stepped outside just then and spoke to her. Gabe turned his attention back to the officers and tried to focus. A few minutes passed and Clara walked by again and got in Sal's car and they drove off. He released a breath. After the officers left, and everyone went back inside, Alex and Gabe immediately pulled Connor upstairs to explain Leo's situation and what had happened.

"Con, when you told Officer Clarke to check your friends for drugs, I wanted to kill you," Gabe said.

"How was I supposed to know? When they had found that baggie, I knew I had to say something to them to appease them. I didn't think they would actually search you guys, and thankfully they didn't. Get that crap and flush it down the toilet please. I don't think they will be coming back but hell, I'm not taking any chances. We have enough booze here to open a liquor store, the last I need is weed on top of that."

"I'll take care of it. Don't worry."

At that moment Bruno walked in again. Gabe instantly wanted to punch him. "I thought you were watching Leo?"

Bruno looked at Gabe and said "I did but then I had to take a piss and get something to drink. I got a little sidetracked with all the little ladies down there. Sue me. I saw that you guys had company outside. Must be nice to get a little "warning" instead of just being shut down like everyone else's parties are."

Gabe fisted his hands. He was ready to lose his shit but Connor intervened. "Bruno, this is the last time you will ever come to one of our parties if you don't back off. You could have caused some serious problems here tonight. Own it."

Bobby walked in at that moment. "I just checked on him and left Henry with him. He puked a few times but he seems much better now. I gave him another bottle of water. He actually seems like he can focus and speak a full sentence now."

"See? No harm, no foul. He'll be fine. We've all been there, drunk off our asses." Bruno began speaking.

Connor interrupted him immediately. "Get out, Bruno. Leave. I'm two seconds from hitting you. We'll take care of Leo tonight."

Bobby and Alex stepped forward, "Let's go Bruno."

"I don't need a freaking chaperone. I'll see myself out." Bruno stormed out of there.

Bobby looked at everyone and blew out a breath, "I'll make sure he gets out."

"Thanks Bobby," Alex turned to Gabe and Connor, "mark my words but this guy is going to be a problem. If not for us, for Leo for sure."

"Agreed. He needs a serious beatdown. I don't trust him. I was ready to lose my shit a few times," Gabe said.

"We could tell, Gabe," Connor laughed. "We'll have to watch out for him. And for Leo. I'll let him stay here tonight and talk to him in the morning."

"I took his phone. It's in your room. I didn't want Bruno to start texting him crap. This way you have a clean slate tomorrow morning. I have to go check on Sonia. Gabe – get rid of that shit before we go," Alex remarked.

"Yeah, I'll do it now." Gabe reached into his front pocket but found nothing. He checked the other one and again found nothing.

Connor and Alex looked at him. "Dude, tell me you didn't drop it?"

"I couldn't have dropped it. The bag was in my front pocket. It was the only thing in there. Fuck." Gabe cursed.

"Ok, let's just retrace your steps. It has to be somewhere and if it isn't then someone picked it up and is probably smoking up somewhere. Let's just make sure it is not anywhere on the floor so Connor's family doesn't find it." Alex calmly responded.

"Ok, I'll check on Henry and have him search the room Leo is in, just in case," Connor stated.

"Fine, only you, Alex, Henry and Bobby know. We have to find it somewhere. If not, you're right. I'll retrace my steps from here to the front lawn. Connor – check the kitchen, Alex and Bobby– check the deck and the front rooms," Gabe spoke sternly.

"On it" "Got it" Both Alex and Connor replied.

All three guys looked carefully throughout the house. Henry checked the guestroom where he was with Leo but found nothing. Bobby helped Alex out by looking in the front rooms of the house. At a certain point Gabe was on the front porch and Kristin came from the side entrance. "Hey Gabe. What are you doing out here? I haven't seen you all night baby."

"Kristin, now is not the time. I don't know how I can make it any clearer but I am not interested."

"Aww, come on Gabe. I'm pretty sure I can remind you how good we were. Don't you remember? It's not fair that you aren't even giving us the chance to see what we could be." She approached him as she said this, her hand caressed his arm while her other hand was on his chest moving towards his abs. Gabe was definitely not in the mood to deal with her anymore and had lost his patience. He pulled his hand out of her grasp, took a step back and looked her straight in the eye. The only way for her to get over him was for him to act like an asshole.

He shook his head, "Listen, Kristen, just in case I wasn't clear until now. We fucked. It was just sex and it wasn't that great. There was no us and there will be no us. Get that in your head." Gabe really hated being such a dick but he definitely was not in the mood. It was better that he was harsh and left her no hope, than being nice, and leaving her with hope that he would change his mind. Kristin's face went from her trying to look all coy and seductive, to shock, and finally a flare of anger.

She was seething. "Fine, Gabe, this was your last chance. I'm done!" And she stormed off.

"Finally," Gabe breathed. He looked around some more.

Connor came outside and as soon as he saw him, he said, "So I take it you finally got Kristin off your back, huh?"

Gabe let out a breath and answered, "I hope so, she wasn't taking the hint."

"Dude, some chicks need that. I'm pretty sure you were clear in the beginning but some of them don't get it and think they can change your mind. She'll get over it. Have you found it?" Connor asked him.

"No, I was just going to check the front yard before she interrupted. I'm trying not to attract attention and get people wondering what I'm doing."

"Good. Let's just check together, we can say we are looking for something else, " Connor said and Gabe nodded. They searched the entire front lawn but to no avail. Connor had locked his parents and sibling's rooms so it couldn't be in there. All four guys checked the guest rooms and the basement to make sure his family wouldn't just find it unexpectantly lying somewhere. They agreed someone must have taken it wherever it had fallen. Gabe and Connor were going to touch base the next morning and have a sit down with Leo about Bruno and what happened.

Gabe and Alex headed home with Sonia in tow, all three pensive and not in the mood to talk. They said their good nights. Alex decided to sleep at home since Sonia was there. As Gabe laid in bed staring at the ceiling, he was having a hard time falling asleep. He was irritated with himself for losing the weed in his pocket, angry with Bruno for putting any of them in that predicament and frustrated with the entire situation. Thanks to Sonia he was able to spend some time around Clara but the situation didn't exactly call for conversation especially with all the people staring at their beer pong game. That, and of course he couldn't seem to form cohesive sentences around her. Not that he would ever admit to that. When he did finally fall asleep in the early hours of the morning, it was with a picture of those green eyes in mind.

10

CLARA

For the most part, Clara was silent as she sat in the back seat of the car. She contributed to the conversation when Sal or David asked her a question, but she wasn't paying much attention. Sal continued to look in the rearview mirror at her, while David kept turning around and glancing at her. They dropped her off with the intent that they would be in touch tomorrow. Thank goodness she was at the karate studio for most of the day, she could avoid Sal until late afternoon or more. Before she got out, David went to walk her to the door but she stopped him.

"I'm fine David, no need."

"Clara, are you ok? You seem extremely deep in thought and we just came from a party. Don't worry about what happened there, they will be fine," David tried to tell her.

Sal looked at her and she knew she had to say something. "I'm fine. I actually had a really good time. Thank you both for coming with me. I am just really tired all of a sudden and yeah, I am just worried about them. My first party and the cops show up." She made sure to chuckle.

"Why don't you come to a party at the university tomorrow night? If Sal can't come, I'll come and get you," David insisted.

Clara stiffened. He knew Sal had plans tomorrow night. "No, thanks, one party is enough for me this weekend. I have karate all day tomorrow so I think I am going to chill tomorrow night. I promised Julia we would do something. Thanks, though. I'll see you soon. Good night Sal, see you at Nonna's on Sunday."

"You got it, good night. Call me if you need me."

She went upstairs and immediately went to the bathroom to wash her face and brush her teeth. Before washing her face, she put her hands on the sink and looked up at herself in the mirror – and really looked at herself. It wasn't something she did often. It wasn't that she never looked in the mirror but she didn't take her time to do so. Her makeup usually took 5 minutes since it consisted of lipgloss, some eyeliner and mascara. Once in a blue moon she would venture out like tonight and put on a little bit of blush. She did like clothes so maybe she took her time a bit more then, but she never looked at herself in the eyes for more than a few brief moments.

For a long time it made her a bit sad to look straight in her eyes. There was a time when she looked at herself in the mirror to remind herself to be strong, to push forward, that everything would be ok. In fact, Tracey, made her look in the mirror every day and made her repeat a mantra until she was once again safe in her family's arms, well, her aunt and uncle's arms at least. She smiled. She remembered the day she looked up from the chair she had been sitting in at the police station, with an officer holding her hand while she waited. Once she saw her aunt and uncle walk through the door, she jumped up and she raced to them. One of her first thoughts was that she wouldn't have to say the words Tracey taught her anymore. So she made sure to not say them again. But habits sometimes were hard to break and still today if she looked directly in her eyes for too long, those words would start coming. She shook her head and headed to her room quietly, not wanting to wake anyone up. She locked her door, sat on her bed and looked outside. She reached into her pocket and pulled out the baggie with the weed and stared at it. *What the hell was she going to do with it?*

11

GABE

The weekend went by quickly. There was another party on Saturday night but Gabe didn't go, neither did Alex, Connor, Leo and a few other guys from the soccer and lacrosse teams. Connor had an intense heart to heart with Leo. It was rare that Leo didn't work the weekend so they took advantage and spent time with him and ensured Bruno wouldn't be there.

On Monday, Gabe walked into school right behind Alex but next to Sonia. He could tell Sonia was nervous although she would never admit it. He showed her the office and both he and Alex waited outside while she did what she had to do. While they waited Gabe kept glancing around.

"Who are you looking for?" Alex smirked.

Gabe let out a breath, "Have you seen Leo yet?" Just as he mentioned his name, Leo popped up from around the corner with Bruno right next to him animatedly speaking.

Leo stopped where they were standing, "Hey you guys. What's up?"

"All good Leo, all good. Where you headed, man?" Alex replied.

"Come on dude, let's go." Bruno said to Leo.

But for once Leo looked at him and replied, "Go ahead Bruno, I'll catch up later." Bruno initially looked at him as though he had sprouted a head but then looked irritated. He left quickly, glancing behind his back.

Leo turned to Alex and Gabe "I'll wait with you two." Gabe smiled slightly and nodded and in the meantime Alex and Leo started to discuss Sunday's football game on TV. While they waited for Sonia to finish up and get her schedule, Gabe tried to not look around. He knew he was trying to find Clara but he didn't want to seem so obvious.

Sonia finally finished and they headed through the hallway, everyone parting aside to let them through, some glancing at them with admiration. Kristin caught his gaze briefly before lowering it and then moving closer to her friends. While he was noticing that exchange, he realized suddenly that Sonia was no longer with them. He turned around and saw Sonia smile and wave good bye while a mane of brown hair turned the corner. He looked at Sonia, who winked but proceeded as usual until they all had to split up to head to their lockers and to class.

Gabe didn't have to go to his locker for his first class so he decided he would go afterwards. His first class passed by quickly and as he was walking to grab his books for his next class, Connor caught up with him. They got to his locker and Connor began to lean on the lockers to his right. Gabe grabbed what he needed from the top shelf and right at that moment Sonia popped up.

"Hey!" she seemed frazzled and he noticed instantly that Connor straightened up from the locker. "I have to go to computer science, can you tell me the fastest way to get there?"

Gabe turned and started to open his mouth when Connor jumped in and said, "I'll take you. I have to go that way anyway."

"Are you sure?" Sonia asked him.

Connor shrugged, "Yep. See you in English Gabe."

"Bye, Gabe!" Sonia exclaimed as they walked away.

Gabe raised his eyebrows and shook his head. He shoved what he no longer needed inside and was about to close the door to his locker when something caught his eye. Taped to the back of his locker, difficult for others to see, was a little plastic baggie. He furrowed his brow and hesitantly reached for it. He looked around without making it so obvious. Ensuring no one was next to him, he grabbed it off the back wall of his locker. He didn't realize that he had been holding his breath but he let it out once he realized it was empty. He looked around again to see if anyone was paying attention to what he was doing. Gabe was certain that this is the baggie that went missing at the party. He stuffed it in his pocket and headed to class.

As he walked to his class he kept searching trying to figure out if anyone looked suspicious or smug but he didn't notice anything out of the ordinary. Gabe couldn't focus during his entire next class. He was convinced it was a message but it just didn't make any sense. The bag was empty so whoever did it wasn't trying to get him in trouble, at least he didn't think so. Although it could be a warning, it just didn't feel like one. He felt like someone was telling him that it was taken care of, and in a way that meant that they had taken care of him and his friends. He usually was the one that took care of other people so he wasn't entirely comfortable with the feeling.

His class ended and he cleared out of the room rather quickly needing to get Alex's perspective on things. Alex was walking with a few people and he looked up and noticed Gabe's strange expression. Gabe nodded at him and they headed into a more secluded area near English so he could also grab Connor. As they saw Connor head down, he looked at them and immediately headed over.

"What's up? Is something wrong?" Gabe lead them around the corner away from prying eyes. He knew that Sarah and Kristin would head to the same class soon as well as others. He pulled the baggie from his pocket and showed it to them. Both guys furrowed their eyebrow and look at him.

"What is that?" Alex asked. He knew well enough that if Gabe was showing him something there was a reason, he wasn't just showing him a tiny Ziploc bag.

"I found it taped to the back of my locker. I'm pretty sure this is the one that I lost at Connor's house the other night, just that this one is empty. "

"Ok, but that is just strange. Why would someone do that? I could understand if it was full, then maybe to get you in trouble. But empty? It's like they want you know that they know you lost it and they found it," Alex noted.

"Well, we figured someone had found it right? It fell from your pocket, they found it and now want to let you know. But still they didn't get you in trouble. Unless, it's a warning that they will get you in trouble. I mean whoever it was, they were able to open your locker dude," Connor remarked.

"I don't know. I am going with my gut on this. I don't think they want to get me in trouble, I think they want me to know that they protected me. But then, why not just tell me so I know who is it."

Alex was thoughtful, "Maybe they will want a favor in the future. Are we sure it wasn't Bruno? We all know that it's kind of something that he would do."

Connor responded immediately, "I was thinking the same thing but Bruno isn't smart enough to open a locker. Plus, Bruno would tell you about it instantly, not play any games. He would want you to know that he saved your ass so he could reap the benefits. Whoever did it, is very smart."

Alex and Gabriel agreed. "It still leaves me feeling uneasy and I'll have to change my combo lock but I think it's someone that wants to protect us," Gabe insisted.

"Ok, well let's keep our eyes open. Whatever happens, we will figure it out. But outside of us three no one knows. Sonia included. I don't want her involved. I've got to get to class, I'll see you guys at lunch, let me know if you see anything fishy and I will do the same," Alex stated and waved two fingers in goodbye.

"Later. Come on man, let's get to English. Mr. Brooks hates it when someone is late." Connor turned toward the classroom.

"Yeah, ok." Gabe kept thinking and looking around if anyone seemed keen on what they were doing. They walked into class a few minutes late gathering the attention of quite a few of the students sitting down. He noticed Kristin looked at him with a hurt expression and then quickly looked at Sarah and looked down at her desk. Sarah on the other hand, looked pretentious and actually smiled as they walked in. But his attention was on the girl sitting in the chair next to his. Clara met his gaze and then glanced at Connor who had said hello to her. She smiled briefly.

"Hey," Gabe said to her trying to get her attention.

She quickly glanced at him, swallowed and responded, "Hi."

Gabe quickly sat down as Mr. Brooks looked pointedly at both he and Connor for being late. Gabe nodded to Mr. Brooks and put his notebook on his desk. Mr. Brooks started to hand out papers with an assignment. He went back to the front of the class and leaned on his desk.

"This is your first major assignment. It is a good portion of your grade and gives you a feel of my expectations and standards. Please pay attention and don't read what is on the paper for right now." He looked around the class. "I want you to write about a specific event that changed your life or feels like it changed your life. For some of you, it's easy to pinpoint as it's something big, for others not so much. I want you to write the event, how it changed you, what you learned, if there is something you do different because of it, the positive, the negative, the good, the bad and the ugly. Just write. Write until you feel like you've gotten your point across, until others feel even a small part of what you felt." Mr. Brooks paused a moment. "This is a work in progress and most of you will revise it multiple times. In a way this opens your own personal Pandora's box and I've noticed that giving it to students in the beginning of the year, allows you to write better pieces on the other topics I have for you. This piece is freeing, if you allow it to be. And therefore, when you write everything else, you get to a point where I really see your creativity come out and that's what I want. I want to challenge you, and I want you to challenge me. I ask that you be honest with yourself. There is no reason to lie to me, I'm not grading you on your experience, I'm grading you on your writing, on how you get your thoughts across. Have courage to not care what people will think when you write this." Mr. Brooks continued, "I'm not going to go through the expectations of length and timeline. You can read that yourselves. The first copy is due in 3 weeks. Today in class I ask you to start your outline, come to me with any questions or concerns that you may have and start to really think about what it is you want to write about. That first topic that comes in your brain is usually the one you should choose. But I know it's not easy and many of you will choose something safer, but I hope you don't make it easy for yourselves because I won't be easy on you. I'll give you about 20 minutes before I walk around and see if everyone is ok or needs assistance."

Everyone in class opened their notebook and some began to write. Others rolled their eyes and you knew they were going to try to bullshit their way through this. Gabe knew what he was going to write about so he quickly jotted down some notes. He was ok with writing about his experience as long as he didn't have to share it with the class. He turned to his left to where Clara was sitting and noticed she began to write something and then crossed it out. She took a deep breath and seemed like she was going to write something and then stopped again. Whatever she was thinking was causing her difficulty. He looked around at the others a bit quickly and they were all intent at writing or pretending to. He looked at Mr. Brooks who was also typing something on his laptop. He quickly wrote a note to Clara.

Hey, r u ok?

And handed it over to her. She looked up at Mr. Brooks and opened the note turning her head toward Gabe. At first, she looked surprised that he asked her, but as he was looking at her, for a brief moment he noticed how lost she seemed to be, maybe even a little bit scared. But then just like that, she blinked a few times and up went a wall. She wrote something on the note and handed it back to him quickly.

Yep, just thinking.

He looked around and wrote back.

You seemed a bit...dazed.

She read it, hesitated a second and then wrote back.

Nope, just lost in thought.

Well, she wasn't one to give a lot of details that is for sure. He decided to change tactics.

Did you have fun at the party?

She looked at it and glanced at him with a hint of a smile.

Yes, you?

He looked at it and wrote again.

Do you always answer questions so briefly?

Clara wrote back quickly.

Well, you are asking me yes or no questions.

Gabe smiled. He continued to look around not wanting to attract attention.

Ok. Well then, I had a good time playing beer pong.

Just as he finished writing it and handed it over, Mr. Brooks started walking around. He looked at Clara and got back to work. He noticed she still wasn't writing anything. In fact, Mr. Brooks stopped by her desk to ask if she was ok. He didn't want to eavesdrop but he understood they were discussing the difficulty she was having today in writing the outline. She told him the assignment would be done on time but she needed some time to think prior to writing out the outline. After about another 5 minutes he told the class to stop and to open to the first chapter of their current book. He lectured for about 15 minutes and asked a few questions until finally the bell rang.

"Chapter 2 and 3 for tomorrow everyone. Feel free to email me if you have any questions about the assignment. But I recommend you start working on it. It seems easy but I assure you that it's not as simple as it seems."

As they started standing up, Connor turned to Gabe and started talking about practice. Gabe then looked down and noticed a small folded piece of paper on the top of his book. He opened it.

Me too.

He smiled and turned to her when he realized that she was already on her way out the door. The girl definitely moved fast. He put the note in his pocket. While Connor and he exited the class-room, he looked up ahead trying to see where Clara was going. Leo caught up with them while they were walking down the hallway, as did a few others. As he walked to his locker he remembered his secret admirer, if that is what we could call them. For the entire period of English he had almost forgotten what had happened. Although he was suspicious and kept looking around surprisingly he wasn't worried. Sooner or later he would know who this mystery person was.

12

CLARA

Clara let out a breath as she rushed from English class. Her chest felt tight and she needed some air. Today was turning out to be a hell of a day. *What was she thinking?* She had gotten rid of the weed but she couldn't seem to get rid of that stupid Ziploc bag. The whole weekend she didn't know why she held on to it. This morning she had gotten here early to practice with Ms. Lawson and to drop off an article for the newspaper for editing and she knew what she had to do. Maybe she should have included a note, but she was glad she didn't. She wanted Gabe to know that someone helped him, but if you asked her why, she couldn't say. If she was brave she would just tell him that it was her. But she couldn't do that. He would start asking questions. She didn't want to go back there. Ever. *Deep breath, Clara.*

She rushed to the bathroom and took a few paper towels and ran them under cold water. She then proceeded to close herself in a stall and put those towels on the back of her neck. She breathed carefully. What a day. Of course she would choose to do something like leave him a message of some sorts in his locker, the same day he decided to write notes to her in class. She chuckled and shook her head. How fucking ironic. And then to top it all off, she has to write an assignment about something that changed her. *Really? Gee I wonder what that could be?* She continued to breathe in and out until she finally felt ready. She threw away the paper towels and stepped out of the stall to wash her hands. As she did a few girls walked in, or more precisely Jamie and Eva. Behind them were a few others who went straight to the mirror. Jamie looked at her.

"Well, well, hi Clara. I heard that you are now part of the soccer team thanks to your little stunt in gym class the other day."

Clara looked at Jamie. "I'm pretty sure I just played some soccer like you did."

"Well, don't think that you can just come in, and get play time on the field. You're going to have to earn it. One gym class isn't going to change that."

"I have no problem earning it, Jamie. I know I can play. Just like I am sure you can play too."

"Well, we'll see, won't we?"

"I guess we will. See you at practice."

Jamie had tried to get in her face but Clara stepped around her and walked out. Eva looked at her and didn't say anything but nodded. She walked out of the bathroom and started walking outside. Air. She needed some air. She heard someone calling her name and looked up. Sonia reached out to grab her arm lightly.

"Hey, where are you headed?"

"Outside, just need some air. I'll catch up with you later ok?"

"Yeah, sure."

She rushed down the hallway and straight outside to the parking lot. She needed a few minutes to herself. First the whole baggie incident which was totally all on her. Then Mr. Brooks' assignment, something that she was going to have to think long and hard about. Gabe writing her notes during class – that just surprised her. Then Jamie's confrontation in the bathroom. She was warned that not everyone would be accepting of her joining the soccer team, she knew that she had to prove herself. She just hoped Jamie wouldn't be a problem. All this and it wasn't even lunchtime yet. She knew this year wasn't going to be easy, but now she knew it definitely would be interesting.

13

CLARA

A few days passed. It was Friday morning and she was almost finished her morning soccer drills with Ms. Lawson. She felt much better after she had just finished an hour with her. She lacked a little bit of focus in the beginning but after about 10 minutes she was able to re-center herself.

"Ok, that's enough for today. You seemed tired in the beginning, but you seemed pretty strong by the end. Go get a shower, I'll see you at practice this afternoon," Ms. Lawson told her. Clara nodded and walked back to the gym remembering her conversation with Vincent from the night before.

"Vince, can I ask you something? I don't want to make a big deal out of it and communicate it to everyone but I know you'll be honest with me. Well, all of you would be but you just take a different approach sometimes. I mean.."

"Clara, just tell me." Vincent looked at her and she calmed down. He was open as a book. Sincere. Calm. "Wait, this isn't about sex, is it? I'm not ready to have this conversation with you if it is. Actually, I don't think I'll ever be ready. You're my sister."

Clara smiled. "No, it isn't about sex."

Vincent relaxed again. "Ok, what is it about then?"

Clara told him about Mr. Brook's assignment. She explained how she had written two different outlines but she wasn't sure which one she would hand in.

Vincent looked at her, smiled and said, "Clara, look at me please." Clara looked up at him. "What are you really afraid of? And I mean really, no bs with me."

She swallowed a lump in her throat and quickly said, "I'm afraid that Mr. Brooks and whoever reads it would think I'm weak. I don't want him to look at me with pity or treat me differently."

Vincent chuckled. "You really have no clue, do you? Even if he did treat you differently I don't think he, or anyone for that matter, would treat you in the way that you think. Clara, do you realize how brave you are? The fact that you are even contemplating writing about what happened to you is a testament of your courage. You were kidnapped. You survived. AND you are here to tell about it. You're strong. And you are damn incredible. He isn't going to walk around on egg shells with you. He is going to be amazed by you. As he should be. Hell, we all are. Stop it with the BS. You want to write about what happened to you, do it. Just write. You love writing, I see it. It helped you. So keep doing it. Maybe writing about it, will be liberating and..I think that is exactly what you need."

"Yeah?"

"Yeah. You know why? Because I think deep down you want to."

Clara looked down at her hands for a second and whispered, "Yeah, I think I do."

After that she had felt much more confident to turn in the version that deep down she had wanted to turn in. They had chatted a few more minutes before heading inside to have dinner with everyone else. They had asked her various questions about school as they did with the others and Laura of course tried to find out about the guys.

It was nice. She felt warm and safe during dinner. More importantly, as she looked around, she felt pride in being a part of this family.

She followed Ms. Lawson and ran inside to grab a quick shower. As she was walking out of the gym, she noticed Sonia leaning up against the wall by the door. "Hey, what are you doing here?"

Sonia rolled her eyes. "I'm waiting for you, what do you think? I knew I would find you here."

They started walking. They had chatted quite a few times this week but to be honest Clara had been busy all week between school, the newspaper, karate and soccer, which was her goal. She had kept to herself quite a bit. The outline was due today and until last night, she was avoiding it like the plague and she may have avoided everyone else in the process.

"Is everything ok?" Clara asked.

"Well you never answered my texts last night so..." Sonia asked.

Clara grimaced. "What texts?"

"The ones I sent you, seriously. Have you even checked your phone? Obviously, you didn't. Listen, I wanted to know if you would come to the soccer game with me tonight. It's away and I don't want to go by myself."

"Um yeah, let me check. You woke up earlier to come wait for me to ask me that?" Clara asked surprisingly.

"Yeah, I know, but I have been fucking bored out of my mind all week so here I am waiting on you. Besides, you were a bit off this week and I guess I just wanted to make sure you were ok and that it wasn't me. I mean, I know we just met and all but I don't know Clara. You've been distracted all week and well..." Sonia seemed nervous.

Clara had stopped walking at this point. "Oh Sonia, don't think that at all. I just had a lot on my mind this week and a lot going on.

But I have to say I'm already better. I spent some time with my family and I think I needed that. I'm ok, seriously."

"Oh, ok. Good. I'm glad you feel better." Suddenly it dawned on Clara that it may have been a tough week for Sonia too. It was her first week.

"Uggh, Sonia. I'm sorry. I suck at this friend thing don't I? It's your first week and instead of banding together I kind of left you to fend for yourself, didn't I?"

It was quiet for a moment until she heard Sonia take a deep breath and then she started to chuckle. "Yeah, well, guess what? You just called yourself a friend, so you're stuck with me now."

She was usually on guard with other girls but Sonia, kind of acted like those walls didn't exist, or rather that she respected them but it wasn't going to stop her.

Clara smiled and responded. "I guess I am, huh. But do you know what you're getting yourself into? I've got a lot of baggage."

"Yeah well so do I, so we are the perfect match, then." Silence followed.

"Are you ok Clara?" Sonia asked her sincerely.

"Yeah, I am. Are you ok, Sonia?" Clara turned the question right back at her.

"Yeah, I am. So, you'll come tonight? There is a party afterwards. Will you come to that too? Alex and Gabe told me about it, but if you're there, then it's bearable," Sonia pleaded.

"Let me check first. And just so you know if you're there then it's bearable too."

"So dinner with your family, huh? I haven't had one of those in a while," Sonia commented.

They chatted a few more minutes on their way to their lockers and their first class. They stopped a moment to talk to Alex. She didn't know Alex very well, but he seemed like a good guy. He just always seemed to be looking at her curiously. While he chatted with his sister, she looked around for Gabe wondering where he was. Although this week had truly been super busy, she realized that she needed to stop being so closed off. She had been in her own world this week. Gabe had tried various times to pick up various conversations with her especially during English but she had been distracted responding more curt than usual. Connor and Rosie had also tried to talk to her at some point and she basically just ran, whenever she could. Found an excuse and ran. She realized she needed to stop running.

As they were about to part ways heading to their different classes, Clara grabbed Sonia by the arm. "You know what? I'll come tonight."

"Yeah?" Sonia shrieked. "Great!"

"Yeah, I have a feeling too many people are going to try to get you to partner up with them in beer pong and I'm not ready to share you just yet," Clara declared.

Sonia pretended to act offended, shaking her head. "Me? Moi? I would never!" She grinned and added, "This is going to be fun! I'll see you at lunch and we can decide on times."

"Deal." Clara smiled.

14

GABE

They had crushed it tonight. 3 to 1. The other team was tough but not as tough as them. He jogged back into the locker room as all the other guys let out a holler. They slapped him on the back. He grinned. Connor looked at him and smirked. It was an amazing game.

"Hey, you coming out tonight?" Bobby said.

"Yeah, I'm coming. I may go grab a bite to eat with my dad, Alex and Sonia but I'll be at the party later."

He had been in a mood all week but tonight it all went away. He loved soccer, truly did and then having his dad there meant a lot. Gabe acted all tough and like he didn't need anyone but the truth was when his dad made time in his busy schedule to come to something like a soccer game, especially an away game, it meant the world. Alex and Sonia were also there. When he had walked out onto the field, he looked at the crowd and saw them sitting there and then he saw those gorgeous green eyes. Clara was sitting right next to Sonia. She had been distant all week, and he had racked his brain wondering if there was something he did or said, but when he came up empty he figured she was going through something. He had barely seen her except for English class where he tried to write her a few notes, but she didn't seem into it until today when she had looked at him and Connor and said hello. Before class ended she had written him a note and tucked it in his notebook. *Good luck tonight.* He'd scored two out of the three goals tonight so he was feeling pretty lucky. He headed out to meet with his family in the parking lot.

"Hi dad."

"Hey, son. Great game, I'm very proud of you. You still ok going out to grab something to eat?" his father asked.

"Yeah, you guys coming too?" as he looked at Alex and Sonia.

"Of course, they are coming.," Ralph objected.

Out of the corner of his eye, he saw someone walking towards them. He turned to the right and there was Clara.

"She's coming too," Sonia said smiling. Alex smirked. *Jerk*, Alex was laughing inside.

Clara looked at Gabe, "Hi." She said softly. She cleared her throat. "Great game. You were pretty awesome out there," she remarked.

"Thanks." Her compliment made him feel 10 feet tall. *What the hell was getting into him?*

She looked around at everyone. "Are you sure it's ok, if I come? I can wait for you guys. It looks like it's a family meal..." she had started blabbering.

Gabe spoke up, "No! I mean, no, of course it's fine. I'm just surprised you're here. That's all. I would. I mean we would love for you to come." *What the hell was wrong with him?*

Gabe's father looked confused a moment but then smiled. "Clara, I'm Ralph. Of course, it's more than ok for you to come. I'm happy to meet one of Sonia's friends. Let's go. I made a reservation. Let's just head out with one car and then I'll take you guys back here. It's not far."

They all piled up in his car and headed to the restaurant. Gabe and his dad chatted about the game in the front seat, with Alex chiming in here and there. Sonia and Clara were discussing something but he couldn't quite focus on both discussions at the same time without his dad noticing. As they got to the restaurant and sat down, Gabe's father pretty much cut to the chase.

"So Clara, I've heard that you are on the soccer team as well. When is your first game?"

As they all turned to her, she blushed a second but then answered. "We already had our first game but I didn't play since I just joined. Our second game is next week. Not sure they will let me play, since I'm relatively new but I'm excited none the less."

"They would be stupid not to let you play. We saw you play that day in gym. You don't mess around," Alex replied.

"Is that the soccer game during gym class that everyone was talking about at Connor's house that night?" Sonia asked. "Not that I doubt you, I just haven't seen you in action yet. To be honest, I can't wait to."

Gabe's father proceeded to order a bunch of appetizers and told everyone to order whatever they wanted as an entree. If Gabe's father noticed that Gabe and Clara were a little awkward towards each other he didn't show it. Conversation flowed pretty smoothly talking about school and soccer. A few people stopped by the table to say hello to Ralph and while he politely said hello, he also made it clear that his time with his family wasn't to be interrupted for too long. At a certain point though Ralph's curiosity got the best of him, "So, Clara. The boys were telling me the other day that you live with your aunt and uncle? What are their names? It's possible that I know them."

Clara froze and looked at the both Alex and Gabe. *Great, his dad just admitted they had been talking about her.* "Yes, I live with them in Belwyn. They are Nina and Frank Salvino." You could tell she waited for the next question like she knew another one was coming, and she may have also known what it was.

"Sounds familiar. What does your uncle do?

"His main thing is that he owns his own construction company. But he also owns a few properties and businesses too," Clara responded.

"Wait, is he S&S Construction?" Gabe's father asked. Gabe has also heard of the big construction company.

"Yes," she replied.

"And your last name is also Salvino." But he didn't ask it like a question, rather as if he was making a statement.

Clara looked at him like she was deciding how she wanted to respond. "Yes, I took their last name when they adopted me a few years ago. My parents died when I was young."

"I'm so sorry," as Alex and Gabe murmured their apologies as well, Sonia grasped her hand and squeezed.

"Thank you, but I know I am very lucky to have them," Clara replied firmly.

"Yes, you are. I work with quite a few children, so I know there are worse circumstances. Where did you go to school before East Cynwood?" Gabe's father asked her.

"I went to Mount Saint Peter's, but I didn't like it there much," Clara answered.

"Well, that gives us something else to compare notes to." Sonia also replied and laughed.

"And before that? Where did you go to middle school? Did you go to public or private?" Ralph was insistent.

Clara looked down and moved both her hands to her lap and Gabe obviously noticed a deep uneasiness in regards to this question. All eyes were on her.

"Um, no I didn't go to a middle school here." Something had obviously happened and he could tell she didn't feel comfortable speaking about it. Although Gabe's father was genuinely interested he also was trying to figure something out. Gabe could tell. So before his dad could ask another question, he looked at Alex and shook his head slightly.

Alex understood immediately and decided to take the bull by the horn and change the subject. "So, uncle Ralph, do you think you have some time to come check out Vilneva University with me and my dad?" Soon Alex and his uncle were involved in a deep discussion about colleges and his future lacrosse career.

Gabe obviously had no idea that Clara had lost her parents. It was something they had in common, to a certain extent. He lost his mom but to lose both? He understood some of it now, her hesitancy, why she seemed on guard. There was probably more to the story but it explained part of it. And hell, if it didn't make her seem even more beautiful, because she was obviously strong. She had caught him staring more than once but he couldn't seem to keep his eyes off of her. There was something about her that intrigued him.

They finished their dinner and Gabe's father took them back to their cars telling them to be careful and not to be late. They exchanged thank you for dinner, Clara especially. "It was a pleasure meeting you, Clara. I'm sure I will see you around soon enough at the house and other games."

Clara looked at him quizzically until Sonia said, "we sleep at uncle Ralph's house a lot. We even have our own rooms. You'll definitely be there at some point."

"Oh, ok. Got it," Clara replied.

All of a sudden, all Gabe could think about was Clara in *his* room. *Fuck. What was happening to him?* He rarely brought other girls to his house but yet now all he could picture was Clara in his home. In the kitchen. Studying with him in the family room. Outside on the deck. And most definitely in his bedroom. *Fuck.* This girl was getting under his skin and he didn't even know her that well. He shook his head and resolved to be a bit stronger.

"What do you guys want to do? Are we heading to the party or did you guys want to do something else?" He would have preferred to hang out with just the three of them. It would give him the chance to get to know Clara better and figure out what it was about her that had him thinking crazy thoughts. But he and Alex had told the others they would be at the party.

"Well, I would love to just chill but you are the captain of the soccer team and you just won a game against a pretty tough team, so we have to at least make an appearance." Alex's thoughts mirrored his own.

"Yeah, let's go, before I change my mind." As Gabe said that he glanced at Clara, and he saw Alex smirk.

They headed to the party and as soon as he walked in, people cheered, pulling him to the side to do a shot. He looked back and Alex had moved closer to the girls to ensure that everyone knew both Clara and Sonia were with them. They didn't know Clara well yet, but she was being a friend to Sonia and although there were times she seemed distanced, she seemed genuine so until further notice, she was with them. He said hello to everyone and took a shot. Right after someone proceeded to hook him up with a beer. After a few minutes he looked over at Alex and the girls, and Bobby quickly took notice. "Want me to see if they want something to drink? I know you won't let just anyone serve the girls."

Gabe laughed, "Sure, thanks Bobby."

Gabe talked a bit with Henry, a senior, an awesome goalie and his co-captain. It was thanks to him that barely anyone made it through to the goal tonight. He glanced at Alex and the girls, Bobby had arrived and slapped Alex on the back. He then hugged Sonia and just as he was going to hug Clara she moved behind Alex and pulled Sonia back to ask her something in her ear. Bobby frowned but then Alex said something to him to make him laugh. He knew that Alex had noticed, because Alex moved to take Clara's spot and stood slightly in front of her. She then said hello to Bobby, but Gabe could tell she wanted to avoid the hug. *Huh. Ok. Was it Bobby? Or something else?* Alex looked at Gabe quizzically. Bobby proceeded to grab them drinks, Gabe chatted a few more minutes with Henry and a few others until Alex and the girls proceeded to go towards him.

"Outside?" Alex asked.

"Yeah, let's go, it's a bit crowded in here."

As soon as they sat down Clara's phone rang. She looked down and answered. When the other person started talking, she looked at Sonia, told her she would be right back and stepped away. After a few minutes she came back, and he heard her say, "Yes. You guys don't have to worry. I'm not going to say that, and you know it. I'll text you when I get home, tell Vince if he wants I can wake him up while he's sleeping." She hung up and sat down next to Sonia.

"Everything ok?" Sonia asked.

"Yep, just my cousins checking in on me," Clara said as she rolled her eyes.

"Wow, there's almost like Alex and Gabe, aren't they?"

"Nah, I think they are worse," Clara responded. Sonia burst out laughing.

A group had formed around all of them. Rosie had arrived and went up to Clara and gave her a hug. They started talking. Behind Rosie were a few other girls, a few looked at Clara and Sonia almost admiringly, others not so much. But he had a feeling Clara and Sonia together would know how to take care of themselves. After a few minutes Connor showed up with a drink and his cell phone in his hand. He said hello to everyone and he looked around until he zoomed in on Clara. He seemed undecided about something, and it concerned Clara.

Gabe couldn't help himself. "What's going on Connor? Something wrong?" He asked it with a bit more bite than he meant to.

Connor looked at him and chuckled. "Sal Capalbo just wanted me to make sure Clara was ok. Undecided if I should tell her or not."

"Oh. Just tell her. She should know that we will watch out for her," Gabe responded.

"We, huh?" Connor laughed again as he went up to the girls, flirting his way around, offering hugs and kisses like he always did. Gabe shook his head but observed intensely when he got to Clara. Connor kind of went in for a hug but then leaned in and whispered something in her ear. At first she stiffened but then she stood up and made her way right behind Connor to where Gabe was standing. She looked at Gabe expectantly.

"Connor said you wanted to speak to me?" *Dipshit.*

"Is that what Connor said?" Connor started laughing and Alex started chuckling along with him. *Glad this is amusing to them.*

"Nah, Clara, I'm just messing with Gabe. I actually wanted to talk to you. Your cousin texted me to make sure you were ok and keep an eye out for you. I told him that we would do it anyway, but I wanted to let you know," Connor concluded running his hand to the nape of his neck. He felt a bit awkward.

Clara rolled her eyes. "Of course, he did. Seriously," She muttered. "I am going to fucking kill them. Sorry about that, but when they get together they feed into each other and well..."

"No need to explain. I can respect it. It's actually cool that he wants us to," Connor replied.

"Yeah, well you don't have to worry about me. Please don't think that now you have to babysit me, or you can't enjoy yourselves or..."

Gabe interrupted her. "Clara, just so you know, Connor, Alex or myself, we wouldn't be looking out for you because your cousins asked us to. We don't take orders from anyone. We're doing it because we want to. You're hanging out with Sonia, we had dinner all together and we are hanging out now. We'll watch out for you because that's what we do."

Clara just stared at him for a moment, and for a split second he saw her tough façade disappear. She cleared her throat. "Ok, well, I don't know what to say to that. Thanks, I guess."

In that moment Sonia appeared, "Is everything ok?"

"Yeah, just my overly protective cousins."

"I'm used to it, remember? I'm going to get a drink. Alex, Connor why don't you come with me?" They walked away leaving Clara and Gabe alone.

"What were you going to say before? When you were talking about them feeding into each other. You were going to say something else, but you stopped." Gabe wanted to know.

Clara looked at him and hesitated. But then surprised him by answering honestly, "oh, well, I usually don't go out that often, at least to parties and with a bunch of friends." And then she started blushing, "not that we're all friends but I mean Sonia and I are at least. You and Alex, well, you're you and everyone I'm sure wants to be considered your friend and just because we hung out tonight doesn't mean that I want you to think that or that I presume we are." She took a deep breath and commented, "I'm really selling myself here, aren't I?"

Gabe laughed. *Damn, she was cute.* "Clara?"

"Yeah?" Clara answered hesitantly.

Gabe smiled, "I'm pretty sure we're friends. Unless you don't want all of us to be?"

"No, I mean yes, of course I want us to be I just don't want you to feel obligated to be a friend just because I am friends with Sonia," she said.

Gabe grinned and replied, "Well, since we are friends, then I should be honest and let you know that we do not feel obligated. Actually, most of Sonia's friends aren't our friends. And to be totally honest, I don't think she considers many people her friend. But for some reason, I don't think you do either."

She nodded.

"So, is that why you don't go out often or is there some other reason?" Maybe she had a boyfriend. Or strict rules. It had to be more than that for her cousins to be worried.

"Let's just say people at my old school were not very nice to me. Or actually most of the girls weren't very nice to me so I didn't really go out unless it was with my cousins."

Gabe tensed sensing there was more to the story but didn't press it. "Got it. Girls are catty, right?"

She smiled. "I guess you could say that."

Right in that moment a bunch of people surrounded Gabe patting him on the back for a job well done at the game. *Right, the game. Totally forgot about it in the last 20 minutes.* Gabe looked apologetically at Clara. Clara smiled, waved and stepped away to join Rosie again. Sonia joined them a minute later. Gabe laughed with his friends, drank a few beers but made sure to look for Clara every so often. He felt good tonight and he knew it wasn't just the game, or getting to hang out with Clara, but it was also because every time he did look for her, it was as if she felt it, and not even a second later, she would look right at him too.

15

CLARA

A few weeks had gone by and Clara was immersed with school work, karate and soccer season. They now had at least one game a week sometimes more. Occasionally she went out on the weekends, but she hadn't been to any recent parties. She had hung out with Sonia a few times with one of those times being with her cousins. Obviously, they welcomed her right in the family. Since then, both Sonia and Clara changed. They both seemed more confident and people sensed it. Sonia often sat with Clara at lunchtime when Clara was in the cafeteria. At her old school the cafeteria was not the nicest place to hang out and even though it was not the same case here she still avoided it out of habit. Since she was often busy after school, she worked on the school paper when she could during lunch.

The girls' soccer team had a few games and Coach had even given her quite a bit of play time. The next game was a home game, so the stands were packed. She was excited that they allowed her to play as much as she did. She didn't disappoint, stealing the ball more than once and scoring a goal. Vincent, Julia, Sal and Sal's younger brother came to the game. Sonia and Alex were there too. The boys soccer team had their own game that night in which they also won. She had to admit that she was a little disappointed that Gabe couldn't be there as well. Well, she could admit it only to herself.

The rough draft to the English essay was due soon. Clara was already done and decided that she may as well hand it in instead of just continuing to rethink it. Vincent was right, she did want to write about what happened to her and it was extraordinarily freeing to do so. She wasn't ready to share it with just anyone but she was confident in sharing it with Mr. Brooks. She trusted that he could not only keep it confidential but that he could assist her in developing her writing skills. In fact, they had found out that Mr. Brooks has written a few books of his own under a pen name, which no one seemed to know, but they figured he was successful since he was always dressed to the nines and drove in with a Porsche every day. A few people at the newspaper questioned why he would continue teaching but It wasn't just about writing, he enjoyed interacting with the students, and motivating them. He wanted to make a difference. That is why so many people respected him and looked up to him.

She put the paper in a folder this morning and brought it with her to class. She sat down in her seat, right next to Gabe. As soon as she sat down, he smiled and handed her a note. She grinned. I guess you could say that was their thing. Almost every day during English they wrote notes to each other.

Hey, we're going to the mall after practice today, did Sonia tell you?

Clara wrote back. *Yeah, she told me. But can't make it.*

He opened the note and was about to write something down but hesitated. He waited a few minutes, listening to Mr. Brooks lecture until he wrote something else down.

Never met a girl that hated shopping.

She shook her head. *I don't hate shopping. I have class tonight.*

Gabe looked over at her with a questioning look. Class? He mouthed. She hesitated but wrote down another note.

Promise you won't laugh.

Never he wrote back.

She hesitated again but then thought, what the hell. *Karate.*

His eyes widened but then he smiled. *Yeah?* She nodded. *I think it's cool.*

They continued writing notes back and forth a few times, making sure to participate in class until he wrote *you seem different today.*

Different how? Clara responded.

Different. You're more carefree.

It was just a note but Clara was a bit taken back by his observation. *Maybe I am. How would you notice that?*

He smiled. He wrote something down but didn't hand the note over. Class was just about finished. Mr. Brooks had asked him a question and Gabe didn't miss a beat and answered right away. Mr. Brooks arched his eyebrow. *Great, he noticed them writing notes.* The bell rang after a few minutes and everyone got up.

Gabe handed Clara the note in her hand. "You coming? I have to rush to my locker."

"No, I have to hand something in to Mr. Brooks first."

"I'll see you later then." Gabe told her.

Clara stepped up to Mr. Brooks desk. "What's up Clara?"

Clara noticed that Sarah was still getting her stuff together. She really didn't want to do this with Sarah here but realized she really didn't have a choice.

"I just wanted to hand this in to you," Clara said handing over the folder.

He looked at her quizzically and took the folder. He opened it and his eyes widened. "Hold on a minute. Sarah, what about you?"

Sarah joined them at the desk. "I just had a few questions about the paper Mr. Brooks." Sarah smiled super sweetly.

"Sure, just give me a minute with Clara and then I can assist you as well," Mr. Brooks replied.

"Sure, Mr. Brooks." And again Sarah was smiling super sweetly at him but she stepped away a few feet.

"Are you sure, Clara? You still have 4 days before it's due."

"I'm sure. I just keep re-reading it and contemplating what I wrote so I figured I should just hand it in," Clara admitted.

"Yeah, sounds like your typical MO," he smiled and added, "Ok, then if you're sure."

Clara glanced at Sarah who looked busy on her cell phone. "I'm sure," she hesitated.

"If I grade it beforehand, we can set up a time to chat about it, ok?" Mr. Brooks reassured her.

She let go of the breath she was holding, nodded and walked away. She glanced once behind her back and noticed Sarah approaching the desk.

When Clara got to her next class she opened the note Gabe had given her. *I notice a lot of things about you.* She felt a slight flutter in her stomach and smiled. She couldn't ignore how his words affected her. She realized he paid her attention but was convinced that once her newness wore off, he would change his mind. It seemed as though every time they locked eyes, he looked straight through to her and no one had been able to do that until now. It scared her but excited her too. She decided to go to the cafeteria for lunch and not the newspaper room. When she got there, Sonia was sitting with Alex and

Gabe today. As soon as she saw Clara she waved and motioned her to come over.

As she was walking to their table, a senior who contributed to the sports section of the newspaper stopped her to chat and asked if she could look over a piece he was writing. He asked for her number so they could set something up, but she told him they would meet a few minutes before their meeting tomorrow. If he felt rejected he definitely didn't show it, taking it in stride. He stuck around a few more minutes to chat, cracked a joke, getting her to laugh and said, "I'll see you tomorrow then." He put his hand and squeezed her shoulder as he left.

As soon as he left she literally took a few steps when, Lucas, a guy from her Science class approached her and asked, "Hey Clara, got a minute?"

"Um, sure. I guess," Clara responded.

Lucas seemed relatively nice, maybe just a little cocky at times. He was on the soccer team and relatively popular, he was also cute with his dark blond hair and blue eyes. The girls spoke about him often. He always asked Clara a bunch of questions. As he spoke, Clara glanced up and noticed Sonia looking at her and then starting to chuckle. Glad to see Sonia found this amusing for some reason. All of a sudden, she felt as though everyone was looking at her and so she could feel her face flush. She looked up at Lucas and tilted her head to the side waiting to see what he would say. She bit her lip out of habit, Lucas smiled.

"So first I was wondering if you knew what you were going to do with your Science project? Mr. Becker is kind of weird isn't he?"

Clara smiled, "Um yes, I guess you could say that. But no, not sure what I am doing yet."

"My sister said his tests are kind of tough too." This was a weird conversation for some reason.

Clara answered, "Yeah, he seems like the type to give difficult tests." Clara inwardly groaned. *Where was he going with this?*

"I was thinking of setting up a study group for his midterm. What do you think?" he asked.

"Sure, I guess." She had a feeling this conversation was going to take a turn.

"And, I was also wondering…" Just as Lucas was going to say something else, Connor, arrived at her side, his arm around her shoulder.

Her heart automatically sped up, like when most people touched her, but this was Connor and she was used to him. *Breathe.* "Lucas, my man. What is going on? Oh, was I interrupting something?"

"Well, kind of," Lucas bit out.

"Well, I have to steal Clara for something important and then maybe you can catch up with her later, huh?" Connor smirked.

"Actually, I needed…" Lucas stepped forward, a bit annoyed that Connor had interrupted their discussion.

"Cool, Clara come with me." Totally ignoring Lucas' attempt to continue speaking to Clara, Connor put both of his hands on her shoulders to steer her towards their table. He leaned in to her ear, "You are very popular today, C. You got all these guys in a fuss. I didn't want to see an explosion take place."

Clara stopped walking, looked up at him and chuckled. "What are you talking about Connor?"

Connor shook his head, "Seriously, you have no clue do you?" He was now standing in front of her, he put both hands back on her shoulders and winked at her and said, "Alright, don't say I didn't warn you. Come on, let's go."

They approached the table and Clara noticed that Connor suddenly tensed up. Gabe was staring right at him and the hands on Clara's shoulders and then he shifted his gaze right on Clara. His jaw ticked and Clara noticed it instantly. Was he upset because of Connor? She didn't think so because he totally came over to save her from Lucas. Plus Connor was in his inner circle. Not that she needed saving but she didn't have a good feeling. But that was nothing compared to Gabe's penetrating gaze on her right now. Now she felt observed. For some reason she didn't feel comfortable sitting down but she did anyway right across from Sonia.

Sonia smiled and glanced to the side. "It was taking you a long time to get to this table. Lunch is almost over, Clara."

"Yeah, maybe you should start having them make appointments," said one of the guys at the table. Quite a few chuckled. Clara wasn't sure if the guy was just making a stupid comment or meant to insult her but she was pretty sure of the latter. She looked over at Sonia who seemed to have a similar look on her face. Clara didn't answer. Alex was opening his mouth to say something to the guy, but Gabe beat him to it.

"Sorry, if sitting here interrupts your flirting sessions," Gabe started, "Maybe you should start your own table and you can have a ticket system or you can set up appointment times, that way you can be better organized. But don't count on Sonia sitting there with your group of boytoys."

Clara's head shot up and looked at Gabe. Everyone at the table became quiet. Had he really just said that? It wasn't just what he said it was how he said it, with a carefree yet smug attitude. This was a side of him that she knew existed, others had spoken about it but she had yet to see it. It was the façade he sometimes showed the world. She could feel tears spring to her eyes. But she was not going to cry in front of the entire cafeteria. She had no idea what she did to get him to say this to her, but she sure as hell didn't deserve it so she responded, "I'm used to dealing with assholes Gabe, I just didn't realize you were one of them."

Tables were quiet, quite a few girls gasped from the surrounding tables, no one talked to Gabe like that. Regret flashed for one second in Gabe's eyes. The people around them waited a beat to see what Gabe would respond but before he could, Clara stood up, grabbed her bag and left.

16

GABE

"**W**hat the hell was that?" Sonia hissed. Alex looked at her and shook his head. "Don't, Alex. That was out of line. I'm going make sure she's ok." She shook her head and got up, took her tray and headed in the direction in which Clara just left.

Gabe watched Sonia rush out behind Clara. He lounged back in his seat and pushed his food tray away. He had lost his appetite. She had not only called him out on his bullshit but called him an asshole in front of the entire cafeteria. Everyone was waiting. They wanted to see what he would do. They wanted fireworks. But he wouldn't react in front of them. He was going to say something but Alex beat him to it. "Show's over, folks. Keep eating, you've only got 10 minutes left so move on."

He looked over at Alex and noticed Connor with a confused look on his face, questioning him. Gabe sighed. *Shit.* He didn't know what came over him. Seeing all those guys trying to flirt with her made him see red. From where he was sitting she didn't seem to mind it either. With Lucas she seemed like she was even flirting back, tilting her head and biting her lip. She even fucking blushed. Then he saw Connor's hands on her, it was the tip of the iceberg. Connor who flirts with everyone and she didn't even step away. He thought she was different but maybe she wasn't. *Stop and think for a second.* Deep down he knew that wasn't true. She wasn't like that. His gut clenched, he couldn't get the look in her eyes out of his head.

Alex nudged Connor. "Dude, are you coming to the mall with us?"

Connor quickly caught on, "Nah, I have to do something with my sister today. Maybe we can hang later."

They started talking about a bunch of other things and soon the other guys at the table caught on and continued talking and cracking jokes for a few more minutes. Gabe contributed very little to the conversation, his jaw ticking. He noticed quite a few faces kept glancing in his direction, including Connor. Soon the bell rang signaling that lunch was over. Alex went to Gabe distancing them from the majority of the crowd, but Gabe shook his head. "Not now, man."

"Ok, but I have to say I'm kind of with Sonia on this one. You sure?" Alex asked Gabe.

Connor noticed them talking and walked by, not stopping like he usually would have done. Gabe would see him later at soccer practice. He sighed. He needed to get his head on straight. He walked away from Alex and continued with the rest of his classes. Toward the end of the day, he was walking down the hall and he saw Clara walking down the hall from the opposite end. Their eyes locked, as they always did, but there was tension. Hurt flashed in her eyes for a second, but then she locked her jaw, tilted her chin slightly up and a wall slid over her face. *Damn it, if that look didn't turn him on too. She was strong and was showing him she wouldn't stand for his bullshit.* Neither of them slowed down but they kept staring at each other both turning slightly to get a good look at the other. When he turned his head to continue looking forward he noticed Jamie and Kristin taking note of the entire exchange. He proceeded to the remainder of his classes but was quiet for the rest of the afternoon.

School ended, and he headed to practice. As usual all the guys were joking around but when he walked in they could sense the mood he was in and toned it down and it actually became pretty quiet.

Connor sat down on the bench near him, "Hey." But he didn't say much else.

Coach came into the room, "Come on, let's get out there. Hustle ladies, hustle." All the guys started to head out, Gabe and Connor bringing up the rear. The silence between them was uncomfortable. Gabe felt more than once that he should start to say something but nothing would come out.

"I sure hope that you weren't referring to me as one of those boytoys," Connor said quietly.

Gabe swung his head towards him and sighed. He stopped walking and put his hands on his hips, "Con.."

But Connor interrupted him. "Let me say something first." Connor stopped walking and faced him. "I'm not one of Clara's boy-toys and I sure as hell would hope you would know that by now. I went to help her from an awkward situation. You have to realize that Clara is not like what you insinuated, and I'm pretty sure you do, I think that is one of the reasons you like her. But, dude, I've never seen you like that with a chick that didn't deserve it. Sonia's right. It was out of line. She's new and she's gorgeous." Connor held up his hand seeing that Gabe was going to open his mouth, "let me finish. On top of all of that, she's kind and isn't like most of the other girls. Did you think guys wouldn't notice? So, you either get used to, grit your teeth and stop acting like an ass or you claim her, so everyone knows not to mess with her."

Connor looked at him expectantly. "Connor, I'm sorry, man. I just. I don't know. I'm trying to be careful with her and you know me I'm usually not like that. I couldn't give two shits. But, I saw red. Here I am going slow and then there she was just ...."

"Just what? Having a conversation with 2 other guys? Then walking away with me who went to go save her from Lucas? Yeah, they were probably trying to hit on her but I'm pretty sure she was just talking. That's it. I don't know what you think you saw, but that is what happened."

Gabe grabbed his hair and groaned, "Fuck." Connor laughed. Gabe apologized to Connor, "I'm sorry man."

But Connor answered, "Gabe, I think you should be saying I'm sorry to her." Gabe nodded.

"What are you guys doing down there? Stop the chit chat and get the hell up here to practice." Coach yelled. They both headed to the field, grabbing different colored jerseys. Connor looked over and grabbed Gabe's jersey and gave him the one he had. Gabe looked at him.

"Figured you'd want to get some of that pent up frustration out on the field," nodded towards Lucas who now had Gabe's opposing team's jersey. Connor smirked and remarked, "this should be fun." Gabe laughed. And it was fun.

17

CLARA

Clara arrived at karate just in time to get changed and take class. She made sure to stretch a bit more than usual. She was extremely tense after the incident with Gabe. When she walked out of the cafeteria, Sonia had come after her. To be honest, she was surprised that Sonia followed her, considering Gabe was her cousin. Pretty much whatever Gabe and Alex said was law, especially in their grade. Even most of the senior class respected those two. But like a true friend she came after her, wanting to make sure she was ok. She also tried to apologize for Gabe but Clara told her that wasn't for her to do. She was used to guys being assholes so it wasn't anything new to her. She just didn't expect it from Gabe but it was what it was. To make it worse, everywhere she went people eyed her, waiting for something to happen, some whispered as soon as she approached or left any of her classes.

Jamie made sure to make a few hurtful comments in the locker room. "Guess someone is already on her way out," as she pushed up against Clara. Coach Lawson had walked in at that moment yelling at everyone to get on the field.

Jamie then goaded her on the field, so Clara looked at her and responded, "Why don't you show me what you've got on the field today?" Clara used all her hurt and anger and channeled it in practice today. Both Coach Lawson and Coach Rossi complimented her on her playing today, which angered Jamie even more. Moira had rolled her eyes at Jamie, while a few others chuckled and then patted Clara on the back for a job well done.

But now here she was in karate. She didn't know what to do about what had happened, but she knew that right now she didn't want to think about it. 10 minutes before the end of class, she felt him. She looked at her reflection in the mirror and sure enough Gabe had just walked into the studio. He looked at her and went to sit down in the back row. She continued with her practice but could feel his eyes on her the entire time. Her heart was going a mile a minute. She didn't know what to think so she continued as if he wasn't there. Sensei noticed the initial tension so when class was finished, he went to Clara to ensure everything was ok.

"Clara, is everything alright? Who's the guy?" Sensei Colin observed.

"A friend from school," she responded.

"A friend, huh? Are you sure because you seem a little nervous. Want me to scare him off?" he asked her.

She smiled. "No, he..he's fine. We just have to talk about something."

"Ok, I'm sticking around a few extra minutes just in case. Or you can just use one of your moves and show him who's boss," he said as he reached out and squeezed her shoulder.

Clara put a few things away, took a deep breath and walked off the mat, making sure to bow before stepping off. Gabe stood up. Clara put on her shoes but she didn't want to talk to Gabe right here in the studio. She started walking towards the exit into the hallway and then stopped to look at him. He let out a breath as though he had been holding it, nodded and then followed her out. They walked a little down the hall, until she turned around and dropped her duffle bag on the floor. She hadn't even bothered to get changed. She looked up at him. He was so handsome with his wavy hair, his chiseled jaw, with those killer lips. But his eyes, they were stunning, he let down his wall, plain for her to see.

"Clara, I'm sorry. I.." he stopped for a second looking for the right words. "I'm sorry Clara. I really am. I didn't mean what I said at all."

She looked at him with her arms crossed over her chest. Clara was honestly surprised that he apologized so quickly and suddenly all the hurt and anger just faded. She nodded, dropped her hands and said, "I just..I just don't understand what I did for you to say that and I'm not like the girl you insinuated. At all." She quietly yet firmly replied.

He answered frantically, "I know you're not. At all." He stopped and hesitated before admitting, "I guess I was jealous."

She looked at him with confusion on her face. "Jealous of Aaron and Lucas?" she asked incredulously. She didn't understand why he would be jealous but the fact that he came all this way to apologize, meant a lot to her.

He said remorsefully running his hand through his hair, "I know, not my proudest moment for sure. I shouldn't have acted like that."

He shook his head as though he was looking for words to say, while she nodded and then moved a step closer. His eyes widened and he ran his hand through his hair but then took a step closer as well. She moved closer to him and put her hands on his chest. It was as though her body was moving of its own accord. She leaned her forehead on his chest, and all her tension eased, her shoulders relaxed. He had been holding his breath but as soon as she touched him, he let it out and slowly wound his arms around her while she did the same. They stood like that a few minutes. She moved back just a little to be able to look at him, "I'm sorry I called you an asshole."

"No, don't be sorry for that. I'm pretty sure I deserved that, but you, you didn't deserve what I said. Any of it. So, I'm the one who should be sorry. And I am."

She nodded and was about to step out of the embrace, when all of a sudden, he pulled her back to his chest. "Is this ok?" She didn't really answer but just hugged him back. This was unusual for her, she didn't allow many people to hold her but with him it seemed like the most natural thing in the world. The fact that he asked demonstrated that he in fact noticed quite a few things about her. She remembered her note from earlier today and smiled.

18

GABE

As Gabe held her close, he felt the tension from the day just drain from him. He also realized that being this close to Clara right now, he had a bit of difficulty breathing. He kept letting out his breath like he needed to catch it. The fact that she allowed him to hug her, to hold her, he knew was important. He didn't know why but he knew that sooner or later he would find out.

He held her another moment but then pulled away, "Want to grab some pizza? Or something else to eat? I'm presuming you didn't eat but if you did we could, I don't know, do something else? Coffee, maybe?"

She smiled. "I didn't eat yet, no. I'll have to let my family know. But weren't you going to the mall?"

"Yeah, I decided not to go. I came to see you instead."

Her face flushed. "Well, let me call my aunt and get changed really quickly."

"Ok, I'll wait here, or better yet, I'll wait inside."

She pulled away and nodded, and picked up her duffle bag, taking out her phone and walked inside headed towards the girls' changing room. He sat down and texted Alex letting him know he wouldn't be meeting up with them.

Did you apologize?

Gabe texted back. *Yes.*

Alex was quick to respond. *Good.*

Gabe shook his head settling in a bit more comfortably in the chair, but he didn't need to. 5 mins later, Clara walked out. He swore she lit up the whole studio as she did. Quite a few turned to look at her. Her cheeks were a little flushed, adding to her beauty. He stood up, reached for her duffle bag and they headed out.

"I had just settled in, thinking for sure, you would take at least 20 minutes. Never saw a girl get ready in less than 10."

She smiled at him and it was like a fucking sucker punch. "Well, this is what you get tonight, plus I'm a little hungry," she responded all sassy. He opened the door to head outside and put his hand on the small of her back.

"So, we can walk to the pizza place right up ahead or we can go to a different place, if you don't like that one."

"Let's go there, the pizza is actually pretty good." They headed there and sat down at a booth in the back corner and ordered rather quickly.

"So, how long have you been doing karate?" Gabe asked her. And that is how their conversation began. The talked about her karate, and his soccer. His father and her aunt and uncle. He was a sponge, soaking up every word she said. They talked about school in general and their classes until they got to the subject of the paper for creative writing.

"I'm surprised that you are taking that class."

"What, creative writing?" Gabe shrugged. "I like Mr. Brooks, he has passion which most of the teachers lack. I knew about this paper and that it would be hard but, I don't know, I figured why not. He's cool and I don't dislike writing as long as I don't have to share it with everyone." Clara nodded. "You obviously love to write since you joined the newspaper, is that why you're taking the class?"

"Yeah, I had heard about him too. I didn't know about this paper though," Clara responded.

Gabe replied, "He makes a lot of students rewrite the paper over and over again trying to get them to be as honest as they can. Some think he doesn't see through all the BS but he does. Did you think it was difficult to write?" What a question. Clara looked down at her hands. Whatever she had written about made her nervous.

She looked up, "Actually, I thought it would be but once I started, it just poured out on paper."

Gabe smiled, "Yeah, for me it was difficult considering it was about losing my mom."

Clara reached over and squeezed his hand, "That must have been hard. I'm sorry about your mom, Gabe."

Just as she was about to pull her hand away, he turned his hand and pulled hers back and held on to it, not letting it go, "thanks," he said in a hoarse voice. She looked down. "Clara, would you look at me?" and she did. "I'm not going to ask you what you wrote about. Believe me, I want to but I can tell it's hard for you. But when you're ready, I'll be here to listen."

"Thank you," she whispered, holding on a little tighter to his hand. Gabe changed the subject without a hitch and without even realizing it, another bit of time had passed, it was already late. Clara had received a text asking if she was ok.

"They're protective of you, aren't they?" he asked Clara.

"Yeah, they are," Carla said.

"Good, they should be." She looked at him and smiled. He shrugged, "I get it, you're their niece. I'd be protective of you too.

Let's go, don't want to get on their bad side and keep you out too late. Did you drive? If not I can drive you home."

"Yeah, I drove," Clara responded.

"I'll walk you to your car then."

They walked out of the pizza place and headed towards her car. Gabe wanted to grab her hand but wasn't sure. He had never been so hesitant before. They had finally gotten to her car and she turned around. Damn, she was beautiful. The way the streetlight illuminated her face, it literally took his breath away. He rubbed at his chest and cleared his throat.

"Thanks for the pizza," he said.

She laughed. "I'm pretty sure that should be my line, so thank you."

He lifted his hand and moved a strand of hair behind her ear and then moved his hand down along her arm and grabbed her hand gently. She shivered. And hell if that didn't make him happy. He looked down at her. He wanted nothing more than to kiss her but he knew he had to move slower with her compared to other girls. It also wasn't the time, not in the parking of a shopping center.

"Well, thank you for letting me bring you to get pizza then. I wasn't sure you would talk to me." But she had. She was forgiving and good. He continued, "We didn't talk a lot about today but I feel like I need to say again that I am sorry. I didn't mean those things that I said," he stated.

"Thanks for coming here to apologize. How did you know what karate studio I was at anyway?"

"I kind of narrowed it down. But then asked Sonia to help me. Not sure how she found out but she did." He sighed and pulled her to him and held her. She wound her arms around him. He smiled, this felt right. After a minute or so, he pulled away, held on to her hand, and opened her car door and let her in.

"I'll see you at school tomorrow."

He watched her until she pulled out of the parking lot and then he headed to his car. Everything felt right again.

19

CLARA

When she got home, her aunt and uncle were up, totally trying not to seem like they were waiting for her but she could tell they were. Hell, they were all up except Laura who was away at college for the week. As soon as she walked in, Julia looked relieved, ran up to hug her and headed to bed. Clara had felt that hug was more than a hug good night. She then went to her aunt and gave her a hug.

"Hi."

"Hi, honey. You ok? You seemed rushed when you came home from school and like you were in a bad mood. But you seem ok, now. Karate helped?"

Clara had sat down. "Yeah, I guess you could say that."

At that point, Vince walked into the room, saw her and said, "You good, Clar?"

"Yeah, I'm good," she smiled.

Vince and she had then started talking about school and a few other things and her aunt chimed in here and there. At a certain point he nodded and got up to go to bed. She had then decided that she too should go to bed. When she went to hug her aunt good night, her aunt Nina held on to her an extra second.

"I'm glad you're getting out more. Just be careful ok? And don't overdo it. You do so much, soccer, karate, the newspaper. You should have fun, more fun."

"Hey now, not too much fun," her uncle Frank replied. Both of them laughed.

"I know, I'm trying and I am. And yes, uncle Frank I won't have too much fun, don't worry." Her aunt winked.

When she went upstairs, she didn't head to bed immediately but went to Julia's room instead. Julia still wasn't sleeping so she went inside.

"Hey, Jules, you ok?" Clara just wanted to make sure.

"Yeah, I'm ok. Why?"

"I don't know, that hug downstairs just seemed different."

Julia hesitated, "I was just..."

Clara raised her eyebrow, "You were..." and motioned with her hand to continue.

"I was just, I don't know, worried. I know you have gone out a few times and now that I met Sonia when you say you are with her I am ok. But tonight when all of a sudden you didn't come home and changed plans. I just got worried. I don't know. Just don't go any-where by yourself, ok?"

Then it dawned on Clara, Julia was worried someone would take her again. She went to sit down next to where she was laying down on the bed. "Jules, look. I know you aren't used to me going out but I promise you, I'll be careful. I do karate so I know how to protect myself and I take more precautions. I assure you that I am always careful, ok?" Julia nodded, a little teary eyed but she looked relieved at the same time. They hugged and just like her aunt down-stairs, Julia held on to her an extra second.

"Hey, how about we go to the movies this weekend. Just you and me. Whatever you want, ok?" Clara said.

Julia nodded. "Thanks."

"I love you little sis. Make sure you dream happy dreams, k?"

Julia smiled, "love you too. Good night."

Clara had then gone to bed, thinking about her family. Although she was considerate, she sometimes forgot that her kidnapping had effects on them too. It took her a while to fall asleep, her thoughts drifted between her conversation with Julia and her night with Gabe.

The next morning she was thankful that she didn't have soccer practice because she pressed snooze twice. She usually got to school about 10 or 15 minutes earlier. Obviously most people didn't forget what happened yesterday. As soon as they saw her, a few looked around, others whispered.

She headed to her locker and to her surprise Gabe was leaning up right next to it. The hallway was a bit quieter all of a sudden.

"Hey, what are you doing here?" Clara asked him.

"I thought that was obvious, I'm waiting for you."

"Oh," she could feel herself blushing but what could she say to that? She became tongue tied all of a sudden. Gabe looked at her and smirked. He knew the effect he was having on her, she shook her head and looked around in the process.

"So it seems everyone is waiting for you to chew me out or for us to make up or something. Are they always like this?" Clara asked him.

She could feel many eyes on her and she had no idea what to do. Gabe looked around, narrowed his eyes at a group who then rushed by after seeing that he wasn't pleased that they were staring. "I don't know. I never had someone call me an asshole before in front of the cafeteria. But I also never cared if they did so...does it bother you? They're just trying to figure out what happened after yesterday since now we're talking."

She nodded and pulled her books from her locker.

"Hey," he said quietly. She looked over. "Want to slap me in front of everyone and I'll beg for forgiveness?"

She laughed. "NO!"

"Then, don't worry about them. They'll get over it. They are just dying to know what happened. This is about us and we're good, right?" He almost seemed like he was worried they weren't.

"Yeah, we're good," she closed her locker shut and turned to go towards her first class. He stepped up right beside her and they walked down the hallway together.

"What's your first class?"

"Ugh,Math."

Gabe laughed. "Nice way to wake up, huh?" Clara looked at him and rolled her eyes. "Did your aunt or uncle say anything last night? You didn't get in trouble, did you?"

She shook her head. "No, they totally were waiting for me but I think they were just surprised. I don't go out often."

"Yeah, you've said that before. One day you'll tell me that story too. But I'm glad, that they were ok, that is."

Connor was heading towards them and stopped to talk. He and Gabe were speaking about their soccer game and Clara had stepped a bit to the side to say hello to Rosie who had walked by. Right at that moment, Bruno was heading down the hallway and joking around with a few other guys. They were tossing a football around but the other guy totally threw the football a bit harder and Bruno had to step out to catch it and rammed into Clara. Clara almost fell over, until she felt two hands grab her, steady her and gently move her out of the way.

"Hey! Watch where you're going," Gabe said, gritting his teeth as he realized it was Bruno that had ran into her.

Bruno laughed and then smirked at Gabe, "Chill out man, just having some fun. Didn't mean to hurt anyone," until his gaze settled on Clara. "Although we got to stop running into each other like this. Obviously that body wants to run into mine." Clara glared at him.

Gabe clenched his fists and took a step closer to Bruno shielding Clara a bit while Connor stepped to the other side of Clara, slightly in front of her in a protective stance. Clara could feel the tension in the air and it seemed that Bruno was about to say something else when Leo stepped up to the group, shielding Clara totally and diffusing the entire situation by punching Bruno playfully.

"Bruno, stop causing havoc, will you? I have to ask you something," and pulled Bruno by the arm away from the entire situation. Bruno smiled but before he turned to look straight ahead, he winked at Clara and made sure to smirk at Gabe. The bell rang signaling the beginning of classes. The entire exchange took only a minute or so that only those close by had realized what had happened. Henry had been walking by and looked at Gabe shaking his head.

Gabe turned toward Clara, "Hey, you ok?" he asked softly.

"Yeah, I'm fine. Thanks for catching me. Totally did not see him."

"Let me walk you to class."

"No, no. it's ok. Then you'll be late."

"Are you sure you're ok?"

"Yeah, there's just something about him. He gives me the creeps."

Gabe grimaced, "That's because he is a creep." Clara swallowed and nodded nervously. "Clara?"

"Hmmm?"

"Hey, if he ever bothers you or steps out of line towards you, you'll tell me right?"

She looked at him. "What? What are you talking about?" she laughed nervously. "I have to go to class or else I'll be late. I'll see you later."

She had to get away to breathe for a second. There was something about Bruno that occasionally reminded her of old memories and she didn't want to think about that time. As she walked away she didn't notice Sarah observing what had happened with a keen interest before walking into her class.

20
GABE

Gabe stared quizzically at Clara as she walked down the hallway. *What the hell just happened?* Something happened to justify her reaction. He had to get to class now but he would find out about it later. This girl managed to send him in a tailspin. But something was wrong with her. He headed to his first class, Chemistry, but he couldn't concentrate on much. He kept thinking about her. And Bruno. He didn't know why he felt that the guy was sooner or later going to do something reckless or out of line. It was like he was waiting for it. Leo seemed to have distanced himself from Bruno and totally saved the situation today.

Henry sat next to him in his second class. As soon as he saw Gabe he shook his head. "I don't know why, but I have a feeling that sooner or later, I'm going to have to have your back with a certain douche. Prick rubs me the wrong way. I can't believe he is on the football team."

That was the thing with Henry, he didn't talk much but his observations were usually spot on. And because of that when he spoke everyone listened.

"I know, man, I know. I feel it too."

"Not sure what is going on with you and Clara, but she's in his line of sight. Watch out."

The teacher came in at that point and they turned toward the front of the classroom. His classes dragged until finally he headed to English. He felt this need to make sure Clara was ok. Heading to his seat, he sat down and waited for Clara. She usually arrived at the last minute, which she did today as well. She was a little tense but seemed a bit better.

You ok? He wrote in a note to her.

Yes. He kind of expected her to be short but he had hoped that he had gained some ground with her and he wasn't one to quit.

You sure? Please don't BS me, because you weren't fine before. He handed the note over and she sighed and wrote back.

I know, I'm sorry I freaked. I feel stupid now. He read it and shook his head.

You're not stupid. I just want to understand. She read it and went to write something but kept hesitating. He grabbed the note again, paid attention a few minutes to what Mr. Brooks was saying and wrote down something else.

I'm here, Clara. She read it, looked at him and nodded.

Bruno reminded me of someone from my past.

He stared at it finally feeling like he was getting somewhere. Being careful he wrote back.

Someone not good? She looked at him and nodded.

I'm not going to ask you to tell me about it yet. But one day I will.

She took a deep breath and mouthed *Ok. Ok,* he nodded and mouthed back. He wrote down another note but kept it close. They paid attention to the rest of class, fortunate to stop when they did as Mr. Brooks called on both of them. 5 minutes prior to class being over Mr. Brooks asked for all their first draft papers to be handed in, he walked around the room collecting them. When he got to Clara's desk he instead placed her paper down, He had already read it and graded it. Right there in the top right hand corner was a big fat A.

"Clara, I wrote down a few things in the margins for your next draft but it was excellently written. Great job."

Clara's cheeks flushed, "Thanks Mr. Brooks," she murmured.

Gabe got closer to her and whispered in her ear, "I don't think anyone gets an A on the first draft. That's incredible."

She looked at him and said quietly, "Thanks." She was beaming, she grabbed her paper and put it in her backpack. Right at that moment the bell rang. They all got up and headed towards the door.

Connor reached them both, "Was that what I think it was? Did you hand in your paper early?"

"Yeah, I did."

He grunted, "Want to help me pretty please with a cherry on top?"

Clara laughed. "I'm not kidding, I hate writing," Connor added.

Gabe looked at him, "Dude, it's a writing class. If you hate writing why are you in there?"

"Not sure, figured it would be better than reading Shakespeare."

Clara chuckled again and Gabe grinned, patting Connor on the shoulder, "Get used to it. We technically just started so there's much more writing to cover. I got to go to my locker and get to class. Clara, see you at lunch?"

"Yeah, I have to go to the newspaper room at some point but I may just go after practice instead or during study hall."

"Ok," he then took her hand and pulled her a little to the side as if he was moving her out of the way but instead stuck a note in her hand.

She quickly caught on and tightened her hold on the note and grinned, "See you later guys."

"Bye, Clara." They both responded.

Gabe went to run to his locker and Connor shook his head. "Dude, I feel the need to repeat myself."

"About what?" Gabe asked.

Connor grabbed his shoulder, leaned in and said, "Stop pussy footing around and claim her." He shook his head, walked a few steps backward and pointed at Gabe. Gabe grabbed the back of his neck and grimaced. He was totally pussy footing around.

21
CLARA

Clara felt like between yesterday and today she was totally out of it. Mr. Brooks had reached out to her with an extra newspaper assignment. He said if she could write her paper so well, she should do some more interesting things. She was excited about it but it cut her lunch short and so she was rushing after that and because of rushing around, she had misplaced her paper from his class momentarily. She found it this morning in the newspaper room but she could have sworn she didn't bring it with her during lunch or when she went back in the afternoon. She was probably wrong. Also, yesterday, during soccer practice the coach wanted her to try a new play with Jamie. Clara expected Jamie to throw a hissy fit but instead she didn't complain and didn't even give her haughty looks.

She just said, "Ok, coach," looked at Clara and continued, "let's do this."

Moira, looked at Jamie suspiciously as well as Amelia and both of them said, "Really?"

"Yeah, why not? Let's go."

The play had been awesome, they had to practice it a bit more but if it worked then it would be a great way to score a goal. Clara had felt in the twilight zone. Not that she was complaining but the entire day had been very weird. Today, as she walked down the hall to lunch she felt everyone was looking at her, more than usual.

As she opened the door to the cafeteria and walked in, every table one by one started whispering and looking in her direction. It would be amusing how each person stopped, became silent, and then started whispering. But this was about her. Her heart started beating frantically. They knew. She felt it. She stopped, thinking over what to do when out of nowhere her backpack was lifted from her shoulder. She gasped and looked to her right.

"Come on, let's go." Gabe lifted her back pack and carried it with him. "Do you have your lunch or are you buying?"

"Wait, wh..wh..what?"

"Did you bring your lunch or do you need to buy something? And keep walking." He said the last part quietly and looked at her. When she looked at him, his eyes were telling her to trust him.

"Um, I didn't bring anything today so I should..I guess I should buy something." Alex was right behind them and Connor peeked out behind him smiling and winking. They headed forward and grabbed some food. Her stomach was in knots of course so she didn't really want to eat anything but she went through the motions. When they went to pay she put her hand in her pocket but Gabe stopped her. His hand on top of hers sent a zing through her. *Did he feel this too?*

"I've got this. Let's go sit down." He had both backpacks on his shoulder and grabbed both trays and handed one to her as they walked towards his table. She looked over and saw Rosie who looked concerned and in fact, Rosie went to stand up to go towards Clara but Clara shook her head slightly. "Later" she mouthed. Rosie nodded and sat back down.

They got to the table and Sonia was already there, she smiled a stiff smile, "Hey, guys!"

Clara sat down right in front of her, with Gabe to her right and Alex to her left. Clara understood then, that they were stating the fact that she was under their protection. Sonia reached out and squeezed her hand, and a moment later Gabe put his hand on the small of her back and leaned close to her ear.

"Breathe, Clara. And laugh like none of this is affecting you. Act like you have no idea what is going on, Ok?" she nodded. As he pulled his hand away and put it on the table she grasped it for a brief moment, tightly and then let go. "I've got you."

If he only knew how those words affected her. She looked at Sonia and leaned in as if telling a story with a smile on her face. Sonia looked at her straight in the eye, nodded and then laughed.

Connor was sitting right next to Sonia and in front of Gabe shaking his head, "Damn, Clara, you've got this school in an upheaval. Damn best spectacle I've seen in a while." She looked at him. He wasn't saying it with malice, he was just truly amused.

Alex answered, "They don't know what to do with themselves now that she sat right here smack in the middle of Gabe and myself." Connor smirked. Sonia chuckled. Alex lowered his voice and said to her, "We have your back but you've got some explaining to do later on. And I'm not letting you off easy."

Clara let out a breath and responded, "I know." She looked at Alex and for a split second, she understood him better. Alex, more than the others didn't trust easily and not telling him anything about her past, well that didn't sit well with him. She understood it but that shit went both ways since she didn't trust easily either. He was concerned for her but he was more worried about Gabe and Sonia. She respected that. He nodded, took a deep breath and seemed to relax a bit.

Gabe nudged her at that moment. "Eat. Do you ever eat?"

"Of course, I do. I just snack a lot," Clara responded.

"Well, you don't eat enough," Gabe answered back.

"You sound like my aunt," as she rolled her eyes.

"Smart woman. Pretty sure I should meet her someday," he said teasingly and he arched an eyebrow. It was almost phrased as a question, like he wasn't certain she wanted him to. For an instant she realized that once again although he was her hero in this moment, acting all tough he also had a vulnerability about him. For a moment she saw through all the BS and everything he showed the world. She saw him.

"Maybe, if you play your cards right," she teased. He opened his mouth as if he was going to reply but then thought better about it, shook his head and grinned.

They all acted as if nothing happened for the remainder of lunch. A few minutes before the bell rang, Alex got up and went in between Clara and Gabe leaning down over them and said, "All of you, meet me outside before going to your next class." Slowly they all filed outside and followed him around a corner where he stated, "I don't think Clara should go to practice. I already know Gabe won't go so Connor is it ok you skip too, or should you cover for Gabe?"

Clara was about to answer and say something but Sonia beat her to it.

"Um, why should they skip? Aren't we pretending that this isn't affecting her?" They all turned to Alex who was looking at Gabe.

Alex was stepping up as the leader right now and for a very good reason. "I think today she shouldn't go to practice because none of us can be there to watch over her on such short notice. And we don't know the truth."

Clara understood what Alex was saying and what he wasn't saying. He wanted to know the truth before he decided that they protect her. She took a deep breath and replied, "Alex is right, I should explain my story, the real story as I'm sure that there is some crazy stuff going around." She looked down and she had to remind herself to breathe.

Sonia grabbed her hand. "Hey, whatever it is, we'll figure it out. OK?"

"Yeah, well, I don't want you guys to get dragged into this. Not that there is anything to get dragged in to because it is in the past but I do have a story. I do think you should know so I'd like to tell you but I understand if after..."

"Stop. Just stop." It was Gabe who spoke fiercely yet quietly. "Clara, we want to know what happened because it involves you but we're not going anywhere, ok?" She lifted her head up and looked at everyone.

Connor spoke up, "you're kind of stuck with us now C."

Sonia spoke again, "I'll drive home with you today. Our parents are away so we'll go to our house right after school." Clara nodded. It was truth time.

22

GABE

They were in Sonia and Alex's TV room in the basement. Clara was standing with her back to everyone staring outside the patio doors with her arms wrapped around herself. She looked cold so Gabe had given her his sweatshirt. Sonia had gone upstairs to make some coffee for herself and Clara. It had started raining outside so Clara's practice had been cancelled while Gabe and Connor decided to skip theirs. Sonia and Alex had grabbed some drinks and put them on the ottoman. Sonia went up to Clara and handed her the mug of coffee. She hesitated next to her because she didn't know what to do but then she stepped away. Throughout the afternoon they had heard bits and pieces of Clara's story or versions of it. Gabe himself, tried to tune out what they were saying. He wanted to hear it the first time from her personally and understand what was true. Finally, Clara started talking and everyone quieted immediately and sat down.

"I was about 9 years old I guess. 9 and three quarters I kept saying. I was with my parents on the way to some modelling interview. My mom, she thought I could be this hot top model or at least on the road to be one." Clara laughed and shook her head but didn't turn around. "I hadn't been doing it very long, nor did I do it often. My mom was very selective. I didn't really want to go to this one, but I wanted to make her happy. This particular modelling gig was in Chicago and we couldn't afford 3 plane tickets so we drove. They had told me it was a long drive from where we lived outside of Philadelphia to Chicago. We left early that morning and I was so sleepy, I remember that. I think the plan was to drive all day and then rest in the hotel at night. My mom packed us lunch. She had made these sandwiches and cut a bunch of fruit. I can still picture my sandwich," Clara almost whispered the last part until she cleared her voice and continued. She still hadn't turned around.

"It was dark and it started to rain. They told me we were almost there. I think my dad was just tired and wanted to get there because he was driving a little faster than usual. I remember them bickering because my mom was sure we were lost. We probably were. We weren't on a highway but on a bunch of winding roads. I remember that one moment I was looking outside the window trying to see if I could see the stars and the next minute, well, the next minute we had crashed against a tree. I called for my mom and dad, but they didn't answer. I could smell smoke." Clara then turned around and a hand tightened around Gabe's heart, crushing the wall that surrounded it. Silent tears were running down her cheeks but she paid no attention to them. She looked haunted. Gabe got up from the sofa to go comfort her but that seemed to wake her up. She swung her gaze to him and held up her hand, "No, I have to finish, please. If I stop I am not sure I'll be able to continue." He nodded and looked over at the others. They were waiting patiently for her to continue, when she did, he turned his gaze back towards her and sat down.

"A man came and he had a boy with him. I thought he was going to help me. I remember that first time I looked at him," she shuddered, "he wasn't nice. I knew, I just knew he wasn't a nice man. He scared me. That was the last time I saw my parents. He took me and left them there to die. He even robbed them. He kept telling me not to worry, that he was taking me with them. I..I didn't know what to think. I didn't know if he was going to call the police, I didn't know what to do and I was so scared. But in my gut I knew that I shouldn't make him angry. My head hurt, thinking about it now, I probably had a concussion but I didn't say anything. I didn't speak. For days I never said a word. I fell asleep in the car and had no idea where we were. He took me to his house and there was a girl. Her name was Tracey. When she saw me her eyes widened and I remember she looked at Paul. That was his name Paul Whiting. Then she glared at the boy. His name was Cain. She seemed more upset with Cain. Anyway, she acted all tough in front of Paul. But as soon as she took me to her room to tend to my head, she was nice. She was always nice when it was just the two of us. She hugged me and told me she would figure it out, but that I had to listen to her. I couldn't speak, I couldn't cry. I couldn't do anything but I remember nodding and I did what she said. Anything that she said for those entire two years, I listened. She found my dad's driver's license somewhere and gave it to me, so I would have a picture of my dad. That's how I know Paul robbed them too. I hid that license and looked at it every single fucking day. She told me to, so I wouldn't forget and so I wouldn't lose hope. I was with them for probably 2 years give and take." She paused, tears streaming down her face at this point, "I tried. I tried to not lose hope but somewhere along the way I did." A sob broke out and Gabe couldn't take it anymore. He jumped up from the sofa and pulled her in his arms. He held her, murmuring words of reassurance. She hugged him back just as tightly.

The others looked shocked. Sonia's hand covered her mouth and her eyes were watery. Connor looked pale and Alex just kept shaking his head. Gabe was sure they had heard stories today but never imagined that she had been taken for 2 years. "You don't have to tell us anymore, if you don't want to. At least not right now. I think that's enough for today."

126

Connor nodded but Alex looked stricken and asked, "Clara, I'm sorry I was so hard on you at lunch," he shook his head. "I…How did you? Nevermind, Gabe is right."

But Clara still holding on to Gabe turned her head to Alex. "You want to know how I got away?" Alex nodded. "Cain. Cain let me go. Weird thing was that he wasn't nice to me at all during those 2 years. That night he was strange yet really mean and after he yelled at me, he hugged me and told me to run. The police found me after that, someone had put a call in. I think it was him but I can't be sure."

Alex nodded and then Sonia asked "And Paul? Where is he? I'm sorry if I'm asking that but what happened to him?"

Gabe held her tighter, "Guys, I think that's enough."

Clara pulled back to look at him and then looked at the others. "It's ok. I think answering the questions is easier then telling the entire story. From what they told me there was a fire and they found him dead." Gabe sat down on the sofa and pulled Clara down with him. He didn't know what to think. He was angry, sad, shocked but in awe of this girl that had been through so much and yet was so strong. He sensed there was much more to the story. It wasn't that simple, he felt it. But he wasn't going to push her. But this explained her barriers, her uneasiness.

Connor finally spoke up, "What about Tracey and Cain? Where are they?"

Clara smiled a sad smile. "I don't know. I begged the police to look for them, especially Tracey. I had my aunt call the police station in Chicago every week for over a year, but they couldn't find her or Cain. I still call to ask." She shivered. Gabe held her tighter.

He wanted to ask a question, but Sonia beat him to it. "I have to ask, I have to know and then no more questions, but did they hurt you?" she whispered.

Everyone was quiet and seemed to be holding their breath while they waited for Clara's answer. "Yeah, Paul did. He hurt all three of us but Tracey and Cain took the brunt of it. Tracey especially would always shift his attention to her. He liked to play mind games with me. He would hit me and then make me feel like it was my fault. He would lock me in dark rooms a lot. Sometimes in the room I shared with Tracey, or the bathroom. But sometimes it was worse places than that, the closet, the basement, even the shed outside. Out of the three of them I was probably the lucky one." She shuddered and closed her eyes. Gabe so wanted to pull her onto his lap but wasn't sure if that was pushing it. She was already tense as she was.

Alex cleared his throat and glanced at Gabe. "How did everyone at school find out part of your story?"

"This is what you wrote about isn't it?" Gabe asked her and Clara nodded. *Shit.* Gabe cursed under his breath.

"Once Mr. Brooks gave the paper back to me I put it away but then I couldn't find it when I got home. But then yesterday when I got to school I found it in the newspaper room. I thought I was just distracted. I could have sworn I didn't bring it with me in there but there it was. I thought I was just not paying attention until lunch."

"Someone took it, read it, and put it back so you'd think you just misplaced it," Alex said, shaking his head.

Connor spoke up, "Who do you think it was?"

Clara hesitated but then responded, "I am not really sure." Alex nodded.

Connor spoke up, "Well, hopefully we'll find out for sure one way or another.

Clara put her head in her hands and ran them through her hair. "So now, what do I do?"

Surprisingly it was Alex that spoke up first, "It's what *we* do." Sonia clasped her hand as Gabe continued to have his arm around her. She was no longer in this alone. "First we come up with a plan. We have to figure out who was behind this," Alex declared.

Sonia commented, "We're going to need food for this. Let's me go get some snacks. Do you want more coffee Clara?"

Clara had long forgotten her mug on a side table when she turned around. "Um, yeah that would be great."

"I'll help you upstairs. I'm hungry myself," Connor said.

And that is what they did. They had a plan in mind. Alex would have to use Zoe's interest in him to see if she had heard anything. Zoe was one of Alex's hookups that hung out with Sarah's crowd outside of school. Knowing Zoe, if she didn't know she would do anything to find out in order to get in Alex's good graces. Although she wasn't directly mean she chose to stay quiet when Sarah or Jamie acted the way they did. That was one of the reasons why Alex wouldn't really give her a fair shot. In his mind, she was a coward and guilty by association but she was pretty and so when Alex had an itch, she was always ready to scratch it. Connor would talk to Leo who was dating this cute Spanish cheerleader. She didn't hang out with Sarah but since Sarah was a cheerleader she knew a lot of what happened. Alex also told Connor to be strategic when he picked his girl of the week. Everyone chuckled. And finally, all three boys had to distance themselves from Clara for a few days. Sonia put her foot down and refused. That was fine with Gabe, Clara needed a friend by her side. Hell, he wanted to be by her side. But he figured that once they distanced themselves whoever had done it or whoever knew the person that did it, might start bragging about it. Hopefully it wouldn't take too long, just a few days. He wasn't sure what was going to happen once they found out who it was but Gabe knew that they wouldn't get away with messing with her, he would make sure of it.

23

CLARA

It had been difficult in the beginning to speak her story out loud. Writing it had been liberating and much easier, but saying it, that had been entirely different. She was afraid of their reactions. She didn't know what to expect, she didn't think they would think negatively of her but she was afraid they would pity her. The last thing she wanted was to see pity in their eyes. But she didn't see that emotion at all. She knew they were surprised or perhaps shocked would be a better word, she saw anger when she spoke about Paul hurting them, and there was something else especially when they realized she had been kept for 2 years. Clara wanted to tell them more. She wanted to tell them about how she learned to pickpocket, but then she would have to tell them about the weed she took to protect them. That would lead to whole new series of questions and she was already emotionally and mentally exhausted. But she knew she had to say something soon especially to Gabe.

After they formulated their plan on finding out who started the gossip mill, they hung out a little more, changing the subject. She had stayed rather quiet. At a certain point she had pulled away from Gabe to snuggle into the couch, pulling up her knees. Gabe kept glancing at her like he didn't know what to do. She grabbed his hand and looked at him. He held her gaze, and smiled a small smile, that smile that was meant just for her. She went to let go of his hand but he didn't let her. He leaned back, holding on to her hand but giving her space. There was a part of her that wanted that space, she needed it to regain focus after her admission. But there was another part of her that wanted to be held in Gabe's arms. When he hugged her she felt protected. But she couldn't ask him. Could she? A little voice whispered to her that she could. But her steely resolve prohibited her from doing so. She was never like this. Other than her aunt and uncle and maybe a few cousins, she never liked being held.

They had turned on the TV although they weren't really paying attention to it, Connor had left a little while earlier. After a while, Clara started to stand up, "I've got to get going too." They all nodded but didn't say anything. *Ok, she thought to herself.* She guessed her story was a bit much for them too and they needed some distance as well. She put on her shoes, and was about to take off Gabe's sweatshirt.

"Keep it for now, it's raining outside," he said.

"Thanks," she whispered.

They all headed upstairs. She put on the hood to the sweatshirt and went to grab her bookbag. Alex and Sonia, had put on their shoes and seemed to be heading out as well. Gabe came up and grabbed her book bag and put out his hand like he was waiting for something. She looked at him quizzically.

"Are you guys going out?" Clara asked. Sonia chuckled.

Gabe was looking at her expectantly, "What?" Clara asked.

"Your keys Clara," Gabe told her.

"W..Why?"

"So I can drive you home," Gabe replied.

"Did you really think that we would let you go home by yourself now?" Alex asked her.

"I don't understand..." Clara said to them.

Sonia spoke up, "I had warned they were just as protective as your cousins, Clara. We're coming to bring you home and they are probably going to barge inside and introduce themselves to your family."

"But, you guys don't have to. I know I just laid a bunch of baggage at your feet and there is even more to tell, but you guys don't have to feel bad, or act any differently."

"The keys Clara. We can talk more in the car," Gabe replied shaking his head, "just give in, please. We're coming with you. Period."

Clara let out a sigh and handed over her keys and nearly stomped her way to her car. He was being bossy and she wasn't sure if she liked it. Ok, she kind of liked it but she felt like she was in the dark about something. Gabe started driving, with Alex and Sonia behind them in Alex's car.

"I presume you know where I live?"

"Of course I do." He looked at her and smiled and just like that any irritation she felt went away.

She sighed. "Can you please explain to me what is going on, Gabe?" She turned slightly in her seat to get a good view of his handsome features.

"Look, a lot happened to you today. I wouldn't feel right just being like, 'ok, that was rough. See you tomorrow.' You probably won't say anything to your family about what happened today but you shouldn't be alone and you shouldn't have to pretend the entire time. Besides, I wasn't ready to let you go just yet, ok?"

Clara nodded, "Ok."

He grabbed her hand. "Whenever you want to talk, I'm here to listen."

"Gabe, there is more that I have to tell you."

"And you can tell me when you're ready, Clara. If you want, which I hope you do. I'm still trying to take all that you told me in. I'm just amazed by you."

"Well, I'm not used to all of this," as she motioned to him and to Alex and Sonia behind them.

"Well, you better get used to it," he said quietly and held on to her hand while he drove.

They pulled in shortly after into the long driveway to her home. *Home*, she thought. She told him where to park her car and both of them proceeded to get out. She rounded the car, thinking Sonia and Alex were just turning around.

"Thanks for driving me home, Gabe."

"You're welcome, Clara," he murmured with a twinkle in his eye.

When she saw Alex and Sonia get out of the car, she rolled her eyes. "You guys are really coming in?"

Sonia laughed while Gabe grinned, but it was Alex that replied, "Of course. Are you embarrassed about us or something?"

"No, it's just I never..." Clara sighed, "never mind. You guys are seriously coming in?"

Alex nodded, and Gabe just gazed at her with those eyes. A tingle shot through her. She was overreacting, and she knew it, but she was nervous.

Sonia grabbed her hand, "It'll be fine, come on."

They walked inside. Her aunt had started making dinner and Julia was at the table doing her homework. Her aunt looked up, "Hello girls," and then looked behind them and tilted her head a bit, "and boys."

Clara went to give her aunt a kiss and then pulled away and Sonia swooped in, "What about a hug for me?"

Clara shook her head and laughed. "Aunt Nina, this is Alex, Sonia's brother and their cousin, Gabriel. We all go to school together." They all greeted her while Clara went up to Julia and sat down next to her. "Hey Jules," giving her a kiss on her temple, Julia grinned, "homework?"

"Yeah, I finished my essay earlier. Will you read it?"

"Of course, I will," Clara replied.

"Hey, don't I get a hug, Julia?" Sonia asked. That was the great thing about Sonia. When she came to the house the first time, she included everyone, even Julia. Most other girls wouldn't. Julia stood up and gave Sonia a hug. Sonia pulled her along, "Come on, let me introduce you to my brother and cousin."

The boys said hello. Gabe glanced at Julia and then at Clara. "You guys resemble each other a bit."

"Really?" asked Julia.

Clara chuckled. "She loves hearing that."

"I wonder why," Gabe murmured.

And then Clara felt a bit awkward. She had no idea what to do but thankfully her aunt saved the day. "Why don't you go to the family room for a bit and I'll finish up dinner. Uncle Frank and Vincent should be home soon. Why don't you guys stay for dinner?"

"We don't want to impose Mrs. Salvino," Gabe replied.

"Hush, you aren't imposing. I wouldn't have said anything if you were. Go watch TV or something. It will be about an hour. I'm happy to have you all over for dinner."

They headed to the family room downstairs, Gabe grabbed her hand when they went inside pulling her closer to him, "Is this ok? That we stay for dinner?"

Clara looked up at him, "Of course it is," she smiled, "But I'm warning you, my uncle may not be as friendly as my aunt is. Let me go check and see if she needs any help and I'll grab us some drinks." Clara headed back upstairs and walked up to her aunt, giving her another hug. She mumbled, "Are you sure it's ok they stay for dinner? You didn't have to ask them to stay, they would have left, they just wanted to meet everyone."

Her aunt pulled away, "Of course it's ok. Honey, I'm happy that you brought some friends home."

"Yeah, but 2 of them are guys. Will Uncle Frank be ok?"

Her aunt Nina laughed, "he'll be fine. Surprised, for sure. You know he will break their balls."

Clara let out a sigh but then laughed, "Ok, well we'll see. I am going to grab some drinks. Do you need help?"

"I'll help her," Julia said. "I'm done anyway. I'll set the table."

Her aunt swatted her away, "Go back to them. I'll call you when it's ready." Clara headed downstairs with drinks and they hung out until dinner was ready. Gabe looked around occasionally but most times he was looking at her. Every time she found his gaze on her, she tried to seem like she wasn't affected by him and she hoped she succeeded but every time his intense stare landed on hers, she almost forgot to breathe.

24

GABE

They had just gotten into Alex's car and were heading home. Clara had a great family, and everyone made them feel right at home. It was obvious that her uncle and Vincent were protective of their family.

"Well, that was interesting," Alex remarked, "if looks could kill in the beginning one of us would be gone for sure."

Sonia replied, "I think they were trying to figure out which one of the two of you was interested in her. Her uncle seemed to chill once he found out who our parents are. I guess for once we can be thankful for their high profiles." Gabe however, remained quiet and contemplating.

"Are you going to be able to do this, Gabe?" Alex asked him.

He looked over at Alex. "Do what exactly?"

"Stay away from her for a few days. All joking aside, after several minutes, there was no doubt of the two of us which one is interested in her. Will you be able to stay away from her at school?" Alex was pushing him.

"I'll have to, won't I? This is the right way to go, it will be quicker to figure out exactly who it was. I'm glad you'll stick to her side though," he turned his head to look at Sonia who was in the back but moved up in between their two seats to speak closer to them.

She nodded, "How could I leave her? Did you hear her today?"

Gabe murmured, "That's what I keep thinking about. I'm just so in awe of her. I can't get over what she went through."

"Agreed," Alex replied, "I was kind of a hardass on her, not so much what I said but how I said it. I feel like an asshole. But I listened to what everyone was saying today. I don't think she wrote the full story. Everyone knows she was kidnapped but not for how long."

Sonia immediately chimed in, "Yeah, I listened to what the girls were saying in my gym class. The gossip obviously kept growing and the story kept changing. Some of the stories were a bit crazy. But there is one girl from her soccer team that defended her. Amelia, I think?"

"Rosie stuck up for her too today and told a few people to go to hell," Alex chuckled, "I had never noticed her before, but that girl is actually fierce. We should have asked Clara what she wrote exactly in the paper."

"I have it," Gabe replied as he looked out the window.

"You do?" Sonia asked.

"Yeah, she gave it to me," Gabe replied, "What she wrote doesn't matter, the crazy stories are out there but they should die down, especially since Sonia is with her. Even if we show a divide, they won't go against her because of us. They know we wouldn't allow that to happen to Sonia. Then when Clara is back with us, then it should die down even more."

Alex turned his gaze towards him, "But is she strong enough to wait it out?"

Gabe sighed before responding, "After everything she has been through, yeah, I think she is. This is nothing compared to that."

"Agreed," murmured Sonia.

"Plus we'll check in on her after school," Gabe remarked.

"Are you going to read the paper?" Alex asked him.

Gabe looked out the window again, "Yeah, I will. But it doesn't matter what she wrote, at least not for me. Let's hope we find out quickly who it was."

"Then what happens?" Sonia asked.

"Not sure yet, Sonia, that part I haven't figured out yet, but I won't let them off easily."

The following morning, they headed to school. Sonia drove separately. As soon as Gabe and Alex entered the halls, people made room for them to pass, a few started whispering. Clara was up ahead, he would notice her anywhere. She was with Rosie, thank goodness.

"Hey Rosie," both Gabe and Alex said.

Gabe nodded at Clara while Alex spoke, "Clara." Clara looked at Gabe and nodded. Both slowed down but did not stop and many seemed to notice. Sonia walked up, making a funny face at the guys.

Gabe walked ahead, Henry looked at Clara and looked at him quizzically. "Everything ok, man?"

"Yeah, why?"

Henry shook his head, "Nothing, I'll see you later in class."

Gabe nodded. He looked to his left and noticed Kristin who had just finished looking at him and then looked at Clara. She smiled. He looked up ahead and noticed Alex had wasted no time in pulling Zoe to him and whispering something in her ear. She melted instantly. Connor was coming down the hallway with a girl and he stopped to talk to Gabe. While he did, the girl instantly caressed Connor's arm. He looked a bit tense but turned his full-blown smile at her, "Hey babe, can you leave me to talk to Gabe? I'll find you after class."

She pouted but responded, "Ok, promise?"

"Promise." She walked backwards for a few steps smiling and turned around and headed down the hall.

At that moment, Sonia, Rosie and Clara were coming down the hall behind them. Gabe was so tempted to turn around, he wanted to make sure she was ok. He turned slightly checking out Clara from the corner of his eye, Sonia was turned around looking at the girl that had just looked away from Connor.

"Hello, ladies" Connor said. "Chin up, Clara" he murmured.

She grinned, "Thanks Connor," she said softly.

But the girls kept walking. Connor glanced at Sonia but kept a straight face. At the same time, Sarah and Jamie were walking by and for some reason both girls decided to stop to talk to Gabe and Connor. They noticed instantly that Clara and the girls didn't stop, leaving Jamie to smirk as she looked at Clara.

Sarah cozied up to Gabe putting her hand on his arm, "Hey Connor! Gabe, I was thinking of having a party after your game on Friday, my parents are going away. What do you think? I wanted to make sure that you guys would be able to come, meaning Connor, Alex and you, of course. I feel like lately there's been distance between us and we don't hang out, like ever."

Gabe looked at her, trying to read her intentions. He had to literally grit his teeth to not move back. Kristin, walked by stopping dead in her tracks when she noticed that Sarah had her hand on Gabe's arm.

She walked up to them, "Hey, what are we talking about?" Kristin asked.

"Oh, hey, just about the party I told you I wanted to have this weekend. You will come won't you guys?"

Connor spoke up, "We should be there especially since you're asking so nicely, count us in."

Gabe stepped back, looking at Sarah, "Yeah, we should be there," as he smirked and tugged on a strand of her hair. He looked at Kristin and then Jamie, "See you girls later. I've got somewhere I've got to be."

Connor smiled and winked, walking away in the opposite direction of Gabe. Gabe looked up at that moment and noticed Clara watching from afar with Sonia but then turned around and walked away. Sonia was giving him a cold stare before heading after Clara. He headed to class, thinking about Sarah's invitation. The girl was friends with Kristin and had no trouble wanting to get his attention or flirt with him. *What a great friendship* he thought to himself. But the look on Clara's face gutted him. This was going to be much harder than he thought.

25
CLARA

Rosie looked at Clara. "What is going on?" This was the second time she asked, the first being when the guys just walked by, the second being now, seeing Sarah, Kristin and Jamie interacting with Connor and Gabe.

"Nothing. The guys are being jerks, that's all," Sonia replied.

"Bad timing to act like jerks. Are you ok Clara?" Rosie murmured.

"Yeah, I'm fine. So, what is everyone saying?" Clara had to ask.

"I don't think you want to know all the stories, some of them are really out there. But, were you really kidnapped when you were little?" Rosie asked hesitantly.

"Yes."

Rosie swallowed and nodded replying, "Ok, then let's just say there are different versions of that."

"I can imagine," Clara replied dryly.

"It doesn't matter, Clara," Sonia reassured her, "It will die down. This has probably been the most interesting piece of gossip in a while."

"Probably since last year. When Mark Tealman's mom was caught with Josh Greenberg's older brother at someone's bar mitzvah none the less," smiled Rosie.

Sonia laughed, "I heard about that one. She'll be fine. Clara's a fighter, there are a lot of people just rolling their eyes at the stories and defending you. Your soccer team for one."

"Really?" Clara almost stopped dead in her tracks.

"Yeah, I even heard Amelia yesterday in the locker room defending you. Not everyone is like Jamie. You're an asset to that team and you're nice," Sonia responded.

"She's right. A few seniors from the newspaper defended you yesterday, I heard them myself. My friends think you're awesome to overcome something like that. Sonia's right, it will die down, in the meantime stick with us. The guys though, I'm just freaking disappointed," Rosie commented.

"It'll be ok," Sonia said.

"Yeah, I don't blame them. I have a lot of baggage to deal with, so it doesn't surprise me," Clara voiced. Sonia looked at her quizzically for an instant and then narrowed her eyes at Clara. "I'll see you guys later. I have to head to math."

"I'll see you in Spanish, Clara," Rosie remarked. They all split ways, she noticed Sonia texting on her phone as she was walking away. Her phone buzzed. Clara pulled it out before walking into math.

Get out of that head of yours. This is an act and you KNOW it. Stop it.

Got it.

Don't you one word me. It's me. I'm the one who refused to pretend because I didn't want to leave you alone. DON'T one word me.

Clara smiled. *It was actually 2 words but ok. I know it's an act.*

Are you sure? Because I feel a but coming...

Just seeing J, S and K talking to them just didn't feel right.

I know. Believe me I know. Sonia then added. *Just have faith, ok?*

Clara took a deep breath. *I know, I know, it's just, I'm not used to this and so I doubt it sometimes.*

I get it. You have trust issues. But then Sonia continued. *So do I. I can understand with others but trust me, ok?*

Clara read that sighed. *Deal.*

She walked into class feeling better and sat down, knowing a few people were looking at her with pity and whispering. But they didn't matter. Rosie was in her next class, and she was ready to narrow her eyes at anyone who tried to look at her with a hint of malice. But her third period came along, and she knew she had to pretend again. She took a deep breath and walked into Creative writing. Gabe was sitting there, and he glanced at her.

He hesitated but then said, "Hey."

"Hey," she answered, and turned to look straight ahead. Mr. Brooks, turned his gaze to her and his eyes showed a bit of concern, but he hid it quickly. He turned his attention back to class and began his lesson. After about 20 minutes he handed out a sheet of paper and says, "Pop quiz, today."

Everyone started murmuring because he was not known for giving pop quizzes. "Now, I have graded your papers, and I will hand them back to you at the end of class. Here's your quiz. You have 20 minutes. Go."

Everyone focused immediately on what they had to do. It didn't take Clara long, she lived for this stuff but a few of the others were struggling. Class finally ended with everyone turning in their pop quizzes and getting their papers in exchange.

When Clara brought up her pop quiz Mr. Brooks said, "Clara, do you mind waiting a few minutes? I need to ask you about an article for the newspaper."

"Sure, Mr. Brooks." As everyone left the room, Clara observed Gabe out of the corner of her eye. He glanced at her, he was tense. Connor was the last one to leave. Before he left the room he glanced at Mr. Brooks and then at Clara, questions in his eyes. She smiled reassuringly.

"I'll see you later, Clara. Mr. Brooks."

Mr. Brooks looked at him for a second before looking at Clara. He studied her for a moment and then said, "He's worried about you." Clara felt like it was more like a statement so she didn't answer but shrugged.

"As I guess he should be. I walked into the teacher's lounge today and they were talking about you. They had heard the rumors going around the school. Are you ok?"

Clara nodded, "Yes, I'm fine."

"May I ask how everyone found out?"

"I think someone took my paper. I couldn't find it when I got home and then found it in the newspaper room the following morning but I didn't bring it in there."

Mr. Brooks gaze hardened, "Ok, who?"

"I don't know," Clara replied.

"But you have an idea?" She nodded. "Look," he took a deep breath, "someone invaded your privacy and that is unacceptable. Let me know if there is anything I can do to help. I have to say I learned about you before you started school. Since you'd be in my class and working closely with me in the newspaper I was brought up to speed by the school psychologist. You are so not what I expected. That paper was written by someone much wiser than their years. But now, you should be living your life like a carefree teenager. Have you told your family about this?"

Clara shook her head, "No, I haven't."

"Maybe you should. Whatever is going on, I'm here should you need anything and I know your coach is here for you too."

"Coach Lawson?" Clara asked.

"Yes. Anyway, relook at your paper, as I mentioned there are a few changes you might want to make in the margins but the truth is, it's an A and I've never given an A on the first draft."

"Thank you, Mr. Brooks."

"Go ahead to your next class. I'll see you tomorrow." Clara nodded and headed out. As she walked to her next class her cell phone buzzed. It was Gabe.

Gabe: *Are you ok?*

Clara: *Yes, I'm ok.*

Gabe: *What did Mr. Brooks want?*

Clara: *He knows about the rumors.*

Gabe: *And???*

Clara let out a breath and responded. *He asked questions, offered support. Nothing to tell.*

Gabe: *Ok, are you going to be ok the rest of the day?*

Clara: *Yes, I will.*

Gabe kept insisting. *R u sure?*

Clara: *Yes, I'm sure. Are you ok? You seem tense.*

Gabe: Do you have karate tonight?

Clara: *Yes, I do. You didn't answer my question.* This time it was Clara to insist.

Gabe: *I'll see you there.*

Ok. She thought to herself. Her phone buzzed one more time *Look up. Please.* She did and there he was. He looked around and then looked straight at her. They stared at each other and right when he was in front of her he let her see how he felt, plain as day. He was frustrated and concerned, that she could easily see. But she also noticed another emotion mixed in, she just wasn't sure what it was. It was moments like this that Clara felt this connection between them was getting stronger.

She continued to her next class which dragged more than usual until she proceeded to go to the cafeteria. She didn't want to go after what happened yesterday but the others had encouraged her to do so. Honestly, she would have preferred to avoid it if she could but she knew it was like hiding and she should face it head on.

She had told herself that this year would be different and so far it was. She had friends ready to stick up for her, so she had to learn to not only accept their support but most importantly she had to learn to stick up for herself and stop avoiding.

She spotted Sonia and Rosie instantly and went over to sit down. A few of Rosie's friends looked at her a bit skeptically, the others though treated her no differently and immediately included her in the conversation. One in particular, Giada, squeezed her arm to show her support. A few tables looked over and whispered, some noticed that not only did the girls sit separately, which occasionally they did, but they didn't even go over to say hello to the guys nor look in their direction. Connor stopped to check in, he actually did that all day. Gabe and Alex only said hello. While Sonia and Alex were fine, she did show Gabe the cold shoulder. When Clara asked her about it Sonia claimed she did in solidarity. Everyone knew Sonia wouldn't go against her brother especially in public, BUT she could show that she didn't think Gabe was as cool as she thought before.

Besides, it showed that the friendship Clara and she had was solid and not to be messed with and that was a point that Sonia felt especially important on driving home. Clara did notice that there were quite a few people snickering about her, others whispering but there were some that showed her admiration, stood up for her when they heard a smart comment in class or smiled at her sympathetically in the hallways and other places. It surprised her. Although she was used to being a loner, she also realized that, without Gabe's words, or his notes, she felt extremely lonely, she just wondered if he felt the that way too.

26

GABE

A few days had passed. It seems whoever decided to steal, read and let everyone know about Clara's past was keeping a tight lip. The guys had already decided that they would wait until the weekend and if they didn't find out, then they would stop avoiding Clara and Sonia. The entire student body noticed the distance. You could tell they wanted to know what happened. During one particular lunch session, when Clara had left the cafeteria early to go work on the school newspaper, one of the guys called her a bad name.

Alex immediately spoke up, "Not cool prick. Back off."

The guy answered, "Sorry, you aren't hanging out with her anymore so I thought it was free rein."

Connor decided to speak up, "Just because we don't hang out anymore doesn't mean we think it's cool to act like a douche." The guy didn't comment.

One of the guys from the team, Giuseppe, also responded, "Stop acting like a bully a-hole. You know they don't go for that shit no matter who it is."

At least Gabe knew that most of the guys from the team were decent so he didn't have to worry about them teasing Clara. In fact, after that day, the whispering died down quite a bit although he could see that Sarah, and a few others still made comments.

Today he was late getting to the cafeteria. He had been assigned a group project with a few others and they had to set up times to meet and ask the teacher a few questions. He hated this shit. The two girls in his group kept giggling every time he spoke and he had a terrible headache. He was extremely tense today, and in all honesty, he just wanted to go home. He was considering skipping afternoon classes. He could come back for soccer practice. Since he was the captain no one would really say anything. He was contemplating it as he walked to the cafeteria. He was almost there when his phone buzzed. He grabbed it out of his pocket and slowed down to read it.

Bobby: *Dude, where are you? Where is everyone?*

Gabe: *On my way to cafeteria why?* Gabe had answered.

Bobby: *It's Bruno.*

This was turning out to be one of those days. *What about him?*

Bobby: *He's kind of harassing Sonia. Alex isn't here and neither is Connor.*

Where the fuck is everyone? Gabe thought to himself. *Coming in now.*

Gabe walked through the doors. All the guys that usually sat at his table all turned their heads towards him and most of them looked relieved. A few were standing, watching intently deciding when to intervene. Bruno was getting up from the table where Sonia had been sitting the past few days. He patted his pocket and winked at Sonia who looked ready to breathe fire. All Gabe could make out from what Bruno was saying was the fact that he had taken Sonia's cell phone. As Bruno began to walk away from the table Clara arrived and managed to collide with Bruno. Gabe automatically clenched his fists and was about to quicken his pace when something stopped him dead in his tracks. It was almost as if he was watching in slow motion and a sense of déjà vu came over him. It was hard for many others to notice but Gabe seemed to have the best view from where he was standing. Clara maneuvered to her right in a way that she had to push on to Bruno's jacket with the book she had in her hand, making an effort not to fall. Or so it seemed. But then, with her left hand she pulls out the cell phone from Bruno's pocket and slips it in her sleeve. Bruno had no idea. He made a comment to Clara who stiffened for a moment, but she immediately backed up and circled back to the table sliding the phone to Sonia.

Sonia's mouth dropped open and then she smiled at Clara, turning it into a smirk for Bruno who in that exact moment decided to open his mouth saying, "Girl, I am going to say it again, no need to collide with me on purpose. Our bodies can collide all you want, whenever you want." As he finished that last part of the sentence his eyes darted to the table and he noticed Sonia dangling her cell phone.

He checked his pocket and whipped his gaze to Clara who said to him, "That doesn't belong to you." The girls at the table chuckled as did a few guys who noticed the entire exchange.

"Dude, you totally got played!" one of the guys declared while the others kept laughing.

Some others were catching on that they missed something and started asking what had happened, a few people commented, "Bruno totally got played by Clara."

Bruno glared at Clara and pointed at her, "How did you do that?"

Clara looked at him and shrugged, "Maybe you should pay better attention." A bunch of other people started laughing as well. He continued to scowl at her for a few more moments until he turned around. As he walked by a few of the guys laughing, he slammed his hand on the table and walked through the back doors that led outside. Clara turned around looking right in Gabe's direction. Her eyes widened. Gabe narrowed his eyes, glanced at Sonia before he walked towards Clara.

He quietly said, "You and I are going to have a conversation. Weeping willow far end by the tennis courts in 5 minutes." He looked at her in the eyes, arching his brow. She exhaled and nodded. He turned to Sonia, "You ok?" Sonia nodded, seeing the look on Gabe's face, she started to stand up when Gabe shook his head. Clara grabbed her stuff and then turned toward Sonia and whispered something in her ear. Sonia grabbed her things as well and walked out with Clara. But Gabe knew that Sonia was pretending they had left together as to not raise any eyebrows. Gabe headed to the table where Bobby was sitting. "Thanks for texting me man," patting him on the shoulder.

Bobby quickly answered, "You're welcome, a few of us tried to get involved and told him to knock it off, but without you guys here, we weren't sure where we stood. He wasn't exactly listening to us but he was only teasing her until he took her phone of course." A few of the guys nodded.

Giuseppe commented, "I can't believe Clara totally lifted the cell phone from his pocket. Totally played him for a fool."

Another guy mentioned, "I know you don't hang with her any-more, but it was totally cool. No idea how she did it."

Gabe ran his fingers through his hair not knowing what to say, "Yeah, well, I gotta get going now. From now on, Bruno gets near either of them, don't hesitate to call me, Alex or Connor, wherever the fuck they are. I'll see you guys later."

He turned around and headed out, taking a totally different direction then where he told Clara to meet him. He knew his way around this school to get where he needed to be with a few twists and turns. Not that he cared if they saw him going to speak to her but he wanted privacy. He pushed through a door heading outside and walked towards the willow tree. As he got closer, he saw Clara was leaning up against it. He stopped right underneath the low branch which hid them pretty much from view. He was surprised that no one was out here. In the spring and early fall you could always find a couple underneath here throughout different parts of the day. Today was a bit chilly and damp and that was probably why no one was under there. She raised her head and held his gaze.

"It was you." He didn't state it as a question, the more he thought of it the more he had no doubt. She continued to hold his gaze and nodded. "What the fuck Clara??" He ran his hands through his hair and began pacing in front of her. He didn't know what to ask or say first. He looked at her and tears were welling up in her eyes. He exhaled a breath stopping in front of her, "Why didn't you tell me?"

She glanced down a second and then looked at him in the eyes, "I was going to, it just never seemed like the right time."

He shook his head and stood there with his hands on his hips. "Where did you learn to do that?

Clara exhaled a long breath, "Someone taught me during the time I was kidnapped."

"Who?" Gabe asked.

"Cain" she said quietly.

He nodded and started pacing again trying to think. "You should have found a way to tell me," he said again.

She was quick to answer, "When was I supposed to tell you? When I told you guys what happened to me? It was difficult enough to get out what I did. When we went out for pizza? 'Hey, by the way, I'm the one that saved your ass'. I'm sorry, ok? I just, I just didn't want to answer any more questions. It came naturally to me, when the cop said they might search you, I instantly knew that you would be in trouble and I just didn't ...I didn't want that. I didn't want you to get in trouble. I was going to tell you, I just didn't know how." She looked at him, and those damn green eyes undid him. Any anger or disbelief he felt melted away as he looked at her. He approached her and took a deep breath, grasping her hands in his.

Clara's cheeks flushed, looking into her eyes he said, "thank you for trying to protect me." He could tell that Clara was surprised by his reaction.

"You're not mad?" Clara asked him.

Gabe let out a deep breath, "I'm not mad. I'm..I don't know what I am. I have tons of questions for you and we need to talk about this. But you did what you did to protect me and for that I'm thankful. But there are a few things I have to know."

Clara nodded, "ok."

"Why did you put the baggie in my locker?"

She responded a bit hesitantly, "I don't know exactly. I wanted you to know that someone helped you out. I think in my subconscious I wanted you to search for answers and to find out it was me but I didn't have the courage to straight up tell you."

He nodded and swallowed, "Ok. What did you do with the weed?"

She responded immediately, "I flushed it down the toilet." He let out a breath he was holding. He didn't do drugs and he didn't think she did either, but he was relieved by her answer.

"How did you manage to get into my locker? Are you..." He hesitated not sure how to ask if she was able to break in places too without offending her.

"No, I don't know how to pick locks. I actually asked the custodian to help me out telling him it was Sonia's locker. His wife works as a secretary for my uncle, so he knew that I wouldn't do anything inappropriate."

He now had a more important question. "Why did Cain teach you to pickpocket?" She immediately looked down and pulled her hands free. She looked up at him with uncertainness, while Gabe waited patiently. Gabe moved a piece of hair behind her ear and then and cupped her face. He could feel her hesitation again and wanted to calm her. "Clara, there are a lot of things I want to know about you and those two years. And the years after that. I understand it will take time. I'm not going anywhere. What you tell me won't change that. But let me in. Please." Her eyes widened for a fraction of a second looking at him in wonder until she nodded. Those last words had probably been her undoing. He pulled his hands away from her face and went back holding both her hands continuing to wait.

She took a deep breath and began, "Cain taught me to pickpocket because Tracey made him. She didn't want Paul to make me do other things, like he made her do sometimes." She swallowed, and his eyes widened. He cursed quietly. Clara continued, "they figured that he would be happy if I was bringing in money or anything I could get of value. Tracey argued that if I looked clean and pretty then people wouldn't suspect me. It worked. They didn't. That pacified Paul for the most part. So, I made sure to become a pro at it. I could lift almost anything from anyone at almost anytime. I hated every single minute of it. But I did it. If I was able to lift something really good, like a wallet with a lot of cash, Paul was bearable. We could eat something better and sometimes he would take the money and leave for hours. When I did really well he wouldn't have Tracey do what he made her do. Once I was found I never did it again until the weed at the party and getting Sonia's cell phone back from Bruno. I swear."

Gabe shook his head and cursed again. This girl brought him to his knees. Even as a little girl, she was strong. He pulled away, running his hands through his hair and paced. He couldn't do it anymore. Gabe couldn't stay away from her anymore even if he tried. He didn't want to. She opened her mouth and was about to start rambling again. *Fuck it.* He took two strides to reach her, pulled her in his arms and finally kissed her. He could tell she was taken aback by the kiss. In the beginning she was hesitant, and he was worried he had overstepped some imaginary boundary. He was about to pull away when she surged up on her toes, tentatively gripped his shoulders and, kissed him back. As he kissed her, he knew right then that he would never get enough. Right now, it was difficult for him to slow it down and not freaking devour her.

He pulled away slightly and took a deep breath, "Finally." He put his forehead to hers and waited a few moments for his racing heart to calm down. He said, "No more freeze out, no more ignoring each other and Clara?"

She looked up a little dazed, "Yes?"

He smiled, "No more walls Clara, you have to let me in." He grasped her face in his hands, "Please, a little at a time, just let me in."

"Ok," she whispered, putting her hands on top of his, "Ok." she said again.

He let out the breath he had been holding and nodded, "Good." He gave her another soft lingering kiss and pulled her to him and held her for a few minutes until he grabbed her hand. Taking a deep breath, he said, "Let's go. We have to go back, someone is going to look for us for sure and we can't be late to 6th period." Her cheeks were a bit flushed, she looked even more beautiful than usual and she was smiling. He would do anything to have her keep smiling. Anything. He was so ruined. He shook his head and grinned as they headed inside.

27

CLARA

As Gabe walked her to her locker, Clara couldn't stop smiling. She kept trying to stop but her grin kept coming out. Gabe dropped her off at her locker holding her tightly and then pulled away, "If I don't see you, I'll text you before practice."

She responded, "I actually have a game tonight at Malstern prep."

"That's right, I'll text you beforehand, but I'll probably see you there." He pulled away, holding on to her hand as he did, winked and walked down the hall. Sonia was coming from that direction and stopped to talk to him a second before coming to a halt at Clara's locker. Sonia arched her brow, with a huge question mark written all over her face.

She got closer to Clara to not have others overhear their conversation, "Well? Is everything ok? Since he walked you to your locker I take it the ignoring is over?" Clara smiled and put her fingers over her lips. "Hello, Clara. Are you going to answer me?"

Clara couldn't stop the goofy grin. "Yes, all good." Sonia looked at her expectantly, motioning with her hand to add some information. Clara could feel a flush at her cheeks. "It was good."

Sonia replied, "Yes, I got that since you keep repeating it."

Clara looked at her and said with wonder in her voice, "He...he kissed me." Her eyes widened after she had said it.

Sonia grinned, "Fucking finally. Took him long enough." Sonia snorted and added when she noticed Clara's look. "What? Oh come on, Clara. It was about time." Clara shook her head and sighed. "You're going to have that blissed out look all day, aren't you?"

Clara laughed. "What, no. I'll be fine. It was just, it was perfect."

Sonia smiled and then grabbed her hand dragging her along. "Well, I would hope so. Come on, let's go, your class is next to mine."

They went to the remainder of their classes and then she rushed to leave for her game. Surprisingly soccer season was almost over. They had only a few more games left, and they were important ones. She had to get her head out of the clouds and into the game tonight. As she walked into the locker room to get changed, quite a few girls smiled at her or said hello. Instead, Jamie looked at her and scowled as usual. Clara shook her head. They got ready for the game rather quickly and headed on the bus where the coach talked to them. Malstern Prep was not too far. As Clara was getting off the bus, Coach Rossi and Coach Lawson stopped her for a second.

"Clara, we wanted to talk to you a minute."

Clara answered, "Ok."

Coach Lawson called Jamie over too and when she saw Clara, she rolled her eyes, "What's up coach?" Clara could hear Jamie gritting her teeth from where she was but Clara met Jamie's gaze head on.

Coach Lawson was trying to hide a grin, "Coach Rossi, would you like to start?"

"Sure, as you both know, we have lost to Malstern prep for the past 4 years. And they for sure don't let us forget it. They've become what I guess you would call our rival or one of them. So, I need your head in the game tonight, 110%."

Coach Lawson then stepped in, "What Coach Rossi is trying to say is that we've noticed a bit of tension between you two, and while we don't expect you to be best friends, we do expect both of you to work as a team and as partners for the common goal. When you are on that field, any tension, dislike, anything negative disappears. ALL OF IT."

"Can I count on the both of you to do that?" Coach Rossi asked them.

Jamie took a deep breath and answered, "fine."

Coach Lawson looked at Jamie, "Are you sure, Jamie? Don't just say it to say it, I expect more from you since you're the Captain."

"Yes, I'm sure."

"Clara, what about you?"

Clara at a certain point had folded her arms over her chest and she had not stopped looking at Jamie, "I have no problem with that, Coach. But I think you both know that."

Coach Rossi nodded, "Good, then let's show them what we're made of. Let's go." Both coaches walked ahead of them as Jamie and Clara followed close behind.

Clara did not know what came over her to ask, "Are you sure you're ready for this?"

Jamie looked at her and smirked, "You're asking me if I'm ready to play hard ball?"

"No, that's not what I'm asking," Clara replied, "I'm asking if you are ready to start acting like the Captain you should be." Then she walked away toward where some other girls from the team were warming up and got her head in the game as Coach wanted. She just hoped Jamie would be able to do the same.

The game was intense, probably one of the most intense she had ever played. After being 0-0 for a while, Malstern Prep was able to score right before the end of the first half. The girls took their break refueling while both Coaches gave them pep talks.

As she was walking out, Jamie approached her, "Fine. Let's bring them down."

"Alright, then," Clara responded, "well number 15 is strong."

Jamie responded quickly, "the girl with the red hair. Yeah, she keeps taunting me. Think you can handle number 21?"

"Oh, I've got her. I've also noticed that the goalie is stiffer on her right side. She keeps trying to massage her thigh and stretch so if you're going to shoot, do it there."

Jamie looked at her. "How do you notice all that?"

Her answer was swift, "My cousin taught me. He plays soccer." But that wasn't true. It was Cain that taught her to notice these things about others. Jamie nodded.

The team went back on the field and within 15 minutes Jamie had scored. After that though, it was tight. Both defensive sides were holding their own no matter how many shots were coming their way. At a certain point the other team had called a time out and, in that moment, Clara felt him. She looked around, and saw Gabe, standing right next to Sonia. He smiled and nodded when he realized she had noticed him. The time out had ended so she got ready to play. She looked at Coach Lawson, who was staring right at her. She pointed to Clara and to the goal, telling her the next one was hers. Clara nodded. She noticed that number 21 was winded and tired, Clara knew that if she had the ball, that's where she needed to go. The clock kept ticking, defense was able to get the ball away from the other team towards their midfielder. Eva looked around as to where to pass the ball. She hesitated for a moment but then realized Clara was the best bet for a pass. Eva started to move slightly towards Clara, finally passing the ball to her. Clara took the ball, moving fast, dodged around number 21 and took the shot, kicking the ball towards the goal. The ball lifted off the ground, making Clara cringe, but the ball went right in the top right corner securing their lead. Moira, and a few of the other girls ran over to Clara and hugged her. She looked in the crowd where Sonia was yelling like a crazy woman and Gabe hooted and hollered along with her. The other team tried to score another goal, however, East Cynwood held firm. When the whistle sounded declaring the end of the game, everyone started jumping up and down. Most of the girls ran over to Clara giving her a quick side hug.

As she walked up to the coaches, Coach Lawson said, "that right there is what I was talking about. Incredible job, Clara!" She then turned to all the girls, "you all were fantastic, I'm so proud of you!"

Coach Rossi was speaking to a few people off the side when he came over and everyone quieted down. "Girls, amazing job. Today you all played as a true team. Thank you. This win was 4 years in the making but it was a great game. Let's head back home so you girls can celebrate!"

As Clara passed him, he gently gripped her shoulder saying, "Clara, great job today. I was impressed. I knew you had it in you." He proceeded to speak to a few of the other girls as they all continued walking. As they headed towards the bus there was a group of people from East Cynwood waiting for all of them. Clara instantly found Gabe's heated gaze settled on her. Right next to him stood Sonia who looked over at Clara rolling her eyes. Clara had a puzzled look on her face until she looked to Gabe's other side and there stood

Sarah chatting away animatedly with him, or rather to him because he was looking directly at Clara. Gabe said something to Sarah who just gaped at him as he walked away and right over to her.

Clara just stared at him but smiled as he got closer, "hey" Clara said.

"Hey yourself. You were awesome out there," Gabe remarked, as he kissed her cheek and then hugged her. After holding her a moment, he kissed her behind her ear and she shuddered. He pulled away and smirked never letting go of her hand.

Sonia came over and hugged her too and she couldn't stop laughing. "I think Sara is frozen in place," she whispered to Clara.

Clara nonchalantly looked over and Sara was gaping at the three of them but as soon as she noticed Clara, her gaze hardened. "Yeah, well." Just as she was thinking about what to say, Coach Rossi told them to get on the bus. Rules were rules and you were under their supervision until you got back to school.

"We'll follow the bus," Gabe said.

"Oh, I have my car," Clara started saying.

"And your point is?" Gabe grinned kissing her on the temple, "We'll see you back at school."

She got on the bus sitting next to Moira who immediately complimented her and they started chatting with other girls adding to their conversation. As they arrived at school Clara realized that she had never really spoken to many of these girls. Clara never allowed herself to be accepted because she hadn't accepted them. She obviously didn't trust them like she did Gabe, Sonia and the others but it was nice and she was learning to be more open about it. As the team got off the bus, Gabe and Sonia were waiting for her.

"Get in, I'll give you a ride to your car, I have to bring Sonia to hers anyway." Clara climbed in the back seat and noticed Gabe kept glancing at her in the rearview mirror as they were talking. They dropped off Sonia first and Clara moved up front and they both waited for Sonia to get in her car and pull out of her spot.

As soon as Sonia had beeped indicating she was leaving, Clara turned towards Gabe stating, "I'm parked by..." Gabe moved over the console and kissed her. It was a gentle kiss, his eyes open as though gauging her reaction. Clara's cheeks instantly flushed. Gabe smiled and pecked her on the lips, then on the cheek and grabbed her hand.

He cleared his throat, "You were saying, you're parked, where?"

She also cleared her throat, "Um, I'm not far. Right over there, by the bike rack."

Gabe shook his head, "I was hoping you were parked farther away. 30 seconds quality time isn't enough." As he drove he turned his gaze a second to look at her, "you were fierce on that field today. Everyone was amazed by you. Especially me."

As the car stopped Clara responded picking at some imaginary lint on her shorts, "It really wasn't a big deal."

He squeezed her hand saying softly, "Hey, look at me." She did. "Don't downplay what you did. You scored that second goal and secured the win. Everyone probably contributed and did great too."

Clara sighed, "Um, weren't you there for some of the game?"

"Yeah, I was but I didn't notice them because I was only looking at you." Clara could feel herself blushing and became shy all of sudden. What was she supposed to say to that? Gabe decided to cut her some slack. "Are you going to karate tonight?"

Clara answered, "No, not tonight. I have a test tomorrow so between that and the game I've decided not to go."

"Ok, can I call you later?" Gabe asked her. She nodded. "Yeah?"

"Yeah, I'd like that," she admitted. The stayed there a moment and stared at each other. "Ok," Clara said softly.

"Ok, then," responded Gabe. They burst out laughing. Shaking his head Gabe said, "Let me walk you to your car. This was definitely not enough time." He got out of the car while she grabbed her stuff and opened the door. He helped her down from the SUV. They took those few steps to her car and she opened the door throwing in her bags. His hands were in his pockets but he took them out and he pulled her in his arms.

"I probably smell," Clara said trying to have some distance between her and Gabe.

"You don't, but even if you did, I wouldn't care," Gabe replied.

So she circled her arms around him too. She felt so safe and it felt so good to be in his arms. Gabe loosened his hold and peered down at her.

"Thanks for coming to my game," Clara told him.

"I wouldn't have missed it." He leaned down and kissed her again. "I'll call you later, but I'll see you tomorrow."

28

GABE

Several days had gone by. Each day started with Gabe waiting for Clara either in the parking lot or by her locker. Although he typically had never been overly affectionate he found that with Clara he couldn't not touch her. They didn't make out in public, but he did hold her hand whenever possible, and when he said hello or goodbye he made sure to hug her or kiss her on the cheek or sometimes even behind the ear. When it was just them with Alex and the others, then he would even kiss her. Every time he would be somewhat affectionate she would blush or try to contain her smile and he felt like a caveman wanting to pound his chest when she did.

The more days passed the more he was hooked. He liked that she wasn't pretentious or demanding, yet at the same time, if he even tried to get bossy with her, fire lit her eyes and she dished it right back. They both had busy schedules during the week, but they were able to hang out a bit during the weekend with the others at Sonia and Alex's house. Gabe didn't leave Clara's side the entire night and he felt that she wasn't inclined to do so either. What was interesting was the fact that no one seemed surprised by them, it was if they had always been that way.

The week had restarted and both of them had a few tests or projects and with soccer dying down for the both of them, the last few games were extremely important for their season standings, so practices were intense and left them both exhausted. He had texted Clara last night saying he would pick her up and bring her to school today. He wanted some extra time with her. He intended to spend some time with her this afternoon or tonight hoping she would agree. They had both finished practice about 15 minutes ago and he was waiting for her in the parking lot. As a bunch of girls stepped out of the door and spotted Gabe, they looked behind them and were talking and giggling. Moira was beside Clara shaking her head and gave Clara a pat on the back. Even Eva, who wasn't extremely nice, looked at the girls in front of them and shook her head. Clara spotted him and waved to both Moira and Eva, while walking towards his car. She got in and pulled the door shut. She was tense. He could tell something was wrong.

"Hey, you ok?" he asked her.

"Yeah, I'm fine."

"Are you not going to tell me what that was about?" Gabe asked Clara. They had probably something to say about Clara. He could tell something bothered her, but she was trying to either hide it or be strong about it.

"Nothing important. Just the same crap." She replied. He smiled, she wasn't getting away that easy.

"Then why aren't you looking at me?" She swung her head and looked at him. "Tell me."

She blew out a breath. "They were just being snarky, as usual, making sure I heard them."

"Heard them say what?" Gabe asked her with a little bit of bite.

Her gaze grew a bit heated. "You do not give up easily do you?" She hesitated for a nanosecond and then said, "They said you have a hero complex. You like to help people, save them. And that is why you hang out with me. After what happened to me, you feel sorry for me." She looked down, picking at some imaginary lint on her pants.

"Don't look down, look at me," Gabe laughed. "I feel like I'm always trying to get you to look at me." She had by then lifted her head to gaze at him. "And, you believe that?" Gabe asked her.

She replied, "No. Yes. I mean." She took a deep breath. "Maybe a little I do, it makes sense. You could have anyone, you could literally snap your fingers in the cafeteria and a line would form. Seniors included." She snorted. "I'm no one and I have baggage. Being my friend is exhausting, and we're whatever.... As I said, it makes sense." He waited because he could tell she wasn't finished, pulling into the nearest parking lot and he pulled into a spot. He turned his body towards her.

"But.." he started.

"But there's a voice inside my head telling me not to believe it. It's telling me it's not true." She whispered looking right at him. She was letting down her walls, plain as day for him to see. He saw the vulnerability there, understood her pain, but he saw her strength, that confidence that existed in her. She was fighting for it. He grabbed her hands. They hadn't stopped staring at eachother. It was hot in that damn car all of a sudden. He felt the air around them charged.

"They're right, I do like helping people." He said softly, and he could see her breathing speed up slightly as he inched closer to her. "And I do like helping you. I actually really like helping you." She was deciding. She slightly shook her head waiting for him to continue speaking. "But they are so wrong."

"They are?" She asked quietly.

"They are so completely fucking wrong. I don't feel sorry for you. Yes, I feel sorry for what happened to you, but not for you. Of course, I would never want you to go through that pain. But I care

what happened to you because it brought you here to this moment, it made you who you are. You are so strong. You may not think it but look at what you've overcome, how beautiful you are inside and out. Everyone gets scared sometimes, or we doubt ourselves and maybe we even fail but few like you thrive. But I especially care what happened to you, because it brought you here, it brought you to me."
Fuck it.

He slammed his lips to hers pulling her closer. No more waiting. He couldn't wait another second. She gasped initially, maybe from shock and just when he thought maybe he needed to be more careful about kissing her, her arms slid around his neck and her hands found their way to the hair in the back of his head. *Heaven. That's what it was.* After a few moments he slowed the kiss down and pulled away. He framed her face with his hands and kissed her again, slower this time, deeper, leaving little doubt about what he thought about her. Her hands came to rest on his forearms and she pulled away resting her forehead on his. He took a deep breath.

"I've wanted to do that since you walked out that door." She grinned. He pulled his head away slightly to get a better look at her, trying to pull her body closer at the same time. *Damn car.* Her hands fell to his chest. He moved a strand of her hair away from her face and gave her another peck on the lips and on her forehead. He pulled out of the spot and continued driving but grasped her hand as he drove. He was quiet for a few moments, shook his head and looked at her and grinned. She was grinning too.

"Come over to my house a little bit?" Gabe asked her.

She nodded and started to open her mouth to say something but he stopped her. "You have karate later, right? I'll take you, what time is it?"

"It's at.." She looked at him and seemed a bit sheepish. Then she laughed. God, he loved her laugh. "I can't remember right now. Give me a minute, that kiss wiped out my brain cells."

He looked over at her grinning and squeezed her hand. "Yeah. Well, I do have a hero complex I guess that includes super powers too."

She pulled her hand away and swatted his arm grinning. "Shut up." He chuckled and grabbed her hand again and drove home.

When he got to his house, he noticed that there were a few other cars in the driveway. "Wait here," he said. He hopped out of the car, came around the front, looking at her the whole time. He then opened her door and offered her his hand.

She tilted her head and looked at him as she got out of the car. "You didn't have to do that," Clara said as she looked up at him.

"I didn't have to, but I wanted to." He leaned her against the door of the car and kissed her again pulling her into his arms. He pulled away after a few minutes and rested his forehead to hers. It was something he never really did before but seemed to come naturally to him with Clara. He also had to remind himself not to come on too strong even though he wanted her. Gabe had to be patient with her. He opened his eyes and her eyelids fluttered open not even a moment later. Those green eyes pierced his soul each and every time. *Fuck. This girl did things to him. He was so screwed.* He gently kissed her behind her left ear, a place he realized was one of her soft spots. She shivered slightly just like she did now. He grinned, pressed another kiss there and grabbed her hand to lead her inside.

When they went inside they could hear voices in the dining room, leading onto the patio. It was uncharacteristically warm outside for this time of year and they were obviously taking advantage of it. Gabe's father called out, "Gabriel, is that you?"

"Yeah, it's me, dad." He looked at Clara and said, "come with me." He tugged her along towards the dining room. "Hey dad." He also greeted the few gentlemen standing near his dad.

"Hello, son. Everyone this is my son Gabriel. And this is his girlfriend, Clara." He smiled and then looked at Clara. "Hello, Clara, nice to see you again."

"Hi Mr. Caruso."

Gabe shook hands with everyone, without letting go of Clara's hand. He noticed how she didn't bat an eye when his father called her his girlfriend. *Good. She better get used to it.* Liz, his dad's girlfriend came over to give him a kiss and introduced herself to Clara. Clara let go of his hand to do so. Liz took the opportunity to whisper something in Clara's ear and instantly Clara's cheeks flushed.

"Son, you and Clara are more than welcome to join us if you'd like."

"Thanks, but we're going to go sit on the lower patio for a little while, then Clara has a karate lesson."

"Very well, then. Have Elisabetta bring you out some food."

"Thanks, dad."

Clara said her goodbyes as did he and he pulled her along toward the kitchen. Before he turned the corner, he looked back and his father was looking at him with a look of fondness and pride. His dad then smiled and flicked his gaze to Clara and winked. Gabe shook his head. They walked into the kitchen and he gave Elisabetta a kiss and introduced Clara. "I make you both a dish with appetizer. Ok, Gabriel?" she said with a thick Spanish accent.

"Yes, please. We are going outside to the patio. I'll come and get it in a few minutes."

"Nonsense, I bring out. You take Clara. Go, go sit." Her eyes twinkled.

He laughed. "Yes, ma'am."

"No call me ma'am, I don't like it."

He showed Clara outside. As soon as you stepped out there was a big table with an umbrella. He took her past that towards the pool house and down a few steps to a cozy patio. It was near the pool but overlooked some of the backyard. He turned on a heating lamp, just in case, sat down on a corner of the sectional so he could put his legs up. Clara went to sit down next to him, but he shook his head. He opened his legs, pulled her to sit in front of him, making her lean against him so her back was to his front. He wanted to hold her. As soon as he put his arms around her she sighed deeply. "What's the sigh about?"

She turned her head to look at him. "I got in the car upset and flustered and here I am 30 minutes later and it doesn't matter. None of it matters."

He kissed her and replied, "They don't matter. But we do. Right now especially, we are the only ones that matter." He leaned down to kiss her again but then heard footsteps and realized it was Elisabetta probably bringing them some food. He kissed her behind the ear, smiling as she shivered. "The food is here."

Clara abruptly pulled away as Elisabetta was approaching. She got up to help put the dishes on the table. The cook had filled a bigger dish with a variety of different things. Together they fixed everything on the table. Gabe went into the pool house and came out with a few drinks. "Thank you," Clara told the older woman.

Elisabetta patted her on the cheek. "You're welcome. You tell me if you need anything. Send Gabriel." Gabe thanked her as well and sat down.

"I hope you're hungry and ready."

"Ready for what?" Clara asked grinning, putting her hands on her hips.

"We're going to play the question game. Are you up to it?" Gabe looked at her intently but gently at the same time. He meant what he had said days ago, she had to let down her wall but he didn't want to force her either. All he wanted was to get to know her better.

She smirked. "Game on." He hadn't expected that but hell if it didn't turn him on.

29

CLARA

Clara knew that Gabe's question game was his way of getting her to let down her walls a little bit without pressuring her. He wanted her to confide in him and she realized this was a good way to start. That combined with the desire to learn more about him is what prompted her to answer him the way she did. She felt bolder and more confident with him for some reason.

They both sat down on the couch crossed legged facing each other with their food placed on dishes in front of them. Clara started with a question and both of them had to answer. It started innocent enough, favorite colors, favorite foods, favorite music or movies. Slowly they began moving forward without stopping to more interesting and somewhat serious questions.

"How many boyfriends have you had?" Gabe asked her.

Her cheeks flushed. "One, kind of two."

"Why kind of two?"

"Nope, not answering that, you have to answer the question." Clara insisted.

Gabe smirked, "Never had a boyfriend." Clara laughed and threw her napkin at him. He laughed right along with her.

He blew out a breath, "I've had a few. Only one serious one though or I thought she was. But that seems like a while ago." Clara nodded. She knew Gabe was popular, just like she knew a lot of the girls wanted him, some had even had him for a short time or so she heard. She didn't know where they stood, but she didn't feel confident enough to ask.

"Why did you kind of have two boyfriends?" He persisted.

"Nope. It's my turn you don't get a double turn. Don't be sneaky." Gabe grinned, motioning for her to go right ahead.

"Can I ask..who was the last girl you went out with?"

Gabe cringed. "Kristin."

"Now that explains a lot," Clara said.

"Explains a lot about what?"

"Well, she always looks at me funny. Sometimes it's like she hates me and sometimes it's as if she is observing me. It's weird." Clara confided.

Gabe nodded and blew out a breath. "I'm not going to lie to you Clara. To put it lightly we fucked around during part of the summer. A kind of friend with benefits thing. I had told her I didn't want anything serious, but she didn't take the hint until recently. She's not bothering you, is she?"

"No, she's harmless. I don't think that she is probably that bad, but she just hangs out with not nice people."

He looked like he was about to say something but changed his mind and nodded instead. "Your turn," he said.

Clara shrugged "It was one of my cousin's friends this summer at the beach. Nothing serious though."

"Ok, my turn again. Why kind of two boyfriends?" Gabe asked again.

"You are relentless," she said shaking her head and sighing. "The second guy, I was stupid and I thought he was kind of my boyfriend. Or at least he was for me. Instead, it was all a game. He got back together with his ex."

"Why do I sense there is more to the story?"

"Because there is," she answered.

"If you really don't want to talk about it we don't have to. I will never force you to tell me anything but I would love for you to tell me so I can understand you better."

Initially, Clara hesitated but then she squared her shoulders back and responded, "it's not that I don't want to tell you because I don't want you to know. It's because I feel stupid. I liked him, or at least I thought I did. He was sweet to me, and paid attention to me. He told me I was beautiful. If I think about it now, there were signs, but I refused to see them. He ended up getting back with his ex while we were still together. So, I became her target. She and her friends were awful to me, but they never knew that I had fought bullies worse than them. But they were the reason why I left Mount St. Peter's."

Gabe grabbed her hand and caressed her fingers. "The only thing I can say is that he was a stupid idiot to not realize what he had. His loss. Those girls were insecure because they knew that you had something that had caught his attention and they were afraid that you could take it away again." He stopped for a second before continuing, "I can't answer the same question but to be fair I can tell you that I've been there where a girl, the one I considered to be my serious girlfriend, took advantage of the fact that I cared for her and lied to me so in that aspect I can relate."

Clara looked at him and said quietly, "Thank you for sharing that with me. I can't imagine any girl not realizing how great you are and taking advantage of that fact."

Gabe moved a bit closer to her. "Thanks Clara," he whispered not taking his eyes off her. "It's your turn I believe. We have to get through all 20."

She smiled. "Ok." She had so many questions for him but she wanted to get the questions back to being important but not as intense or sad. "If you could do anything right now what would it be?" She asked him.

"That's easy. I'd kiss you."

"Why don't you?" She asked him.

He smiled, "Nope, you can't ask 2 questions in a row remember? Don't be sly. You have to answer your own question too."

She chuckled as he threw her same words right back at her. "Hmmm, I guess I'd kiss you back."

"Yeah?"

"Yeah."

"What am I waiting for then?" he asked grinning. He moved their dishes to the side, leaned in and kissed her first on the lips softly and then with a bit more pressure. He then began placing small kisses across her cheek until getting to her ear. He placed a kiss behind it until he finally pulled away. He moved back, opening his legs and pulling her between them with her laying on his chest. He held her tightly to him.

After a few moments of silence, she tilted her head up and said, "Your turn."

"My turn? Ok, it's not really a question but tell me something about your parents. When we went out for pizza you talked about your aunt, uncle and cousins but nothing about them." She stiffened in his arms and he responded by holding her a bit tighter. He said quietly, "It's just me, Clara. Just tell me something small."

She drew a deep breath, "My dad loved karate. When I was a kid we would always watch those old karate movies together. That was our thing. He's one of the reasons I take karate now. My mom loved to sew. She used to sew me these dresses. The more ruffles or bows the better. When I look at them now I cringe. I can't believe I dressed like that. I was like her living doll."

She burrowed slightly deeper in his chest and he just held her quietly until he began to speak and answer the same question, "My mom loved to read. By the pool, in the sunroom. It didn't matter. We used to read books together when I was younger, I would read one page and she would read the next. One of our favorites was Charlotte's Web and the Wizard of Oz. When she got sick, I made sure to read them with her again."

"I'm sorry Gabe, that must have been so hard."

He pulled back so he could look down at her and shook his head. "It was at the time, just as I'm sure it was for you, if not harder."

"I don't know. There are different kinds of pain but in the end pain is pain." They were quiet for a moment until Clara said, "Can I ask you a question?"

"Well, we are playing the question game," Gabe answered ruefully.

"What about Liz? You never really talk about her. Do you not like her?" Clara asked him.

"No, I do, she's actually really nice. I just don't know her that well." Gabe confided.

"Hmm, maybe she is waiting for your cue." Clara told him.

"What do you mean?"

Clara sighed, "You lost your mom, Gabe and she was a great mom. I think Liz maybe doesn't want to seem like she is there to take her place and is waiting for you to come around. When I went to live with my aunt and uncle, my cousin Vince didn't speak to me a lot in the beginning. I though he hated that I was there. He finally admitted to me that I made him nervous. He was so worried that I wasn't ok, that I was suffering, and he didn't want to say the wrong thing or act the wrong way so he stayed quiet. Maybe it's the same with her. I just met her but if I were to go with my gut, I think she is genuine."

Gabe tightened his hold on her but didn't say anything for a few minutes and Clara began to think she said too much. She hesitantly pulled away a little bit, ending up on her knees in front of him, "Gabe, I'm sorry, it's not my business. I was.."

"Stop Clara, I don't think that at all." He pulled her and adjusted her so she was straddling him. "I just never thought of it from that point of view. She does hold herself back a lot when I am there. I guess it's something I should speak to my dad about. I just, again, I just never realized it. Plus, I'll never be offended by you being honest with me. Never." He pecked her on the lips.

Maybe it was her position, or that after speaking to him the past hour she felt bold, and before she could stop herself, the question was out of her mouth. "What are we? What are we doing?" Her eyes widened when she realized what she had said. *Where the hell did that just come from?* His eyes heated becoming almost black. She immediately tried to backtrack. Cringing, she started blabbering, "Nevermind. You don't have to answer that. It just came out. I meant.."

But then he pulled her closer and kissed her hard on the lips. He pulled away, just a tad so his lips were resting on hers, "shut up," he said grinning and started kissing her again.

All of a sudden, they heard footsteps and "Gabriel, I bring you more food." Clara pulled away and immediately slid to the side of Gabriel. Gabriel let her go reluctantly, his eyes dancing with mirth. He thought it was hilarious. *What had come over her? Not only did she just flat out ask him what she was to him but then she is making out with him at his house on his patio where anyone can show up.* She took a deep breath and swatted his arm.

He chuckled but got up from the couch. "Elisabetta, let me help you with that." He made room on the table as the older woman approached and piled the dishes they had already used. "Wow, Elisabetta, you've really outdone yourself this time."

"Thank you, Gabriel. I bring a little bit of everything. You want more of something, you come, and I give it to you. OK?"

"Thank you." Clara also thanked the woman who looked at her and smiled.

"She seems so wonderful." Clara said.

"She is. She's been with us since I was a kid. She's family." Clara felt awkward all of a sudden, racking her brain to think of something to say so he would forget what she asked. Gabe said, "How about we skip your question for the time being but that means you lose your turn and you have to answer mine. What do you say?" *Crap. Of course, he wanted to skip it. What the hell was she thinking?* She felt so silly. He probably hated when girls put pressure on him and here she was jumping the gun. She just wanted to leave now but couldn't since he had to drive her home. She could text Vincent or Sal. They would come get her in a heartbeat. "Clara?"

Her head whipped up. "Yes?" her voice squeaked. She cleared her throat to respond, "Yes, let's forget about mine and I'll answer yours instead." She tried to look everywhere else but at him.

"Ok, but will you look at me please?" He was grinning, finding humor in her discomfort. *Jerk.* She half glared at him since she felt he was acting a bit arrogant and she felt she had to put her defenses up. He shook his head, "I love it when you get heated up ready to defend yourself. Your eyes light up and even though it's dark and I can't see them as well, they are probably vivid green right now. You teeter on this line of being a bit insecure about yourself but then not wanting to put up with anyone's shit. I like that. It shows me you're modest yet strong, humble yet fierce. You impress me, Clara. So damn much. I just hope that I impress you enough to at least want to be my girlfriend."

Clara's heart started beating a million miles a minute. She didn't expect that declaration. Her heart felt like it was going to burst out of her chest. Since he liked her boldness she decided to say, "Well, I don't think that was really a question. Aren't we playing the question game here?"

He shook his head laughing, "You really like to keep me on my toes." He pulled her closer, "Actually, let's resume the position prior to Elisabetta interrupting us." Before she realized it, he pulled her on top of his lap as if she weighed nothing, so she was straddling him again. He pulled her closer and moved a strand of hair away from her face, cupping her jaw in the process. "Much better. You were too far from me and I couldn't see your eyes. Will you, Clara, be my girl-friend?" She just stared at him mesmerized as he waited patiently.

She whispered, "Are you sure?"

He took a deep breath and turned serious. "Clara, I've been sure since the first time you walked into English class. I was even more sure when we played beer pong and when I saw you play soccer. I'm sure every time you walk into the cafeteria. I was sure when I found out you saved my ass." He pulled her closer, "And I'm damn sure tonight." He was about to say something else but that's when she put her hands around his neck and leaned in to kiss him. She pulled away this time resting her lips on top of his grinning, "Yes. Now shut up."

30
GABE

Typical cold Pennsylvania weather arrived, signaling the end of soccer season which allowed both Gabe and Clara to clear their schedules a bit and spend more time together although Clara worked more at the karate school. She kept herself awfully busy. He admired that she was a hard worker but he sometimes worried that she overdid it. He kept wanting to ask her about it but didn't. At least not yet. Gabe sometimes went to the karate school and sat there waiting for her.

If previously anyone at school had any doubts that Gabe and Clara were an item, they no longer did. He held her hand often, pulled her onto his lap at parties or in the cafeteria, even pecked her on the lips occasionally. But word travelled especially fast after his last soccer game. After he and his team had won, he picked her up and kissed her in front of everyone before heading to the locker room. He wanted everyone to know and he wanted to make sure the guys backed off. Most of the guys knew not to mess with Gabe or Alex but Bruno seemed to not care. Gabe in fact, had one more run in with Bruno and although Clara wasn't there, Bruno made sure to comment on her beauty in a vulgar way. If it weren't for Leo and Connor, he would have probably bashed Bruno's head in.

One night he had dinner at Clara's house for the first time without the others. They were all very friendly with him, Julia in particular. He had just finished saying goodbye to everyone and Clara was walking him to the door. He had made her laugh and Julia come barreling in and hugged him unexpectantly.

"Thank you," she whispered. He looked at Clara who shrugged and understood that he wanted a few minutes to talk to Julia alone. Clara stepped away in the next room and Gabe squatted down to be more on eye level with Clara's younger cousin.

"Thank you for what?"

Julia smiled, "For making her laugh. She never laughed like this before."

"Never?" He asked clarification.

"She laughed but not like she does now with you. Now that I think of it, if she did laugh it was usually when she was with me but not when there were a lot of people. But again, that laugh was never like this one."

"Well then, I'll try to keep making her laugh, ok?"

"Promise?" As Gabe looked at this ten year old girl in front of him, he wondered if she realized how much like Clara she was.

"I promise Julia."

"Good. And if you don't then I'll tell my cousins and they'll come after you."

Gabe laughed and thought to himself, *definitely Clara's cousin,* "I have no doubt." He gave her a hug and waited for Clara to come back into the room, so he could kiss her soundly before leaving.

He was thinking about the whole exchange with Julia when he walked in the door. His father was up watching tv which didn't happen often. But when Gabe walked in he knew his dad was waiting for him, so he didn't waste time and went to sit down right next to him. "Hey son, everything ok?"

"Yeah, everything is good. You're watching tv, you never really do that."

Ralph Caruso laughed, "you know me well. We just haven't spent that much time together lately with this latest case and you've been busy too. I just wanted to check in, spend some time with you. Were you at Clara's?"

"Yeah. You didn't have to wait for me, we do have phones, I would have come home earlier. You're not that bad to hang out with." Gabe said and grinned.

"Clara wouldn't get upset if I stole you away?"

Gabe chuckled, "No, she isn't like that. She loves her family and she knows I love you so... she would be happy we were spending time together." Ralph nodded, pleased with his answer. They spent some time talking about school, soccer, his father's latest case. His father then asked him about Sonia and how she was holding up.

"She is actually doing really well. She doesn't really talk about what happened to her. But I'm glad she's here with us. I figure she will when she is ready. I know Alex is grateful you helped with that."

"They're my niece and nephew, of course I would. I just never realized until you brought it to my attention. She could have come home from boarding school much earlier. But I see that she is doing much better with you guys. She's calmed down. She seems happy," Gabe father said.

"I think she is happy to be back and I think Clara has something to do with that too. She's trustworthy, and genuine and Sonia knows that so she's more relaxed. I wouldn't say that's how she acts with everyone but within our circle she's good. We've got her back," Gabe replied.

"And Clara?" Ralph asked.

Gabe looked at him quizzically. All of a sudden, he sensed where this conversation was going. "What about her?"

"How is she doing in a new school and all?" he asked.

It wasn't the question that made Gabe pause, it was how the question was asked. His father knew something. "She's doing well. She had a rough start but she's ok now. But you're not referring to that, are you?

His dad took a deep breath. "Son, you were having a conversation with Alex in the beginning of the year about her. I could tell that she had gotten to you. But I want you to be careful, not just for yourself but for her too. Clara has also had a tough past. Has she talked to you about it at all?"

"How do you know?" Gabe asked. No point wasting time.

His father seemed surprised. "So she has."

"Dad, you didn't answer my question, how did you find out?"

"After what I heard from you and Alex and then at dinner that night she seemed familiar to me. I was working closely on a different case at that time with the DA and with Tony Blanchard, who was a detective there. So I called Tony the other day and asked him."

Gabe shook his head and got up. This was his father and he knew he was looking out for him, but he felt defensive for Clara. "Why would you do that? You could have just asked me first."

"Hold up. I am not trying to get you upset. You're my son Gabe, it's my job to check on you. What if she hadn't said anything, and then I had jumped the gun. I wouldn't even blame her if she hadn't told you anything yet. Hell, I'm surprised she has. I want you to be careful because I see it, I see how much you care for her already. I just want you aware for your sake and hers. Take it easy, have fun but know that there may be things from her past that will be a road block for her and you need to be sensitive to it."

"I am. She's..she's unlike anyone I've ever met, dad. Anyone. I get why you would ask around about her but can you not do that again? If you have a question come to me, and if I know the answer I'll tell you if I can. But I don't like others..."

His father interrupted him, "I'm going to stop you right there Gabe. Maybe I need to clarify, I didn't ask multiple questions about her. I asked if after she was found, if she returned to the area. I also asked one more question, that's it." Ralph shook his head and chuckled, "Damn, you've become her pitbull. I don't think I've ever seen you like this."

Gabe put his hands on his hips and let out a breath. "I'm not her pitbull. She has been through a lot, this year included and I'm just protective of her."

"As you should be. If you care about her, you should be and I know you do." His father wasn't looking at him like he was crazy. He actually looked at him with pride, just like that night weeks ago when he had brought Clara over.

Gabe had to ask, "What was the other question you asked?"

"I asked what happened to the man who took her and he told me that they found a body burned in the house he lived in, presumably his."

Gabe nodded. "Ok. I know that part too. Did he ever mention the other two kids living there? There were two others too, older than she was. But Clara couldn't find them afterward, she still calls the police station in Chicago to ask about them."

"No, I didn't even know that. Again, I didn't ask a lot of questions, just those two."

"Ok." Gabe remarked.

"So, does that mean you're done shooting daggers at me?" Ralph laughed. "I need a snack, let's go to the kitchen and see what we've got."

Gabe mumbled a sorry and followed him into the kitchen, where they made sandwiches and talked a bit more. His father had a business trip planned and would be away a few days through the weekend but back in time for the holidays next week. He was glad he hadn't come home late and was able to spend this time with him. He still felt a little uneasy about his conversation regarding Clara but he brushed it off realizing it was better he didn't have to hide anything but hoping Clara would feel the same.

31

CLARA

Clara went upstairs after Gabe left to get changed in something much more comfortable. She heard Julia's TV still on and decided to check in on her. She wasn't sure what she had said to Gabe earlier and he did not go into specifics just telling her, "She's happy for you." She knocked on the door and peered inside. Julia's was laying down watching the Nanny reruns. She turned to look at Clara and smiled. "You never get sick of this show, huh?" Clara said leaning on the door.

Julia responded, "Nope, and neither do you. Come watch with me." Clara decided to lay down next to Julia and watch with her. Julia snuggled next to her. As they were laughing, another knock sounded on the door.

They both looked, and it was Laura. "Hey, what are you guys doing?"

"Watching the Nanny reruns," Julia replied.

"I had just stopped to check in and got sucked in," Clara said. "Come on, you know you want to watch too." Laura laughed. Clara moved over, and Laura laid down next to her and they started laughing as they watched the show. They stayed like that maybe 20 minutes as the episode finished and the next started. Neither Laura nor Clara were inclined to get up and leave yet. Laura had left the door open and all of them saw Vince walk by, stop in his tracks and back up.

He looked in and smiled. "What are you guys watching?" They all repeated for the third time their show of choice. "Is this a girls only late night show binge?"

"Nope," said Julia.

"You live in a house full of women, I'd think you'd get used to the fact that you're included in almost everything," Laura said.

"Just making sure, I didn't want to interrupt if you were talking about girl stuff," replied Vince. He decided to lay down at the bottom of the bed, perpendicular to them.

They watched quietly for a little while, commenting here and there on the show and teasing eachother. Clara laughed whole heartedly at something Vince said and they all laughed along with her. It was Julia the first to speak, "I like him." She squeezed Clara's hand. Clara turned to look at her, knowing she wasn't referring to the show but to Gabe. "Is that what you told him tonight?" She asked her younger cousin.

"He didn't tell you?" Julia asked her incredulously. Clara shook her head. Julia hesitated at first to find the right words but then spoke quietly and with conviction, "I thanked him for making you laugh." Laura and Vince were quiet.

Clara chuckled and turned toward her, "I've laughed before."

"Not really," replied Vince. "I mean you did but not like you laughed just a few minutes ago. You never laughed like that."

"Your laugh was kind of hollow before. Now it's genuine," interjected Laura.

"Huh." Clara didn't know what to say, partially because she thought there were plenty of times that she laughed just fine and of course, there were times that she thought she had fooled everyone and apparently not. But maybe that was the point. For a long time she was ok, just going through the motions, day after day, trying to get back to normal. But lately she felt different, she felt like she could breathe.

They were quiet a few minutes and then Laura said, "I like him too." She took Clara's other hand and squeezed.

Vince turned his head, "I haven't kicked his ass with the cousins, so you know I have to like him at least a little bit."

Laura laughed, "You guys haven't even done your typical line of questioning. That's saying a lot." She was quiet a second and then she said, "I think even dad likes him. He still looks at him a bit warily, but he was stricter before with having boyfriends and all, but with you he isn't, and I think that's partially because of who you've become and in part because of how Gabe seems like a good guy."

"How can you dislike a guy that looks at Clara like she's hung the moon?" Vince said, turning his attention once again to the girls. Clara's eyes widened. "Even if dad didn't want you to date, all he ever wanted, was to see you happy. All *we* want, is to see you happy. You've changed Clara, in a good way. You're more carefree. A part of that is thanks to Gabe. And the others too. So why would we go against that?"

"It was like there was a missing piece to your puzzle," Laura said quietly again. Clara squeezed her hand.

"All right then," Clara began to say, "I guess I like him too."

Everyone chuckled, including Clara herself. They spent probably another hour there watching the Nanny, cracking jokes, until Julia's eyes started to close, heavy from sleep. Clara nudged Laura and Vince whispering, "let's go." She kissed Julia on the forehead, as did Laura. They headed out of her room. Laura squeezed her hand, "love you," and headed to her room. Vince hugged her tightly. Clara went to bed and thought about what her cousins said. As she snuggled into her pillow, she fell asleep with a smile on her face.

32

GABE

Gabe was exhausted. He ran his hand over his face. The meeting with his science group took much longer than expected. The girls kept getting off topic. One of the girls named Stella either blushed every time Gabe turned his attention to her or stared at him like he was a science experiment. Instead, the other girl was different. She was calculating. He couldn't wait for this meeting to be over so he could enjoy Clara for 12 days straight. Finally after two hours they made some headway and split up their tasks to be done. Lola kept insisting they should meet during break but everyone said no.

As he was walking towards his car, he started to pull out his phone to text Clara. He wanted to see if she was still at school. She had a newspaper meeting and then another one with Jamie and the coach. Gabe's group had met at a coffee shop near school. As he walked out, Lola followed him, typing on her phone. She caught up to him and said, "Hey, maybe we should exchange numbers in case we had any questions."

Gabe shook his head. "You have my email. We're in a good place, actually, we're probably ahead of schedule. Enjoy the break."

She grabbed his arm. He stilled turning his gaze towards her and pulling his arm away. He arched his eyebrow in question. Her eyes darted behind him and he sensed that someone had approached.

She nudged her chin in the direction to whoever was standing behind him. Lola walked towards her car as he turned around.

Kristin stood there looking at him and murmured, "hey, Lola." Lola nodded and got in her car and drove off. Gabe crossed his arms over his chest staring at Kristin. "Hi, Gabe." Kristin obviously had come to say something. He was immediately irritated.

"Well? Did you just ambush me here to say hi? If you have something to say, just say it. Get it out because I have to go." She had started to lower her gaze to the ground but when he said that, her gaze whipped up to find his.

"You have to go to her, don't you?" Kristin asked him. Both of them knowing who she was referring to.

Gabe didn't like where this conversation was headed. "It's none of your damn business." He blew out a breath and softened his tone. Snapping at her wasn't going to get him anywhere. "Kristin, why are you here? What's going on?"

She looked up at him, "I just had to know. What went wrong with us? Did I do something?"

He shook his head. "Is that what this is about?" he said quietly. "You didn't do anything wrong Kristin. I was honest with you from the beginning and you can't say I wasn't. I told you, it wouldn't be anything serious, no girlfriend status."

"I know you said that, but it seemed as though we were having a great time. The last few weeks we saw each other almost every day, Gabe."

Gabe exhaled. He knew she had begun getting attached, every party he went to she was there. How do you tell someone that they just happened to be at the right place at the right time, readily available? He needed to make her understand without being a dick. "Listen, I did have fun this summer. The last few weeks, we saw each other more often, because there was a party almost every night and we were both there. But I didn't make any promises to you and usually I didn't make plans with you, did I?" He tried to use a softer tone even though he was annoyed. He had thought by now she would have been over it but it was obvious she wasn't.

"No, you didn't," she answered quietly, "I guess I just presumed that you were there for me. Now that I think about it, you never reached out to me first. I thought maybe you were keeping me at a distance and then would realize how good we were together. But I know we were good together. I know we were. You can't deny that part, Gabe."

His phone buzzed a few times in his pocket but they both stayed quiet for a moment. Gabe didn't want to be a dick like he was at Connor's party, but he didn't want to be too nice and get her hopes up. He wanted it done. He also didn't want to bring up Clara, even though she had to know by now that they were together. He didn't think Kristin would take it out on her, but he couldn't be sure.

She looked straight at him, "It's not going to change, is it?"

"No, Kristin, it isn't." No apologizing either, he wasn't going to do that. He had been clear then and he had to be clear now too. His phone buzzed again. He wondered if it was Clara done with her meeting, he went to get his phone.

"At first, I hated her, you know?" He lifted his gaze to her, his attention was now fully on Kristin. She was going there, and he needed to hear her out because after he did he would tell her that Clara was off limits. "I thought she had taken your attention away from me. You didn't think I noticed, but everywhere she was, you watched her and I watched you. You watched her with such an intensity. I kept trying to think of what I needed to do to get you to look at me like that. Every time you get to English class, you're happy, almost excited. It's because Clara is there, I realize that now. I kept trying to understand what was so special about her, what it was that had you so absorbed. I thought maybe ..I don't know. Do you feel sorry for her, is that it?"

His phone buzzed again. WTF? He was about to say something when his phone started ringing. He reached in his pocket and noticed Connor calling him. "Hold on a minute," he said to Kristin. Gabe needed the reprieve, so he could think of what to say back to Kristin. Also, it was odd that Connor would text and then call immediately. Unless it was important.

"Hey, Connor, what's up?"

"Gabe, is Clara with you?" Connor asked quickly.

"No, she was supposed to meet Coach Rossi and Jamie to discuss something. She may be done by now though. Why?" Gabe began to feel uneasy.

"Dude, Claudia told Leo that she overheard 2 girls talking in the locker room. All she could make out from the conversation was it had to do with Clara and doing something to her tonight. She didn't want to get caught so she slipped out and immediately called Leo. He was at work so he didn't answer right away and she went to find him. We've tried calling her but no answer. When you didn't answer our texts, we were hoping she was just with you."

He immediately started walking towards his car, "I'm close by. I'll go check on her now."

"Ok, Sonia and I are on our way too and I already called Alex when you weren't answering. He was coming to find you." Connor hesitated, "Man, I don't have a good feeling."

"Meet you there." Gabe hung up the call and instantly looked for Clara's name to call her. He turned his head slightly to Kristin saying, "I have to go. I can't talk anymore and leave me alone Kristen. It's over." Something was wrong, he could feel it. Clara's phone kept ringing until her voicemail came on, "Clara, it's me. Call me as soon as you get this. Please." He opened his door when Kristin spoke up behind him.

"I may know where Clara is."

Gabe stilled and turned around slowly. Kristin kept fidgeting with her hands. She was nervous, very nervous. "What do you mean you know where she is?" His voice was hard.

She cleared her throat. "I'm sorry. Initially, I was supposed to keep you busy, so I took the opportunity to find out what I needed to know. I'm sorry."

Gabe walked closer to her and raised his voice. "Kristin, stop wasting fucking time. What the hell is going on?" He was never inclined to hurt a girl but right now he just wanted to shake her. Something was going on. He clenched his fists to refrain himself.

She swallowed hard and kept fidgeting, "Sarah and Jamie are playing a prank on her, someone else is involved too but not sure who. Initially, they were supposed to just scare her a bit, but I found out they are pretending to kidnap her. They didn't tell me directly."

"What????? What the fuck is wrong with you? Tell me where they are taking her, NOW." He dialed Alex's number as he was listening to Kristin.

"I'm sorry, I knew it was wrong. I should have never agreed. I'm sorry." Kristin was blabbering, and it was pissing him off. It was wasting time.

"Stop saying sorry and tell me where she is!!" As he yelled at Kristin who flinched, Alex answered the phone.

"Sorry, yes. I heard them talking, they are taking her to the woods behind the pool in Bello park. They were going to leave her there for a few hours in the dark, at least I hope that's all they were going to do. They didn't tell me everything. They probably knew I would have second thoughts. That's all I know, but I can find out more."

"Keep your phone on you in case I need you to find out more." Gabe barked at her. She nodded. Gabe then added, "I won't tell them you told me, but don't open your mouth about it either." She nodded frantically again.

He turned towards his car and yelled into the phone at Alex, "Did you hear that?"

"Yep, turning around now, I'm on my way. What is going on?"

"Sarah, Jamie and a few others are playing a prank on Clara. They're pretending to kidnap her."

Alex cursed under his breath, "What the fuck is wrong with people? This is messed up. Hang up I'm calling Connor and I'll call Sonia too. Leo is with me."

Gabe responded immediately, "Follow me to the woods. Tell Con to doublecheck the school just in case they didn't do it yet. I'll meet you there." His foot hit the gas peddle a little hard as he peeled out of the parking lot heading towards the area behind the pool that Kristin indicated. "I'm coming, Clara." Gabe whispered to himself. His fists clenched.

33

CLARA

Coach had approached both Jamie and Clara with the idea of training throughout the winter for a spring soccer tournament to be held in Florida. It was a great opportunity for them. Clara had overheard Coach Lawson and Coach Rossi speak about having two team captains next year. She had mentioned it to Gabe and he thought that the tournament was probably a way to see if they could work together. When she seemed preoccupied he assured her that if Jamie wouldn't be able to so, then it would fall on Jamie, not her. Both coaches knew Clara wasn't one to start problems, especially Coach Lawson. Although Clara seemed hesitant about her role in the beginning, Coach Lawson had become one of her biggest cheerleaders. Clara had become very fond of her.

Both Clara and Jamie had put off this meeting between them for days but yesterday Jamie approached her in the hallway. They both decided to meet up in the back courtyard in between the cafeteria and the gym to talk and come up with a schedule, then they would meet with Coach. Gabe had a meeting for his group project around the same time, so they agreed to meet up afterwards. She couldn't wait for this break to start. Gabe and the others had planned a weekend in the mountains skiing. Clara had never been skiing so she was excited. Vince and his new girlfriend were coming as well, so her aunt and uncle wouldn't worry too much. But she would be able to spend 3 uninterrupted days with Gabe and every time she thought about it, she smiled. In addition to that, Clara loved the holidays. When you're a kid and you don't have them for a few years, you realize how truly special they are and Clara felt extremely blessed this year. Clara's phone beeped signaling the arrival of a text message. It was from an unknown number.

R u there? Running a few mins behind

Yep, I'm here. Clara answered presuming it was Jamie.

OK. As Clara looked up she noticed someone approaching with a hoodie. Although the person was looking down, she realized the person walking towards her was not Jamie. She knew Jamie's walk, and this wasn't it. The hair on the back of her neck stood up. She stiffened and went to retrieve her phone back out of her bag. Someone called her name, "Clara." Her shoulders slightly dropped as it seemed like a voice she knew but something in the back of her mind kept nagging at her. As the hooded person kept walking in her direction, she shifted her gaze for a second to the right towards the voice, seeing in fact, Jamie or was it? This person had a hood on too. Just as she began to ask she felt someone come up behind her and before she was able to turn around, a sack went over her head and large hands grabbed her from behind.

Taken by surprise, Clara froze for a moment, panic seizing her, but then her brain caught up and her training kicked in. She managed a hard elbow to the person's gut with force. The person grunted. Going with her instincts, she was pretty sure the person was a male. Clara then delivered a swift back kick to the person's knee resulting in them grunting again. If they thought she wouldn't put up a fight, they obviously didn't know her very well. She was able for a moment to extract herself from the arms surrounding her, so she began to lift the sack partially from her face and take a deep breath. But then, someone else pulled the sack back down over her face and pushed her violently to the ground with enough force to daze Clara for a moment.

Large hands quickly wrapped around her hands and linked them together, pulling her up and dragging her a few feet. She knew she should scream but instead, she just listened and needed to think. There had to be at least 3 of them. "Jamie" if she was a part of it, the guy who grunted and the other person walking towards her. She fought with the one restraining her like a wild animal. She could hear someone approaching from the front, so she kicked her right leg out in front hitting someone, who yelped, but not hard enough. Just as she was about to scream, they threw her to the ground again. *Shit that hurt.* She was sure that her leggings were just torn, her left knee burned. She was panting trying to remain calm.

"What the fuck? Stop." Someone else scream whispered incredulously.

"Shut up," said a gruff voice.

She needed to breathe. She felt claustrophobic due to the sack over her head and it was messing with her head. Memories from the past of being locked in small spaces flooded her mind each time she blinked. But that wasn't her anymore. She had to remember that. *Breathe, Clara, Breathe.* With her scraped palms she lifted herself to her knees and hearing breathing behind her, her right knee came up off the ground. She straightened her leg and delivered a reverse broom sweep causing the person to fall.

"Shit!" she heard one of them say.

"What the hell, she can fight!" Another one answered.

She stood up. Catching her breath, she was listening to understand where all three of them were located. She needed to lift the sack and had to do it quickly. She feigned moving to the right instead moving to the left and began to lift the sack over face when a body tackled her. As she fell her gaze shifted down and the sack was high enough where she noticed a tattoo on the person's forearm, but the force of the tackle sent her reeling back and the wind was knocked out of her. She lifted her head and she felt the earth spin on its axis before everything went dark. *Fuck.*

* * *

It could have been minutes or hours when Clara finally came to, she had no idea. She was in a car. Her hands were tied in front of her, the sack, which she was pretty sure was a pillow case, still over her head and because of this they couldn't tell that she was awake.

The person seated to her left, kept fidgeting and tapping their foot on the floor. They were nervous. If she had to guess, it was a girl and Clara was proven correct when she spoke to the others in a hushed whisper. "I'm not sure about this anymore. You guys totally took this too far." *Jamie.*

"Shut up," said the guy through gritted teeth.

"You guys are fucked up. All of you. If I had known what I had to help with, I would never had agreed," spoke another hushed voice. She was pretty sure it was the person driving, and it was a guy.

"You didn't have much of a choice," spoke the gruff voice next to her.

"Well, I'm done after this." The driver spoke again.

"Your debt is paid. But speak a word of it and I'll come after you." She knew this voice. Clara couldn't place it right now but she knew who this was. *Think, Clara, think.*

"Already told you I wouldn't say anything. Don't want your wrath or the wrath of Gabe and the others on my head."

Jamie spoke again, "I didn't think she would put up such a fight. Wouldn't she have like PTSD or something and freeze up? This is not how I thought it would go."

"Stop being so dramatic. They won't find out you helped us and it's just a prank. We needed to put her in her place. After this maybe she'll leave this school too," a fourth voice spoke quietly.

"We're here. No more talking." The leader was the guy next to her.

They pulled up and two doors slammed. Clara was undecided what to do. Even if it was just a prank, she had to get away, but she had no idea where they were. For all she knew she could start running and run smack into a wall. She needed to understand where she was.

As the guy next to her pulled her out of the car and picked her up, the car drove off. The guy holding her smelled of sweat and something familiar. It was getting harder to pretend to be passed out, her mind flooded with moments she fought the past few years to forget. She couldn't help it and she went stiff. Whoever was carrying her noticed instantly and said to the others, "she's awake," dropping her quickly on her feet and lingering too long with his touch. This time when he spoke, he changed his voice. He nuzzled her neck inhaling and making an appreciative noise. Clara tried not to cringe, but it was difficult, and he chuckled. There were 3 of them, unless the driver came back but she didn't think he would, and only her. Since running off was not a smart option she decided to try and get some answers hopefully also delaying their plan if someone was looking for her. *Gabe would look for her right?*

"Where are you guys taking me?" Clara asked. No answer except for a slight shove.

"What is this about?" She couldn't let them know that she had heard it was a prank. "Do you really think you will get away with this?" They chuckled again and responded with a changed voice, "We are getting away with it, aren't we?"

"Jamie?" And although no one answered, she heard it, a small gasp. The guy tightened his gasp as Clara began to dig in her heels and pull herself in the opposite direction. "Listen, just stop for a minute. Just leave me where the car dropped us off. And all of you go. I won't say anything about this." Clara could feel her heart beating frantically and she was slightly panting. She was about to panic, but she was fighting it with everything she had. She didn't want to give them the satisfaction. "Come on, Jamie, what do you want me to do? Quit the team? Is that it? I know deep down, there's more to you."

"Shut up!" the guy said to her tightening his grip even more. She was bound to have bruises tomorrow.

But Clara didn't stop. "Jamie..."

"Enough!" The guy holding her hissed as he threw Clara to the ground again.

"Fuck you!" Clara responded as tears sprang to her eyes. She could feel the panic rising.

"Actually, maybe I will have a little fun. What do you say? It's kind of hot with you tied up and not being able to see anything."

It was then that Jamie interfered, "Let's just do what we said we would do and leave. The longer we stay here, the longer we risk it."

"You're right. But I like taking risks. The rest of you can leave. I'll take it from here."

Clara stood. "This is NOT part of the plan!" Jamie hissed.

"What do you think?"

He must have asked the other girl who disguised her voice and answered, "Do whatever you want. I don't care. It's not part of the plan but if you touch her then Gabe probably won't want her anymore and I'd love to see that happen."

"Guys, this is taking it too far. We had to scare her not seriously hurt her," Jamie argued. The guy grabbed Clara by one of her arms.

"Plans change," the other girl said, "let's go. Unless you are willing to risk it staying here with him?"

"No, I just..." Jamie started to say.

"Then come on. I'm out and I won't hesitate to leave you here."

Clara started shaking her head, "Jamie, please." Clara was overwhelmed remembering when she used to beg to not be locked in the shed or the closet. Tears slowly trickled down her face and she whispered, "please don't leave me here."

"Aww, come on Clara, we're going to have some fun now. Don't be like this. You'll love it and if you don't, well, I know I will." His grip on her wrist tightened. If this guy was going to try to do what he was insinuating, then she would fight back with everything she had and scream until the people in the next town heard her.

You teeter on this line of being a bit insecure about yourself but then not wanting to put up with anyone's shit. I like that. It shows me you're modest yet strong, humble yet fierce. Gabe's words echoed in her mind. He was looking for her. Clara knew it. She needed to waste time and fight back when she could. So that is exactly what she did. She pushed at him and started yelling as loud as she could.

"You're just making it worse. And I don't think anyone can hear you."

Footsteps pounded towards them. "Shit, someone's here. We can't go out that way," Jamie said. She must have turned around.

"Clara??!!" It was Alex.

"Clara!" Another voice joined in. Was it Leo?

Clara started yelling, "I'm he...". The guy grabbed her and put his hand over her mouth trying to muffle her sounds. Even with the pillow case between them, Clara was able to bite his finger and let out another scream. "Fuck," he grunted.

"I hear her, this way!" It was Leo.

The guy holding her froze. He cursed repeatedly under his breath, then threw her to the ground and decided to get away. Footsteps approached her and just as she was about to plead for them to help, a voice rang above all of them, "Go after them. I've got her." They ran past her as someone stopped right in front of her.

Gentle hands grabbed her. She would know those hands anywhere. "Clara" he whispered. Gabe lifted the pillow case over her head, letting out a breath and touching her everywhere as if making sure she was in fact in one piece. Gabe looked at her with such concern in his eyes as he softly said, "I've got you, baby. I've got you." He undid her hands and went to pull her close just as Clara burst into tears.

34

GABE

Connor was driving and kept glancing in the rear-view mirror at Gabe. Alex and Leo were following them, Alex in his car and Leo was driving Gabe's Jeep. Both Alex and Leo had ran after the trio guilty of this so-called prank but had lost them. It didn't matter, thanks to Kristin, they knew Jamie and Sarah were a part of it, they just had to figure out the third person. Sonia kept turning her head and looking at Clara, tears in her eyes and anger on her face. Gabe was sure Sonia felt just like him, helpless. She reached out to give a comforting touch to Clara, but as she touched her leg, Clara flinched. Connor grabbed Sonia's hand and gave it a reassuring squeeze, a tear trickled from Sonia's eye, she turned around, so Clara wouldn't see it. Connor murmured quietly to Sonia. "Hey, it will be ok. I promise." Sonia nodded and held on to his hand. Connor kept speaking to her quietly and glanced in the mirror at Gabe and nodded.

Gabe couldn't worry about Sonia right now. He could only think of the girl clinging to him. His heart fractured in a million different pieces. He held her tighter. She stopped crying at a certain point but was trembling and every so often she would fist his shirt tightly. He kept murmuring reassuring words in her ear. Rage pulsed through his veins, but he pushed it down. She needed him to remain calm and his need to take care of her surpassed any other emotion right now. He was sure that this prank had brought up some pretty bad memories for her. As soon as he had untied her hands, she threw her arms around him and didn't seem inclined to let go. Neither was he.

After a long 15 minutes, they finally arrived at Gabe's house. His father was travelling and would be getting home tomorrow night which meant they had privacy. He carried Clara inside. Alex and Leo arrived right behind them. They all filtered to the basement. Connor put Clara's bag on the coffee table. He and Sonia had found it in the courtyard on the ground.

"Gabe, I think you should tell Elisabetta that you are home if not she may come looking for you and ask too many questions," Alex told him. He nodded thankfully at his cousin, knowing that he was stepping up again because Gabe for sure couldn't think straight. He sat down with Clara in his lap holding her tightly.

He moved a strand of hair off her face. "Hey," he said softly. She lifted her gaze. Those green eyes fucked with his sanity right now. He had to wait a few moments before speaking. "I have to go speak to Elisabetta, I'll be quick." She nodded in understanding. He looked briefly at the others. Alex was observing him. He nodded in reassurance, Connor was quiet with his hands in his pockets, Leo was strangely pacing.

As soon as he moved Clara to the couch, Sonia sat down and grabbed her hand. "We're here Clara."

Clara looked at her and gave her a small smile before turning to Gabe, "Go. I'll be fine," she said hoarsely. He almost wanted to laugh, she was reassuring him when it should be the other way around. He got up and went off to check in with his housekeeper. She insisted on making food for him and his friends. She would leave it on the counter for them to eat whenever they were ready and be back tomorrow.

When he returned to the family room he found Clara on the phone. "Of course. Thanks Laura, I'll see you tomorrow. Love you too. Yep, don't worry I won't forget."

"We had her call her family and tell them she was sleeping over my house," Sonia stated. "Luckily her aunt and uncle went to some fancy Xmas party in Harrisburg and are staying the night. So Laura is covering for her."

Gabe nodded, "Ok, good."

"You ok?" Sonia asked him. He looked at her thinking about how to respond. "It's not your fault, Gabe."

Sonia always managed to see a different layer to him. "I should have been there, Sonia. I should have fucking been there."

"And I could say that my phone should have been on me so when Claudia called me I would've answered. We could have beat them to it," Leo interrupted shaking his head.

Gabe looked at Leo and responded, "You were working. You couldn't have known."

"And you were meeting your study group and couldn't have known either," responded quietly Clara. All heads turned towards her. "I could have fought back more. I should have. I got a few good kicks but I could have done more. That freaking pillow case..." She shook her head, with tears in her eyes, "it messed with my head. I..."

"Clara, stop." Gabe approached her hesitantly.

She kept shaking her head, "No, Gabe. I'm supposed to know how to defend myself." She furiously wiped away the tears.

"It was three to one Clara, the odds weren't in your favor. It wouldn't be in anyone's favor much less someone with your past," Alex spoke.

Connor interjected, "They knew that pillowcase would mess with your head."

Gabe pulled her to sit down. "Can you tell us what happened? We know that Jamie and Sarah were a part of it, but that's pretty much all we know."

"Sarah? So that's who the second girl was. I should have known I just didn't put two and two together. I was trying to keep it together. I didn't want to give them the satisfaction." Clara took a deep breath and began to tell them the events of the afternoon, with the others putting in their parts of the timeline. Clara was upset that she hadn't defended herself enough, but Gabe had to remind her that her fighting delayed them and that allowed them to get there in time.

Connor chuckled, "I would have loved to see their faces when you fought back."

Alex grinned, "I am more than positive that if it were just Jamie and Sarah, you could have taken them easily." The others agreed. "Do you have any idea who the third person is Clara? Other than being a guy? I mean we can try to narrow it down. Eventually, we will figure it out."

"It's got to be someone they both know and probably hang out with." Sonia chimed in, "and then there's the driver."

"Yeah, but the driver had no idea what was going on. He said he wanted no parts of it. The guy told him that his debt was paid but not to say anything. The driver said he wouldn't because he didn't want Gabe's wrath." Clara informed them.

"He told the guy driving that his debt was paid?" Leo asked her. Clara nodded.

"Dude, are you ok? Your wheels have been spinning. Are you going to get in trouble for leaving work?" Leo shook his head but he seemed very odd. He was very agitated. Gabe could tell there was something else.

"Anything else Clara?" Leo insisted.

Clara thought for a second, probably playing back the events in her heads until her eyes widened. "Yes, a tattoo. I saw a tattoo on his forearm when I was able to partially lift the sack. But I can't remember what it was exactly. It was a little red too."

"Like it had the color red?" Gabe asked her.

"No, his skin was red around the tattoo." Clara told him. He frowned.

"It was red because it was irritated. Because it's new." Leo said quietly. He clenched his fists.

"I know him. My head was all over the place and I couldn't figure it out though. He disguised his voice but he seemed familiar."

"It's because you do know him." Leo responded staring right at her adding quietly, "We all do. Especially me."

Clara tilted her head looking at Leo until her eyes widened and she gasped. "Bruno. I..I" she shook her head.

"Motherfucker." Gabe gritted through his clenched teeth. He sprang up from the couch but Alex gently pushed him back down and pointedly looked at him and Clara. *Clara needs me. Keep calm.*

"I've got to go." Leo turned. "I need to do something. But whatever you decide to do, I'm in. I just need to go now." Just like that Leo left quickly.

"Should I go after him?" Connor asked.

It was Alex who spoke. "No, I think he needs to be alone and to come to terms with it. This is someone he knew since he was a baby. And he needs to pick a side on his own. We'll call him tomorrow."

Gabe was quiet until Clara's hand cupped his cheek. He looked down at her. Her other hand was trying to unclench his fist. He took a deep breath and as he stared at her, he slowly calmed down. He kissed her forehead and pulled her closer. He needed to be close to her probably just as much as she needed it now. She kept him calm. The others were quiet. Clara started to say something, "Guys, please I don't want anyone to get hurt over this."

"None of us will get hurt. I promise. But in some way, they will pay. You're one of us. Let's just take this all in and discuss it tomorrow. Jamie, Sarah and Bruno aren't going anywhere." Alex nodded, as did the others, but a silent understanding passed between him, Gabe, Connor and Sonia.

The others went to the kitchen to get food and drinks to bring down as Gabe got comfortable on the couch with Clara in his lap. He asked if she was ok, "I will be," she responded burrowing herself deeper in his arms.

During the next few hours Clara was extremely quiet. There were moments when she would stand staring outside the patio doors and other times when she would sit down and reach for Gabe. They turned on the TV but no one was really watching it. Everyone was actually a bit quieter and a bit restless. She barely ate even though both he and Sonia tried to get her to eat more. But after two bites, she shook her head. Gabe didn't know if she needed space to take in the events of the afternoon, but at a certain point he decided that she needed rest so he picked her up to bring her upstairs.

For a moment, she went rigid but as he carried her upstairs to his room she relaxed. When he tried to place her on the bed, she tightened her arms around his neck, "Sshhh. Let me just lock the door. I'm not leaving you. I promise." She let go and wrapped her arms around herself as he walked to the door and locked it. He turned around and looked at her. He was so angry. All he wanted to do was go get Bruno now and beat his face in. But he knew more than anything she needed him right now. Gabe took a deep breath and headed to the bathroom. He picked up a washcloth and wet it under cool water and then went back into his room. She was sitting against the headboard, with her arms wrapped around her legs and her head bent down. He sat down next to her. "Hey." She lifted her head and opened her eyes to look at him. Those green eyes gutted him. "May I?" She looked at him quizzically as he gently wiped her face. She closed her eyes and sighed. He then grabbed her hand and gently wiped it down and then proceeded to her other hand. He looked up and she was staring at him. It took all his strength to not crash his lips to hers. He threw the washcloth on the night table and tucked some of her hair behind her ear. "When I was a kid, my mom used to do that anytime I got hurt or was really upset about something. It soothed me."

She nodded. "Thank you." Clara hesitated a second and then whispered, "Gabe?"

"Yeah?"

"Would you please hold me?"

It felt like those words went straight to his heart and grasped it in its hands.

"I hadn't planned on doing anything else." He stood up and pulled her up from the bed so he could pull the covers back. He urged her back on the bed, turned on the lamp and shut off the light. He took a moment and stared down at her. She really had no idea how damn beautiful she was. She was wearing a pair of his sweatpants because her leggings were ruined. Clara wearing his clothes, did things to him. Gabe got onto the bed and pulled her in his arms and held her.

Although initially she was stiff, as he began to caress her hair down to mid back she began to relax. He absentmindedly pressed his lips to her forehead every so often. She burrowed her head a bit deeper between his neck and shoulder inhaling deeply.

"You smell good," she said. He smiled and held her tighter as she slowly fell asleep. His phone buzzed on his nightstand. A message from Alex.

She ok? Sonia is flipping out here.

She just fell asleep. She's ok. I think.

Good.

Then another message. *They will pay for this.*

Yes...they will.

They had gone after one of their own, so they would pay. Tomorrow they would figure everything out but for now, there was no other place he would rather be. He was going to hold her until she told him to stop.

35

CLARA

Her eyes fluttered open and when she saw Gabe she paused for a second. As she took in her surroundings, events from last night flooded back to her. She took a deep breath. She didn't move as not to wake him; his arm was still around her waist. She stared at his handsome features and noticed that although she should probably be panicked or upset, she couldn't remember a moment when she had felt as safe as she did now. Without realizing it at first, Clara began to gently run her fingers over his eyebrow, tracing the outline of his cheek and then his chiseled jaw. Just when she was going to start the other side of his face, his eyes fluttered open and he pierced her with his gaze. He slowly smiled and as she went to pull her hand away, he grabbed it and brought it back to his cheek after placing a gentle kiss to her palm.

"Hey," he said softly.

"Good morning," she replied.

Clara could feel her own heart going a mile a minute. He moved his hand from on top of hers to move a stray piece of hair form her face and put it behind her ear.

He pulled her closer. "How are you feeling, Clara?"

She pulled her gaze from his lips and looked in his eyes. "I'm ok." She nodded as though to convince herself. She needed to get a grip, this was not the time to think about making out.

"Clara." He caressed her face again moving another strand of hair behind her ear. "Talk to me." His eyes were pleading with her and whatever control she had to keep her feelings to herself broke.

She sighed. "Honestly, I am not sure about all my feelings yet. I know that I'm angry both at them and at myself." She looked down for a moment until his fingers lifted her chin holding her gaze steady, letting her know he was listening. "I started karate for two reasons. One to be able to defend myself and second to feel closer to my dad. He always made me feel safe, so I wanted to feel like that too but on my own. I should have been able to protect myself, but that stupid pillow case over my head...it made me feel claustrophobic. Every time I closed my eyes, I was 10 years old locked in a dark place waiting for someone to open the door. I should have been stronger." She shook her head as tears surfaced in her eyes and she tried furiously to blink them away. She hated feeling so vulnerable and weak. But Gabe continued to patiently look at her, Clara also recognized that she felt something else too. "And maybe I shouldn't but I.." she stopped abruptly.

"You what?" Gabe told her while caressing her jaw.

"But after all that happened I also feel safe. Even though I feel so angry for what they did, I know that now I'm not hopeless or alone and that's thanks to all of you. Sonia. Alex. Leo. Connor. And you. Especially you."

Gabe cupped her face with his hands and he smiled a small smile. "It's because you're not hopeless and you're not alone. You think that you weren't strong enough but I know that's not true. You amaze me again and again. We are all here for you. Especially me." They looked at each other and he was just about to lean in and kiss her when his phone started buzzing. Gabe shook his head and peered behind his shoulder at the phone, looking like he was deciding to ignore it or not. He turned back to Clara, and then someone started knocking on the door. He shook his head and groaned. "Worst timing." He smiled and turned toward the door asking quite loudly, "what do you want?"

"It's Sonia. It's like 8.30 and I wanted to check on her. You aren't answering your phone."

Gabe looked at Clara and groaned. "We're coming." He smiled and moved to get up but she stopped him. She looked at him, cupped his right cheek and kissed the corner of his lips. She felt him shudder. He leaned his forehead against hers and took a deep breath. "Now that she knows we're awake, she won't stop. We should answer the door because if I don't do it now then we won't be answering it for a while."

Clara grinned. "I know." Clara spoke up and responded to Sonia, "I'm alive and well Sonia, just give me a minute."

Clara told him she needed to go to the bathroom, but when they both got up from the bed, Gabe pulled her back into his arms, "Holding you in my bed last night was amazing. I know maybe I shouldn't say that considering why you were there, but it was." He held her another second, nuzzling her neck and inhaling her, "And you smell really good too."

Clara blushed instantly. *She did say that didn't she?* Gabe pulled away and chuckled as he went to unlock the door while Clara went to the bathroom. It was a bit muffled, but Clara could hear her say, "Is she ok? I am so mad Gabe and so worried about her." Clara smiled as Sonia continued to half whisper to Gabe by the door. She couldn't hear all of what was being said but as she approached them she heard Sonia say, "No one messes with my friends and she's probably the best one I've got."

Neither had heard Clara come up behind them but she pulled the door open wide and looked at Sonia. "You're my bestie too." Sonia flung her arms around Clara asking a bunch of questions. Clara held on to her but turned her head to look at Gabe a bit amused.

Gabe shook his head, "Both of you go down, I'll be down in a minute to make us all breakfast. Let me text Connor and Leo to come over too." Sonia pulled herself from Clara. "Connor is already here. Since your dad wasn't here we invited Connor to stay and texted Leo so he is on his way. I hope that's ok. And Alex already started breakfast. How do you think I was able to sneak up here?" Sonia smiled as she started her way down the hall. "Come on Clara, you have to eat."

"I'll be down in a minute. Go." He grabbed Clara one last time and gave her a kiss on the forehead and then one behind her ear. Clara shuddered, clinging to him a second longer. As she pulled away, she met Gabe's smoldering gaze, surprising him by giving him a hard kiss on the lips. His eyes darkened. She reluctantly pulled away and as she walked down the hall following Sonia she was thankful that this boy was hers.

36

GABE

They had finished breakfast and the girls had gone upstairs to find something to wear for Clara. All Gabe could think about was that Clara was taking a shower. In his bathroom. Thinking of her in his bedroom and much less taking a shower, made it a bit difficult for him to concentrate. He sat at the counter with Alex, Connor and Leo knowing they had to start talking. They hadn't really discussed anything during breakfast and the guys had to think about a plan. He also needed to approach the subject with Leo. Gabe understood that it hit him close to home but if push came to shove, he needed to know what side Leo was on.

"So, what's the plan?" asked Connor.

They all looked at Gabe waiting for an answer. "We wait." Connor and Leo looked surprised. Alex didn't. "We're on break. I want to enjoy it with Clara. They aren't going anywhere and making them wait will drive them a bit crazy. It also gives us time to think of a plan."

"I agree," Alex added.

"Ok. We also have to figure out who the driver was. Even though he didn't know the plan, the truth of the matter is that he could have called one of us, and he didn't." It was Connor that spoke now, and he shook his head, "I just, I still can't get over all of this. What were these three fuckers thinking?"

Gabe hesitated a second and then looked at Leo. "I know this is hard for you since Bruno is involved. But if anyone is going to pay the most, it's him. Not only did he hurt her, but he was planning on doing even more, and I won't let him get away with that. I need to know that you're on board whatever happens."

Leo exhaled. "He crossed a line. If that was Claudia or one of my sisters I...I don't know what I would have done." He stopped speaking a second. "Sorry if I left last night but I needed to think, and I had to speak to my mom. I didn't mention anything specific, but I did tell her that Bruno had changed and that he hurt one of my friends. She was actually afraid to talk to me about it, thinking that I would get defensive and push her away." Leo lifted his gaze and stared at Gabe, "So, I'm in. What he did. What he might have done to Clara, that is not ok." Gabe nodded and Alex grabbed Leo's shoulder in reassurance.

"Do we get the school involved or the police?" Connor asked them.

"I was thinking about getting the school involved but Jamie and Sarah would say it was a prank and they were never going to hurt her. Plus, we all know Sarah's dad and he would get her out of anything, which means that Jamie would get out of it too. In regards to Bruno – that's not the way you deal with someone like him." Gabe answered.

"What about the girls? Do we involve them?" Alex asked.

"No." They all turned surprisingly to look at Connor who had answered. His gaze was hard. Leo looked amused. Gabe tilted his head in question.

"Yes, you do." Gabe inhaled. It was Clara. He turned around on the stool. His nostrils flared. He was totally turned on. There she was in leggings and one of his long sleeve cotton shirts. Her shoulders were rolled back, she lifted her chin. Her arms were folded over her chest. Her green eyes flaring. She was pissed off and she was gorgeous. Sonia stood behind her, with her arms crossed as well, smirking.

"If you think the both of us are just going to sit there looking pretty, well, you obviously don't know Clara or myself very well." Sonia stated.

Gabe wanted to put her over his shoulder and carry her back upstairs but instead he held out his hand, inviting Clara to take it and join them. She raised her eyebrow questioning him. He grinned and shook his head. "Just come here and we'll talk." She hesitated. "Please, Clara?" Her stance softened and her shoulders dropped. She walked over to him and gave him her hand. He pulled her in his lap but before speaking, he put his hand at the nape of her neck, turning her face to look at him. Gabe stared at her a few moments, trying to read her. He then sighed, giving her a peck on the forehead and held her close. Turning to the others he said, "Let's start with Jamie. She has to realize that Clara knows it was her even if she sent that message." Clara had found a message on her phone from Jamie, telling her she couldn't make it to their meeting. It was sent sometime when they were in the car before Clara had come to.

Clara nodded, "She may not be 100% sure that I figured it out but she's pretty sure."

"Pretty sure she is pissing in her pants right now," Sonia huffed.

"Plus, what about Kristin? Won't she tell Sarah and Jamie that we know they are involved?" Connor questioned.

"No, Kristin won't say anything," Gabe replied.

"Are you sure?" Alex asked him. They all looked at Gabe, even Clara had turned her head to look at him.

"Yeah, I'm sure. She's not stupid." Gabe answered.

Clara turned back around and took a deep breath. "Well, I want to confront her on my own. I know she was hesitating and I don't think she meant it to get that far. It doesn't change what happened, but I can get her to admit it." Alex was ready to open his mouth when this determined look came over her and she stated, "I'll confront her and I'll get her to admit it."

"What about recording it? Then make the rest of the team and Coach Rossi and Coach Lawson hear it." Sonia offered.

"There's my little sis adding the touch." Alex chuckled.

"Yeah, they need to know. Team captains should defend the team at all costs. She didn't." Clara stated. Clara seemed to be getting upset so Gabe ran his hand down her back in a soothing gesture until she leaned her head on his shoulder.

They all nodded their agreement but Gabe hesitated a bit, "Honestly it makes me a bit uneasy because we can't be there physically for that. What if she tries to hurt you?" Gabe asked.

"I don't think she will because I want to do it at school, preferably somewhere like the locker room, but if she does, I can take her. I know who I'm up against, it's not like I have a pillow case over my head." She shuddered, and Gabe held her tighter whispering reassurances in her ear.

They continued to discuss their plan. Jamie was simple, once the coaches found out what she had done, all of them were sure that she wouldn't be team captain any longer. If the coaches decided not to do anything, then they would cross that bridge when they got to it. Sarah was a bit more difficult, since she hid behind her family's money and power. Not only did they have it, they weren't afraid to use it. So it had to be something unconventional and humiliating. Sonia was the mastermind behind ensuring Sarah would be put in her place. As for Bruno, the boys were going to take care of him. He still had no idea that any of them had figured out his involvement. Leo was pretty sure that knowing him, he was probably gloating. Everything would wait until they went back to school after break. In the meantime, they were going to enjoy the holidays and their ski trip.

Once they had finished talking, Leo headed home and Alex, Sonia and Connor decided to go finish Christmas shopping and would be back in about an hour or so when they would drop Clara off. Gabe had just gone to lock the front door and when he came back, Clara was outside on the patio. She just stood there, the wind blowing her hair lightly as she looked out to the pool and the back-yard. He took a deep breath and headed out to follow her. He could only imagine what was going on in her head.

"Hey," he said softly as he wrapped his arms around her from behind, "it's cold out here."

"I know," Clara responded and she leaned back into Gabe. After a few moments she told him, "I love spring and summer. The flowers, the colors, the warmer weather. It used to give me hope. But there's something about the winter. The cold, it makes you feel alive." She stopped for a second but then took a deep breath and began, "For some reason I can't stop thinking about this one time when Paul had locked me in the shed. It was so cold that night." Clara paused again. Gabe was afraid to move, heck, he was afraid to breathe. If she was speaking now without his prompting, then she must be over-whelmed with whatever she was feeling. He didn't want her to real-ize that she was openly sharing for fear that she would withdraw. Thankfully, she started talking again, "I can't even remember what happened that day to make him put me there. Tracey wasn't home.

He had sent her somewhere. I remember that for a split second, I saw Cain about to open his mouth. It was so quick I was sure I imagined it. Or maybe I was hopeful but he just nodded and didn't say a word as usual. Paul all of a sudden slapped me so hard and then dragged me to the shed in the backyard. He literally threw me in there. It wasn't really big and it was always crammed with stuff. It was freaking cold and I just kept telling myself that at least I was feeling something because I was alive."

"How long did he keep you in there?" Gabe asked hoarsely.

"Almost all night." Gabe stiffened and held his breath. "It wasn't that bad, I guess. It was cold but that wasn't the first time he had locked me in there, so Tracey had hid a sweater and a jacket for me. But it was the first time that he left me there that long. Shortly after, I heard a bunch of cars arrive and lots of noise. Paul was having a party so being in that shed was probably the better option. Eventually I fell asleep and I found a blanket on me. When Paul passed out from drinking, Tracey was able to sneak me inside. It wasn't until 4 or 5 in the morning and when she opened that door, it seemed as though she was frantic. She kept saying, "oh my God, oh my God," over and over. She kept rambling that she couldn't find me."

"Could it have been Cain to put the blanket on you?" he asked.

She shook her head. "I don't know. I don't think so, he was always mean to me. He barely spoke to me unless it was to order me to do something. So making sure I was warm was never a priority. Hell, if anything he always acted as though I was a nuisance. I usually didn't fight back or say much because it would have been worse if I did. So that night as usual I did nothing. Today I keep thinking about the fact that back then I chose not to do anything for specific reasons but yesterday, I just feel like I could have done more."

Gabe opened his mouth to object but just in that instant, she turned around, placed her finger on his lips and said, "I know what you're going to say, that I did fight back, that I screamed, yada, yada, yada, but I can't stop feeling that I could have handled it better."

Gabe looked at her intensely and kissed her finger. "Can I talk now?"

"Yes, sorry."

"First of all," grinning as he pulled her closer, "I would not have said, yada, yada, yada." Clara chuckled and shook her head. "Second, it's normal that yesterday brought back some memories for you and I'm honored that you shared them with me." He exhaled, "Third, did you not throw in an elbow and a few kicks or were you talking about someone else? You were ready to panic but you didn't, you were able to resist. For me, that means that you were strong. You also were able to figure out it was Jamie, which tells me that you are smart. We talked about making them pay, which shows me you're fierce and not scared. Don't be so hard on yourself."

Clara nodded, "I'm just so angry."

"And you have every right to be. But don't take it out on yourself, let's take it out on them."

"Just, what did I do so horribly that warranted them to do that to me?" she said angrily.

"You did nothing wrong, Clara. That's on them. Some people can't handle when someone like you comes in and disrupts whatever plan they had in mind. But don't let them stop you."

"Ok." She whispered softly. He pulled her closer, so close their lips were almost touching.

"I wish you could see yourself through my eyes," he confessed to her. Her eyes widened slightly. "And I know you said the cold makes you feel alive but there are other things that can make you feel that way."

"Yeah?" Clara asked him and he nodded and smirked. "Gabe?"

"Yeah?"

"If it involves kissing, can we please do it inside? I'm freezing and I can't feel my face."

He laughed, "Hell yes. I know just the way to warm you up before everyone comes back."

37

CLARA

Clara looked at her alarm clock and sighed. It was only 5 am and she had been tossing and turning for a while now. It had been like this the past few days. She'd had a few nightmares and couldn't get back to sleep. Break was over and today was the first day back to school. She dreaded today. She looked over on her nightstand to where her journal was. She smiled. Gabe had given it to her along with a few other things for Christmas. She opened the beautiful cover and her hand caressed the page with his inscription.

> *Clara,*
>
> *Maya Angelou once said, "There is no greater agony than bearing an untold story inside of you." Use this journal to write whatever and whenever you want. I hope one day you can share it with me.... and the world. - Gabe*

Without realizing it, he managed to slowly chip away at her resistance. If she hadn't noticed that she did the same thing to him, she would probably be terrified. In some ways it did scare her. The holiday break had been amazing. She had always loved the holidays and spending time with her family. This year she got to spend it with Gabe and her friends. She had her difficult moments especially the past few days, and Gabe was right there with her the entire time. Clara was still worried that Gabe would get tired of all of this. Not only did she have baggage but he was used to girls throwing themselves at him and being more open sexually. Clara was extremely nervous and although she wasn't a prude, she definitely wasn't ready to take that step.

She began writing her nervous feelings for that day. After a few minutes, she was done but she figured she might as well get up. She sighed, it was going to be a long week. The next several days, were intense; a karate tournament was coming up, the next newspaper was set to come out, indoor soccer practice a few times a week, and of course, dealing with Jamie, Sarah and Bruno. She typically tried to keep herself so busy so she would fall into a dead sleep. Hopefully that would be the case this week too.

She took her time getting ready and finally headed downstairs. Her aunt was already up having a cup of coffee.

"Good morning," Clara said giving her a kiss on the cheek.

"Good morning, honey."

Clara grabbed a homemade waffle from the plate on the counter and ate it while pouring some coffee in a to-go cup.

"You should get two cups ready." Her aunt said to her, grinning. "I waved for him to come in but he shook his head," as she pointed outside the window to where Gabe was waiting in the car. Clara stared for a second, a small smile on her face. She turned to get another to-go cup but her aunt had one ready.

Clara grabbed a banana for herself and a few waffles for him, "I'll bring him some anyway. I'll see you later."

"Have a good day, honey. We're going out to dinner with the Santino's in case I don't see you. Just text me when you're home so I know you're ok. Love you"

Clara nodded. "I will. As always. Love you."

Clara headed outside with her hands full. Gabe opened the door from the inside and Clara handed over his coffee. "That's for you," Clara said as she climbed in.

"Thank you," he said putting his coffee in the cupholder and with that same hand, cupped her cheek and leaned in halfway for a kiss. Clara didn't hesitate and covered the other half. The kiss was simple but as they looked at each other, heat between them instantly flamed. Gabe shook his head while he put the car in drive.

"Not that I mind, but what are you doing here?" Clara asked him.

"Well, I thought that was obvious, picking you up," he grinned.

She rolled her eyes, "you know what I mean."

"I woke up early and figured I'd come and get you. I know you have mixed emotions about today," Gabe said hesitantly. "Besides, isn't it a boyfriend rule or something, that I should pick you up, whenever possible?"

"Is it? Well, then it's a good thing I came bearing another gift," as she pulled the wrapped up warm waffles and gave them to him, "sorry, no syrup."

Gabe stopped at the light, took the waffles and kissed her below her ear, "I don't need syrup, but thank you." He whispered before starting to eat.

"You're also here because you're worried," Clara stated.

"Yeah, I am." Gabe admitted.

"Do you think they will try something today?"

Gabe exhaled, "No, I don't. But they don't think you'll be in school anyway, and I don't know what they'll do when they see you. I think they will probably go on as usual so no one suspects them, but who knows. But I never thought they would try to fake kidnap you either and they did, so I wouldn't put anything past them." Gabe's hand gripped the steering wheel tightly as he spoke.

"Ok." Clara looked out the window.

"Hey, look at me." She turned her gaze to him so he continued, "You're my girlfriend, it's my job to worry and to protect you. I don't think they will try anything, especially Jamie. I think she's afraid so she'll stay away. Sarah, on the other hand, I'm not so sure that eventually she will try something else but not today."

Clara nodded and furrowed her brow, "Wait, you said they don't think I'll be here today, why?"

Gabe looked at her before turning his gaze back to the road. "Kristin called me last night after I left your house. She said she heard you weren't coming to school anymore and since no one has seen you around, they figured it was true. She said she was sorry that you had made this decision. Honestly, I think she was more worried that I would take it out on her." He grabbed the coffee and took a few sips.

Clara was silent soaking in what he said. "Why would she think that?" She asked him with a bit more bite than she intended to but she couldn't seem to control it. Rationally, Clara knew that it should bother her more what Kristin said, but right now she was focused on the fact that Kristin called him. It bothered her. She was trying to feel confident but failing miserably.

Gabe pulled over and looked at her. "It's either wishful thinking or Sonia. I kind of evaded the question. I told her that we wouldn't do anything towards her as long as she kept her mouth shut." He cringed for a second. "Again, I think she is afraid of how I'll act towards her, how we will all act towards her. I've barely answered any of her calls or texts during break so that's a guess."

"So, she's tried to contact you during break?"

"Yeah. I think.." Gabe started to say.

"I heard what you think Gabe but I don't trust her. She likes you a lot so I think she's trying to get in your good graces again."

"I don't think so. I'm pretty sure she's figured out it's over."

Clara fiddled with the cup of coffee in her hands before she looked up at him, "Yeah, well, you're not exactly an easy guy to forget." She exhaled and looked out the window, "let's just go. Whatever their reactions are, let's just get this over with so I can confront Jamie today." Gabe paused a second probably thinking of what to say or do. "Gabe, let's just go. Please." So he reluctantly pulled back into traffic. They were silent the entire way there.

When they got out of the car, Alex and Connor were waiting for them by a tree. Sonia wasn't with them which meant she was inside. All of a sudden, she felt like an outsider to their group. She was super annoyed, they were planning payback for something done to her and she wasn't even a part of it. She slammed the car door with a bit more force than intended. Alex's eyebrows shot up. Gabe approached them, "Hey."

"Good morning," Alex greeted both of them.

"Hey guys." Clara gave them a smile. "Sonia with chimp #2?"

Alex grinned, "Chimp #2?"

"Yep. Figured we needed a few code names. Chimp sounds good to me." Clara responded as she looked around. "Well, I have to go to my locker and then I want to see their faces when they realize I'm still here. Just tell me if there's something else about me I should know so we're all on the same page. Have I changed my mind? Am I thinking about it? Or I'm finishing out the year and then I'm out of here?" She looked expectantly at all three guys, in particular at Gabe who cringed and rubbed the back of his neck and he was about to open his mouth to reassure her. She didn't want his sympathy. At all.

While Alex kept looking back and forth between them, Connor was looking at Clara and he was concerned. For her.

Clara felt bad and was about to apologize when she heard, "Gabe?" It was Kristin. *Fuck apologizing.* Clara turned around and stared, from where she was standing Kristin hadn't seen Clara yet. *Wait for it.* Kristin shifted her gaze to Clara and her eyes widened.

Clara smiled sweetly, looked at Gabe and said, "Just let me know what page I'm supposed to be on, ok?" Clara was NOT sticking around for this. She grabbed her bag and practically stomped away. It was Connor that lifted the bag from her shoulder and took it. "I can carry my own bag, Connor," she stated as a matter of fact.

"I know. But I'm afraid of you hurting someone with it so let me help you. I'm not going to ask if you're ok, because you're obviously not." She looked at him remorsefully. "Don't. Don't do it. You have nothing to apologize for. You've had a lot happen the past few weeks and you have every right to be upset and more. I half expected you to go ape shit back there on Kristin. Just, everything will be ok, just breathe, Clara. Or hit something, that may make you feel better too." He grinned.

She sighed. "You know for someone who is considered a player or a ladies man, you're pretty sensitive."

Connor laughed. "Thanks, I guess? Where are we going? To your locker?"

"Yeah, you don't have to walk with me."

"I want to. I'm here for you, C. Gabe's my best friend but I'm here for you. You're my friend too."

She bumped his shoulder with hers. "Thanks, Connor. That means a lot to me."

38

GABE

He closed his eyes and inhaled. Talk about wrong timing. When he opened them he saw Clara walking away with Connor. *Shit*.

"What do you want Kristin?" Alex asked her. Gabe turned around.

"Yes, Kristin, what do you want?" Gabe said exasperated.

"I just..." She looked between Alex and Gabe hesitating but then seemed to gain some confidence, "I just wanted to check in. I told you Gabe, I feel awful." She looked around trying to see who was paying attention. She lowered her voice, "I didn't think she would be here today. I thought you said.."

Gabe looked at her and responded with a hard tone. "I didn't say anything Kristin. It's none of your business or anyone else's for that matter."

"You're right. I'm sorry. I was just surprised, I guess." She looked remorseful and Gabe felt bad for responding so harshly.

"Listen, just.." But Gabe didn't get to finish before Alex interrupted.

"We actually have to go, I have to talk to Gabe a few minutes. Maybe we'll catch you later," as he clasped Gabe on his shoulder to steer him away from the situation.

"Thanks, man." Gabe said.

Alex was quiet for a few moments as they walked until he brought Gabe to a bit more quiet area. "Listen, I get that you don't want to be jerk but you're forgetting what Kristin did. Yes, in the end she told you what was happening but we got to Clara JUST IN TIME before Bruno did who knows what. Do I have to remind you of that?"

"No, I'm just trying to appease her in case we need her again." Gabe answered.

"Ok. I can understand that. But I still think you need to be careful. I don't trust her and neither should you," Alex reminded him.

"I don't trust her."

"Good, because I think she has an ulterior motive and I think that motive is you."

Gabe was thinking for a second, "That's what Clara thinks too."

"Well, I think Clara is right. Kristin may just be trying to cause friction between you two and honestly Clara is already upset, so it's working. Just keep that in mind," Alex responded.

Gabe exhaled, "Yeah, ok." He wanted to find Clara. He looked at his watch, there was no way he'd make it to his locker and class on time if he went in search of Clara. But she was upset, he couldn't leave her like that. Frustrated, he said goodbye to Alex and almost sprinted to his locker. He quickly grabbed his books and pulled out his phone to text Clara.

Are you at your math class already?

He began to head towards her locker hoping she was still there. He was totally not paying attention, walking fast and looking down at his phone when he ran into someone and nearly knocked them over. Gabe shot his arms out to stop them from falling but by doing it so quickly, he basically pulled this person closer to him. When the person gasped, he looked down and there was Kristin. *Fuck, what was going on this morning!* He tried let go but she held on tighter.

Gabe grabbed Kristin's hands to pull them off of him but fate seemed to be against him because right then, Clara turned around and her gaze landed on them and it seemed as though he was holding Kristin in his arms. Gabe quickly let go and stepped back but Kristin stepped closer. "Don't touch me Kristin." He walked around her moving towards Clara as Kristin tried to grab his arm again. Gabe shook her off intent to get to Clara, who began to walk down the hall. Connor witnessing the entire exchange, looked at Gabe shaking his head and followed after Clara.

The bell rang. "Clara," he had almost reached her dodging around people and went to grab her arm. She looked over her shoulder at him and once she realized what he was going to do, she stepped to the side.

"Clara, please," Gabe implored, "Let me.."

"Don't Gabe. Not now. Please?" she looked at him and her eyes pleaded with him. "Go to class." The bell rang and Clara stepped in. Gabe didn't follow her, he stood there for a moment feeling defeated. What the hell was happening? Today, she needed him the most and he felt like everything was going wrong.

Connor, who had stepped to the side walked up to him and said, "Leave her alone man. Give her some space and talk to her later."

Gabe glared at him ready to open his mouth. Connor raised his hands, "I'm trying to help you, dude."

"Really? I didn't realize I needed your help." Gabe answered him hastily.

"I've got to get to class and so do you. I'll see you in English. But calm down, man." Connor turned and left.

Gabe walked to his next class glancing in the classroom at Clara who was staring outside lost in her own thoughts. She had shut him out. He walked to his classes and sat down but barely paid attention.

When he finally made it to English, he saw Kristin and Sarah out of the corner of his eye chatting it up with a few others but ignored them and sat down, trying to look busy. The last thing he needed was for Kristin to speak to him and then Clara to walk in. After a minute, Connor walked in and sat down in his usual spot.

"Listen, Connor, I.." Gabe began to apologize but Connor interrupted him and moved closer.

"Don't. It's me, man. I've known you since I was 7. I get it." Connor then turned his head to look at him and Gabe felt a huge 'but' coming, so he raised his eyebrow. "But," Connor continued, "she's holding a lot inside. More than she lets on. My little sister is like that so I recognize it. I always joke around, but if I'm worried, then..."

Gabe exhaled looking around ensuring no one was listening, "So what do I do? Because, I am worried."

Connor looked pensive for a moment before stating, "She needs to give you different answers so ask different questions, and give her some space to figure it out. As for the others. Do what you always do when they mess with someone we care about. RAISE FUCKING HELL. With everyone." He smirked. Mr. Brooks was setting up a laptop when the bell rang. Clara still wasn't here. Mr. Brooks started doing roll call when Connor's phone vibrated. Connor frowned and showed the message to Gabe.

Writing for the newspaper. See you at lunch.

Gabe grabbed his phone to check but he already knew that Clara hadn't texted him. He took a deep breath and grabbed a chunk of hair. She was upset. He, on the other hand, felt like a piece of shit – angry for various reasons, helpless and jealous that she texted Connor. He knew he wasn't being rational. He knew it. Most likely she was in the room designated for the students that were part of the newspaper, he had to talk to her. Gabe went to get up, but Connor clamped a hand on his arm and shook his head. "Don't, dude."

"Connor and Gabe, is there something you would like to share with the class or can you pay attention now?" They both apologized and looked straight ahead.

Gabe waited a few minutes before asking Connor very quietly, "why not?"

"Because that room is her territory," he looked forward, "it's like her sacred ground, don't bring tension there."

He sat there and listened to Mr. Brook's presentation, or so he thought but he couldn't recall anything from it. He grabbed his phone a few times to text Clara but didn't know what to write. *In person*, he kept telling himself. Class finally ended and he got up. Connor was about to say something when Kristin approached with Sarah.

"Hey guys, how are you?" Sarah said, "I was just speaking to Sonia about you guys. We were thinking of hanging out next weekend."

Connor raised his eyebrow, "Really?" and then it was as if he remembered something and instantly was about to recuperate, "where were you guys thinking?" Gabe stayed silent.

"Well, there's the annual event at the country club so we thought we'd all go. It's on that Friday. It may be a bit of a drag in the beginning but then we can move it to the golf course..." She intently left it as a huge question mark at the end. She then started to look pensive, "Sonia and I have to coordinate how many people we can actually bring since there's Alex too and if he brings a date. Kristin, what if you become Nathan's guest?"

Kristin whipped her head to answer Sarah, "What?"

"Never mind, we'll figure something out. So I'll talk to Sonia, then?"

"Sure," Gabe answered staring directly at Sarah who seemed oblivious to his mood.

She clapped her hands ecstatically, "Perfect! Come on, Kristin, let's go!"

Kristin was going to say something else but thought better of it and walked away. Gabe turned to Connor. "Raise hell, huh?"

Connor grinned. "Yep,"

"I need you to do something for me. Sonia had warned me to go with the flow with whatever I heard."

"Shoot, what is it?" Connor asked him.

"I need you to tell Sarah to find a way to NOT invite Kristin."

"Ok, I'm on it. Want to tell me why?"

Gabe smirked, "I have an idea, but Kristin seems to be getting in the middle of things so I need her out. Tell Sarah that I specifically asked for her not to be invited."

Connor nodded, "You got it, bro."

Gabe smiled as he sent Sonia a quick message. *Time to wage war.*

Welcome aboard.

39

CLARA

The day dragged, she avoided the others all day. Especially Gabe. He had texted her throughout the day but she hadn't answered. She needed some distance so it was easy to hide out in the newspaper room. Gym proved a bit more difficult since she had to pretend that she didn't know Jamie was involved. Because she didn't go to English, she got to gym a bit earlier to speak to Coach Lawson. Clara told her that Jamie and she hadn't met and that it was making her anxious. "Coach Lawson, could I say that you asked about it to put a bit of pressure on the subject?"

"Of course, Clara, actually I am putting pressure. This tournament is a great one to do and I think with the both of you we have a great chance. I thought you had met. Tell her I told you to speak and I want a schedule done by EOD tomorrow. Thanks for bringing it to my attention."

"You're welcome and thank you." Clara decided she was going to do this her way. She was no longer confronting Jamie in class, she was going to do it after school. Now she just needed a few girls from the team to be there too. She approached Moira as soon as she came into the locker room. "Moira, can I talk to you a second?"

"Hey Clara, sure. What's up?"

"Well, Coaches Rossi and Lawson want us to do that tournament and Jamie is dragging her feet. I need to meet with her a few minutes after school, but I was wondering if you could stay in the area. I need a witness. I don't trust her, you know."

Moira looked at her sympathetically. "Yeah, I know. This tournament is important for all of us. Where are you meeting with her?"

They spoke quickly about the details. She asked Amelia the same thing and she also agreed. Step 1 and 2 done. Now step 3: convince Jamie to meet with her. It was hard when she just wanted to smash Jamie's face in the wall.

"Jamie, we need to talk about the tournament."

Jamie looked at her and hesitated, "Yeah, of course. Sorry about that day but time got away from me."

"Yeah, whatever. We can meet after school today."

"Today? Well, I..."

"Listen, Coach Lawson asked me about it and I didn't know what to tell her. She wants a schedule in place by EOD tomorrow and we don't have gym tomorrow. It will take us 10 minutes."

"Shit. She asked you?" Jamie questioned her.

"Yeah, go talk to her if you want but she was not happy." Clara told her as a matter of factly.

"Yeah, ok. Right after school is fine. How about.."

Clara interrupted her, "how about the back parking lot. I am parked there and I noticed you were too. I'll bring a notebook, it will literally take us not even 10 minutes."

"Fine. Ok." Jamie conceded. Step 3 finished.

Clara knew she had to keep one of the others in the loop, she couldn't depend on just Moira and Amelia. So she sent a group text to all of them. She knew she should text Gabe directly but she was being stubborn. She knew it but right now she didn't care. As the day passed quickly, her anger grew. She was mad. At all of them. Jamie. Sarah. Bruno. Kristin. Gabe. Alex. Even Sonia and Connor. Ok, maybe not Connor after this morning. But the others. Screw them. She was taking this situation in her own hands and doing it her way. At least this part of it.

When the day was finally over, she moved towards the parking lot. Both Moira and Amelia were on their way. Jamie was already there, leaning on her car.

"Ok, let's get this over with," Jamie stated.

"Sure," Clara answered as she kept an intense stare on Jamie's face.

Jamie seemed uneasy. "Anyway, I was thinking Tuesdays and Thursdays for indoor practice."

"The gym is occupied those days. I asked. Only days are Mondays right after school and Wednesdays only for an hour. We could use the turf field for Friday weather permitting." Clara answered her. It sounded arrogant.

"Yeah, ok, then I guess that's ok. We may need more practice leading up to the tournament. I can send an email to the coaches and let them know that this is the start, taking out the holidays etc. What else?" Jamie was nervous. Clara crossed her arms over her chest as she moved closer to Jamie.

"Well, we can skip all this BS and talk about how you and the others decided to pretend kidnap me and leave me in the woods behind Bello Park."

"Wwhat are you talking about?" Jamie stuttered.

"I was awake in the car and even though you were whispering I recognized your voice. You were sitting right next to me, tapping your foot on the floor repeatedly. You were nervous."

Jamie nervously laughed, "what are you talking about? I didn't come to meet you that day."

Clara glared at her. "I KNOW it was you. I actually have no doubt. Whatsoever. I pleaded with you in those woods. Remember? You hesitated but you didn't stop it."

"Clara, seriously. Why would I do that?"

"Not sure. To scare me? To get me to leave school? To get my PTSD to kick in? Didn't you say something about that? That you didn't think I could fight?"

"Clara, I don't know what you're talking about. Just stop."

But Clara didn't. She took a step forward, "Did it make you feel better to see me with a pillow case over my head? Were you able to sleep at night when I begged you not to leave me?"Jamie was pale and quiet. "But you did leave, didn't you?" Clara pushed her a little bit. "You left me with the guy who wanted to hurt me more. My bruises for you weren't enough? Or the crying? You left me. All by myself. To save yourself. Aren't team Captains supposed to protect the team?"

"Clara, I.." she shook her head. Clara pushed her again.

"Tell me, Jamie, how did it feel? Did it make you feel powerful?" Clara stepped closer again as Jamie stepped back.

"I don't know what you're talking about!" Jamie hissed.

And then Clara decided to use the one piece of information that she had figured out today. She could be wrong and all of this would blow up in her face but she went with her gut. "Lucas told me Jamie. He was driving the car. He couldn't give me all three names so guess whose name he gave me?" Clara smirked.

Jamie's face turned ashen. "What? No, no he's lying." She started shaking her head.

"Is he? He has a picture." Clara was totally making this part up but it worked. Silence. Clara's gaze never wavered.

"Clara, I.. I didn't mean for all of that to happen. I.."

"What the fuck?" Jamie turned and there was Eva with Moira, Amelia and Lidia, a senior.

"Seriously Jamie?" Moira asked and then turned to Clara. "Let me get this straight. Jamie with other people decided to fake kidnap you then left you in the dark in the woods?"

Clara nodded, Jamie looked down.

All 4 girls turned to Jamie but it was Eva that spoke. "Jamie, how could you? What the hell? That is low even for you! Why?"

"Probably so she would quit the team. Or school all together, am I right Jamie?" Gabe asked her. Clara's head whipped around, he was right behind her with Alex, Connor, Leo and Claudia.

"It's true. I heard her speak in the locker room with someone else but I didn't know who it was. I went to get Leo." Clara smiled at Claudia and nodded in thanks before facing Jamie and the other girls again.

"Guys it was just a prank," Jamie laughed but seemed very unsure of herself.

"But you left me there, with a guy who threatened to hurt me. He insinuated that he would rape me and you left." Clara said sternly. Moira and the others gaped at Jamie.

"I don't think he would have done what he said. He was trying to scare you." Jamie said to Clara.

"Maybe. Maybe not. You hesitated Jamie. You knew that he might do that but you still left. I begged you." Clara claimed.

"I wasn't going to just leave. I would have gotten help for you just in case he had decided to take it too far. I would have texted someone."

"Bullshit." All eyes turned to Moira. "You would have texted someone and given yourself away? Seriously?"

Clara continued, "Even so, by the time you had found some way to let someone know I needed help, he could have done who knows what to me. You shouldn't have left me there. Period."

"Agreed," Moira stated as the others also murmured their agreement.

Jamie exhaled and turned to the other girls, "It was supposed to be a stupid prank. For me it was just to put her in her place. It wasn't supposed to end up like that." She looked at Clara, "I didn't expect you to fight back. I seriously thought you would just freeze. You heard me. I tried to remind them to just leave you and to go. But they wouldn't listen. I left because I thought I could get you some help, some way. I just didn't know how. When I saw Alex and Leo looking for you, I was relieved but I obviously didn't want to get caught." She paused, "I didn't mean for you to get hurt, especially physically or in the other way that he threatened."

"Other than Lucas, who was there?" The question came from Eva.

"I, I can't tell you guys who the other two were. I just can't. If I do, then..I just can't ok?" Jamie whispered the last part.

"You do realize that sooner or later we will find out who it is, right?" Alex asked her.

She nodded, "I know. But it can't come from me."

"You're not our captain anymore," Lidia said. "I won't take it to the principal because I'm sure that nothing will be done as usual. But you're not the Captain. Step down or we'll take it to Coach. You are seriously a piece of.... " Lidia turned around and left.

"Guys, I'm sorry."

"Sorry, doesn't cut it. And you shouldn't be saying sorry to us. You should be saying it to Clara," Moira said. Tears were coming out of Jamie's eyes and she wiped them away.

Eva approached Clara and Jamie a bit closer, "For what it's worth, I'm sorry Clara for what they did. It was so wrong."

Jamie looked at Clara, "I, I just.."

"Just leave, Jamie. Go home for now. You've said enough." Amelia went and hugged Clara, "Are you ok?" Clara nodded and Amelia turned to Jamie, "I'm with Lidia, step down or we take it to Coach." She squeezed Clara's hand and walked away.

"Clara, please, I'm sorry. It got out of hand." Jamie pleaded with her.

Clara just looked at her and shook her head, "Just go." Jamie's eyes widened and then Gabe opened his mouth, "Say a word of what happened here now, and any consequence will be worse. Clear, Jamie?"

Jamie nodded repeatedly and quickly left.

Moira stared at Clara and shook her head, "I'll have Eva talk to her. She won't say anything. I'll see you tomorrow Clara." Moira kept looking at her and hesitating as if she wanted to say something but then she left. Eventually all that remained were Gabe, Alex and Connor. Clara took a deep breath. And another. She was going to cry and she didn't want to. She shouldn't feel sorry for Jamie. She shouldn't after all that happened towards her. She felt Gabe's hand on the small of her back and she stiffened for a second until she folded herself into his chest. He ran his hand up and down her back.

"Are you ok?" he asked her. She instantly stiffened. For some reason that was the wrong thing to say.

Flashbacks kept flowing in her mind of when she was found and that was ALL people asked her. "Are you ok?" She understood that they didn't know what to say but after days of hearing the same thing she hadn't been able take it anymore. One day, she started running until she was so out of breath she had to stop and she found herself in front of the karate school. She ran back home and told her uncle she wanted to go. He put her in the car, brought her back there and signed her up without asking any questions. Uncle Frank understood that he had to give her some power to take her life back.

Clara closed her eyes briefly and when she reopened them, she pulled away from Gabe and glanced at the others before she said, "No, I'm not ok. I'm not fucking ok. Just stop..." She was becoming frantic and as she shook her head she declared, "stop asking me that."

She backed up as Gabe spoke, "Clara, just..."

"I can't Gabe. Not right now. Just leave me alone," She responded. "Please." She kept shaking her head and ran off towards the other end of the parking lot.

As she turned her head she saw Gabe staring at her and Alex's hand on his shoulder. Connor looked at her questionably. She shook her head and ran. He nodded in understanding and turned towards Gabe.

* * *

Home. Thank goodness she found Rosie in the parking lot and she was able to take her home. She was silent most of the drive so she told Rosie she wasn't feeling well. When she went through the door and heard silence, she let out a sigh of relief. There was no way she would be able to hide her mood from everyone. She changed into something comfortable and headed downstairs to the family room. Her phone beeped.

Sonia: *Are you ok?*

Clara: *Honestly? Not really. Gabe call u?*

Sonia: *Yeah he did but Rosie called me first. I'm on my way.*

Clara: *Gabe tell u to come over lol? I'm fine.*

Sonia*: He told me what happened. I'm not coming 4 G. I'm coming 4 u.*

Shortly after Sonia arrived. They both slumped on the couch close together. The TV was on and they pretended to watch it for a little while. Sonia just held her hand for what seemed like the longest time.

"Want to talk about it?" Sonia asked her.

"I guess I should, but no, I don't feel like it," Clara remarked. They both laughed. Clara sighed. "I feel like if I put it in words, I'll just sound crazy."

"We are crazy. But try me out. I'm known to be a great best friend." Sonia responded.

"That you are." Clara sighed and waited a few minutes before beginning. "I'm tired. I haven't slept well in days. I've had nightmares and flashbacks. Not every night but close. I guess what happened just brought back some bad memories."

Sonia turned to her and grasped her hand, "I know there's more that you have to say but why didn't you say anything? I think that's normal. You could have told Gabe that. You should. He would probably climb through your window and slay your dragons while you slept," Sonia laughed.

Clara looked away from her. "I'm not used to this," Clara whispered as she leaned back on the couch. "Yes, I have an amazing family that loves me but I always try not to burden them. For the most part I've always put up this front that I was OK. One look from Gabe and I feel as though I'm stripped bare. No walls left to defend myself. And it scares me." Clara paused before continuing, "What if I get used to all of this and then he realizes I'm too much hassle? Because lately everything is like a whirlwind inside of me. And I don't know what I feel. I don't know exactly what I need. It's like I want to depend on him and I don't. I'm constantly fighting this war inside trying not to need him so much." Tears slipped from her eyes before she continued, "Because I do. I need him and it scares me shitless. I know he isn't like the other guys I've dated. I know that. But this morning I felt like an outsider not knowing all that was going on. They did this to me and you guys have this plan to get them back and I don't even know it! Then Kristin calling him and talking to him at school, the way she approached him this morning? And then later in the hallway. You weren't there, she was all over him." She groaned, "this green eyed monster came out, I swear I would've gauged her eyes out if I could. What the hell?"

Sonia gave her tissue and held her hand, "So, you're tired, cranky, overwhelmed, angry, a little insecure and to top it all off, you're feeling possessive. Am I right?" And after a beat of silence they both started chuckling.

"I told you I was feeling crazy."

"You're not crazy, Clara. You're overwhelmed but this time you have people backing you up. It's like you were walking on 2 feet and now you're caterpillar and have a lot of feet."

"That has to be the strangest analogy ever, Sonia."

Sonia laughed and Clara leaned her head on her shoulder. "Yeah, strange but it makes sense, right? I'm sorry because I should've told you what my plan was but when we discussed it you said you trusted me and I thought it was one less thing for you to think of." Sonia paused a few moments and added, "I know I don't often talk about what happened to me or about my relationship with my mom. But it's because I've decided to focus on what I do have. I have an amazing brother and cousin, my dad is getting it, my uncle fights for me and now I have a few extra friends and a fucking rocking best friend that I never thought I would have. I'm not saying to ignore what you're feeling, because I think that's what you did in the past. Now it's all coming to a head, good and bad. You're afraid that it's going to scare people away but it won't."

"Anyone tell you should be a psychologist when you're older? Where the hell did that come from?" Clara lifted her head.

"While you were at soccer practice I've been watching Dr. Phil," Sonia said grinning.

"You're pretty good at this best friend stuff."

"Thanks. I've always been a bitch to most girls so that means a lot." They both laughed.

"It's hard to rely on people that aren't family. Friends can choose not to want to be with you and stop being your friend," Clara confessed.

"I know. I get it. Its going to take time getting used to it. The guys took care of things when everything went down with me and I'm glad they took it off my plate. Look at it this way. What if I were in your shoes? Would you just sit back?"

"I would have beaten the crap out of them," Clara said hastily.

"Wow," Sonia laughed, "but see, you would do anything to defend me, right? You're genuine and pure so you fight back the simple way. With words like you did today by confronting Jamie. With fists to defend yourself or someone you care about. Gabe, Alex, and I have learned to fight back differently with certain people. There are times we've had to be cunning and sly. I think in a way we don't want to show you that side of ourselves. I guess we're worried that you would look at us differently. We also know that it might weigh on your conscience. Even if they are the bad guys. But you're one of us and we can't just pretend it didn't happen. I know that sometimes people say the best revenge is to move on. But Sarah and Bruno, they would try something again, I know it and so do the guys. They need to be taken care of."

Clara wiped her eyes and nodded. "I wouldn't think less of any of you for getting back at them. They started it."

"Just like we wouldn't think any less of you for what you're going through. See?"

"Touché. I just don't want anyone getting hurt."

"And we don't want you to get hurt again."

"You're really tit for tat you know that? I take back the psychologist comment, maybe a lawyer would suit you better," Clara joked.

Sonia grinned. "You better now?" she asked as she hugged Clara.

"Yeah, I am. Thank you for being here."

"Where else would I be?"

They watched TV for about an hour or so until Sonia was sure Clara was better. Clara walked her to the door and Sonia hesitated, before saying, "Call him," but then added, "Or don't yet. Do whatever you need to do for you. He's my cousin and I love him. But I know how overbearing they can be. They just don't always realize it. But whether tonight or tomorrow, you need to set it straight with him because in the end he's doing it because he cares. But me, I'll always have your back. Don't forget that."

40

GABE

Gabe was trying to read a page in his biology book for probably the 7th time when Sonia had just texted him letting him know she saw Clara.

Gabe: *Is she ok?*

Sonia: *She needs you*

Gabe: *So what do I do?*

Sonia: *You wait*

Gabe quickly answered. *For what?*

Sonia: *For her to come to you*

Gabe: *How can u say she needs me and then tell me to wait*

Sonia: *Trust me, k?*

Gabe groaned. He ran his hands through his hair. All he knew was that something was going on with Clara, he needed to speak to her and she needed him as much. This wasn't like him, he didn't wait. He always met things head on making him seem sometimes bossy or cocky. He tried not to act like that with Clara. But at times, such as now, it was proving difficult. As he was contemplating his next move his phone beeped with another message.

Clara: *Are you upset with me?*

Gabe: *No. Never. Are you angry with me?*

Clara: *Not really. It's complicated. Can you come over?* She didn't have to ask twice.

Gabe: *B there in 20.*

Clara: *Be safe*

Gabe: *Always*

Gabe got there in record time. Once there he walked up to the entrance closest to the family room, where she had texted she was. Before he arrived at the door, she opened it and as he approached, she flung herself in his arms.

It doesn't get better than this. He hoisted her up so her legs were around his waist and inhaled her scent. "I'm sorry," they both whispered at the same time as they held on to each other. He shut the door and carried her inside.

"Are you alone?" She nodded squeezing him tighter. Heading to the family room, he sat down on the sofa, never putting her down. She was now straddling him. After a few minutes, she rested her head on his shoulder and started running her nails through the hair at the back of his neck. At a certain point, he grabbed her hand and groaned, "I can't concentrate with you touching me like that."

He could feel her grin. She placed her hand on the side of his neck just moving her thumb back and forth. "Clara," he warned. She kissed his neck before pulling away to look at him. Just like that the heat between them flared, "We have to talk." She nodded her agreement and bit her lip. "Ah, fuck it," he said as he slammed his mouth to hers and she responded.

As he kissed her his hands slowly skimmed the hem of her sweatshirt. When he realized she was wearing a tank top underneath, he started lifting it, just lightly caressing her. But Clara pulled away from him, unzipped the front of her hoodie and shrugged it off. Her arms went back around Gabe's neck and she kissed him hungrily. It felt amazing. He lowered her onto the couch fitting between her legs and continued kissing her. They had made out before, but this time it was more urgent. There was this need on both their parts. Gabe wanted to mark her as his, but he kept reminding himself to slow down. He continued kissing her for a few moments before pulling away and nibbling on her neck and collarbone. He was convincing himself to pull away until she hooked her leg around his waist and he groaned. His hand moved from her waist, to her thigh and back up until he grazed her breast as he dove in for her lips. She moaned and squeezed his shoulders hard. Gabe pulled away from the kiss but moved her leg tighter around his waist, "Clara, look at me." She opened her eyes and he shivered, putting his forehead to hers, both of them breathing heavily. "I want nothing more than to continue this," as he trailed kisses across her cheek and down her neck, "but we have to talk first." He moved his way back up to her lips, until she slipped out her tongue and gently licked his lower lip. His eyes rolled in the back of his head, "Fuck." Gabe kissed her hard again, tilting her head to angle his kiss. Her hands moved from the back of his neck where she was running her hands through his hair to his jaw. It felt like heaven. Minutes went by. Gabe didn't know how, but he managed to pull away, and placed his forehead on her shoulder trying to catch his breath. Even though she was out of breath herself, she half giggled. He lifted his head grinning. "I should use this as a tactic to get you to talk more."

"No need for this tactic although I probably wouldn't mind it," Clara smiled softly. *Fuck, she was beautiful.*

"Are you sure?" Gabe said as he arched his eyebrow.

She sighed, "how about we just talk? But let's stay in this position. So I don't see your face, because honestly, your eyes mess with my concentration."

"My eyes? Seriously?" He shook his head. "But ok to whatever you said." He settled his weight on top of her but to the side, so as not to crush her so it was like she was holding him.

"I have to learn to just talk more." She paused. "So you can push me a little but please stop asking me if I'm ok. Ask me something else but not that. Please."

"Ok." He answered hoarsely.

She nodded. "When Sonia came over earlier we talked for a while and she said I was tired, cranky, overwhelmed, angry, a little insecure and to top it all off, I was feeling possessive. That is a direct quote, by the way."

He grinned and answered, "Ok, wow. Well, how about you talk to me about why you're tired."

"I haven't slept. In days. Since our trip to the cabin to be exact." He went to lift himself up to look at her, but she held him down firm. "I've been having bad dreams," she whispered. He stiffened but just listened as she continued, "sometimes, I wake up and I'm just afraid to close my eyes again. Other times I try to sleep because I'm so exhausted, but I end up tossing and turning for hours until I finally fall asleep again for an hour or so."

"Why didn't you tell me?"

"Because I try to be strong. Because I figure it has to pass sooner or later. Because I don't want to be a burden. And because I don't want you to think I'm crazy."

"Clara.." But he stopped himself. Right now, it wasn't about him convincing her of what he thought, she needed to let her thoughts and feelings out. "I don't think that. At all. All you had to do is tell me and I would hold you while you napped, or climb through your window."

"Sonia said you would probably do that. And slay my dragons while I slept."

"Every last one of them." He kissed her jaw and just like that, she relaxed and they talked about her feeling cranky, overwhelmed and angry. They talked for a while or rather she did most of the talking and for once, he didn't interrupt, he just listened, and asked more questions. He kissed her jaw or took her hand from around him and kissed that. He held her tighter when it became difficult especially when explaining one of her nightmares and told her to cry when a few tears slipped out. After a few minutes of silence Gabe told her, "And all of this is making you feel insecure? About us?"

She hesitated, "Kind of. When we went to school today, I just felt outside of the group. It was as if you all knew what was going to happen except me. That didn't sit well with me, Gabe. This is my fight and while I understand and appreciate that you guys are fighting for me, it's mine and I can't be on the outside. I'm either in your group or I'm not, not just when it's ok to be. And as I am saying all this I feel unsure, because well, I haven't been a part of the group long, you could turn around at any moment and say, 'you're out.'"

"Is that what you're waiting for? For me to do that to you? Or one of the others? To say we've had enough?" She nodded. "So you don't talk about it because you want us to think you're strong, which we do regardless." He stopped a second, "And Kristin and the fact she won't go away doesn't help, does it?"

Clara tensed up and shook her head. "Especially after today and how she acted."

He closed his eyes a second and said to her, "Baby, can I look at you now, please? I need you to see me when I say what I'm about to say." Clara slowly loosened her hold on him which he took as a green light. He lifted his head and smiled. He sat up and fixed her so they were facing each other for the most part. Her legs were over his legs and he held her hands. He took his time to start talking until she was ready by lifting her head and looking at him. *Finally.*

"I'm used to taking charge and sometimes with you I either do it too much or not enough and I, or actually you and I, have to find that balance. I love that you don't just sit there and take what I give you, that you let me have it when I deserve it. But you're mine and I just want to protect you. The guys and I, and Sonia too, we thought we were doing you a favor by not telling you everything and there are still things we have to decide. We figured you had 100 thoughts through your head, we didn't want to add any more. You're one of us. It doesn't matter that you're new. It's because it's you. You're genuine and pure. You don't care about who our parents are or our money or status. You don't want anything in return, you just want us and well, we just want you. We don't care about your past, Clara, we all have shit in our closet. Yours happened to come out sooner but slowly you'll learn more about all of us. But sometimes we fight dirty, and I don't want to taint you with all of that. Maybe I don't want you to look at us like we're the crazy ones."

Clara nodded, "Sonia mentioned something like that. But I wouldn't think that of you."

He caressed her cheek, "You have every right to be angry and overwhelmed with all that happened. You also have the right to be upset with me. But please stop pushing me away because you're scared. Yell at me. Tell me to go to hell. Whatever. When I came to the parking lot today and you were facing Jamie head on, you were so fierce. I was so fucking proud of you not just because you got her to admit it in front of the others, but because I know it wasn't easy. Part of you wanted to run and the other part of you wanted to bash her head in the windshield of one of the cars, am I right?"

She chuckled and nodded. "How do you know that?"

"Because when I'm not an ass, I actually pay attention. A lot. It's kind of obsessive actually. I'm afraid of scaring you sometimes." She looked up at him with her beautiful eyes, he cupped her jaw and she placed her hand over his, leaning into his touch. "Every time I look at you, you take my breath away. Every single time. When you kiss me, it's like I stop breathing and breath too hard all at once. I never get enough. I don't want Kristin. Or anyone else. I just want you. I thought I was clear on that." He sighed, "With Kristin, I was just doing what I thought was best in case we needed her again. But I can see now that she tries to take advantage."

"I don't want to be insecure, just hearing that she called you multiple times and then when she approached this morning. I was tired and cranky but I wanted to be like, back the hell off. And then, when I looked up in the hallway and she was in your arms, I.." Clara stopped speaking a second but then added quietly, "I guess I just worry that I'm not enough. She can satisfy your needs and I'm just not ready to, you know, do that yet and she's more than readily available to jump in your bed."

"Is that also why you were feeling possessive? Of me?"

Clara blushed and looked down until Gabe nudged her. "Hey, look at me, please." She lifted her gaze again, "What happened in the hallway, was me not paying attention because I was looking for you. I texted you and I just wanted to get to you in time and I ran right into her. Literally. She took the opportunity to hold on tight and not let go. I don't know what's going on in her head. If dealing with her makes you feel this way, I have to set clearer boundaries so she understands. But I know you're not ready and I understand and I respect it. It's one of the things I like about you. But I want you. Hell if I want you and only you, OK?"

"Ok," Clara responded softly.

"But can I admit something to you?" Gabe's eyes darkened, "Baby, hearing you feel all possessive about me, I find it hot…."As he slowly closed the gap between them, "it kind of makes me want to beat my chest like a caveman." Clara began to shake her head and Gabe cut off her giggle with a deep, long kiss. He finally pulled away, breathing heavily, "Told you, every damn time. You're the one that does this to me, with just a kiss." He took her hand for a brief moment and held it on his chest above his heart which was beating rapidly. Gabe then stood up pulling her up as well. She looked at him quizzically. He laid down on the couch placing her in his arms comfortably so she could put her head on his chest.

"What are you doing?" she asked him.

"You look exhausted so I'm going to hold you while you sleep. I don't think your aunt and uncle would like to find me in your bed. So the couch it is. We can talk more later. Just try to sleep, Clara, I'll slay all those dragons for you."

She looked up at him, with emotions swirling in her eyes but then placed her head in the crook of his neck and inhaled, "You still smell good."

He smiled and inhaled her, "So do you, baby, so do you. Now sleep."

The following day after school, Gabe had told Clara that he had a soccer meeting and Lucas would be there. It was the truth but she realized it was random so she refused to leave, saying she would wait for him.

He handed her the keys to his car, and just as he was about to leave, she stopped him and gave him a lingering kiss. "Be careful," she whispered. He held her with one hand on her waist and his other hand at the nape of her neck holding her gaze. She knew what he was going to do next. For the most part. He pulled away and nodded.

Turning around, Alex waited for him and began walking beside him towards the gym.

"You coming?" Gabe asked Alex.

"You asked me earlier if I was coming, which tells me I should come. Even though it's just a soccer meeting, right?" he said sarcastically.

"Of course." Gabe walked into the gym. Henry, Connor, and Giuseppe were there and looked right at Gabe as he walked in. Lucas was messing around with Dale and wasn't paying attention. *Perfect.* Gabe walked right in and went right for Lucas, who only realized what was happening when Gabe was a foot away but it was too late. Gabe grabbed him by the collar and punched him right in his gut. Lucas toppled over clutching his stomach and Gabe proceeded to throw an uppercut to his jaw. Lucas fell back. Dale seemed ready to try to break them up, but Alex pushed him back and held him there.

"Gabe! What the..." Lucas tried to speak.

Gabe grabbed him up off the floor, and shoved him up against the wall. "I heard you didn't want to tell me because you didn't want my wrath. What do you think? Was that a good idea?" He punched him again.

"Gabe, I'm sorry. I couldn't say anything. You don't understand. I couldn't.." Lucas started begging.

"But you could. Instead, you left her there. With them." Gabe saw red. He threw Lucas to the ground. "And even if you were scared, you could have come to me afterwards. You should have."

"Gabe, I texted her and Connor. When I realized she was ok, I figured they just pulled a prank."

Another punch to his face and Gabe glared at him. "She wasn't ok and God knows what would have happened if we didn't get there in time." Kick to the gut and Lucas howled in pain. "But you are a part of MY team, MY team. You betrayed ME. I don't give a fuck what you were scared of. You made a choice. And it was the wrong one."

Gabe went to throw another punch. It took Henry, Connor and Giuseppe to stop him and hold him back.

"I'm sorry." Lucas pleaded.

"You should be." Gabe was breathing heavily, and broke apart from Connor and Giuseppe. "I'm fine. I'm done." He pointed his finger at Lucas, "Know what's good for you and shut up about what happened today and be ready, you are going to help me with Bruno when I need it."

Lucas nodded, "Ok," he grimaced as he tried to stand up. Alex let go of Dale who went to help Lucas, but Alex pulled him back. "That goes for you too Dale, keep your mouth shut."

"Fine." Dale responded as he went to help Lucas.

The others turned to follow Gabe out of the gym. "What was that?" Henry asked Gabe. Gabe looked at him and smirked looking at Connor, "I'm raising fucking hell, that's what that was."

41

CLARA

Clara was going to wait inside Gabe's car but she knew that Gabe was confronting Lucas and so she was a little worried about that. But there was also something else, at weird times Clara felt as though someone was watching her. She brushed it off, this payback business was getting to her for sure. As she was getting in the car, she noticed Rosie and Giada coming her way, so she stopped to chat with them. While she was listening to something Giada was saying, she felt Gabe's gaze on her from the side. She looked at him and glanced down at his hand, her eyes widened a fraction but she was able to rein in her concern. Gabe put his hand behind his back so the other two girls wouldn't notice as they approached.

"Hello ladies. What are you doing hanging out in the parking lot?" Alex asked them.

"We were heading to Starbucks but saw Clara and stopped to say hello." Rosie answered.

"Well then, let's go. I could use a coffee." Alex responded smirking. Rosie smiled.

"Great! You guys coming?" Rosie asked everyone. The others murmured their consent but Gabe's gaze never left Clara as he waited for her answer.

"Sorry guys, I have to go to karate," her eyes never leaving his, "baby you still ok taking me?"

She knew the word baby would have the desired effect. His eyes flared. "Whatever you need." She smiled that smile meant only for him.

Giada sighed, "You guys are gross. Let's go please." Everyone chuckled, as they all moved to hug Clara. Alex gave her a kiss on her temple and whispered, "Go easy on him."

"I will," she said quietly. He nodded and everyone left. Before leaving, Henry looked at Clara and then said to Gabe "I'm here when you need me." Gabe nodded.

Clara and Gabe stood there staring at each other until Gabe stepped closer so that she was leaning with her back on his car. "So, baby," he smiled, "you ready to go to karate?" He closed her in as he put his hands on either side of her. *God, he was so freaking handsome.* It was cold out but he had on a lighter jacket, his jeans hung low on his hips, and his thermal shirt was tight and outlined his chest and broad shoulders.

She shook her head. "I have to take care of a few things first."

"Like what?" He moved closer.

"Like taking care of your hand baby," she said quietly. Gabe groaned. Clara laughed kissing him on the side of his lips but then sighed. "Come on," looking at him pointedly.

"Alright, let's go," and he held his hand out for his keys.

"Nope, I'm driving."

"Aren't you a little feisty today?" Gabe grinned, "First, you called me baby and now you're acting bossy."

As they got in the car, "Gabe, I am going to show you bossy if you don't start talking." She put her seatbelt on and turned to him, "and show me your hand." She held out her hand and then added, "please." He shook his head in fake annoyance but showed her his right hand. "Gabe! It's all red and.." She closed her eyes a second. "I figured you would hit him once but this looks like more. Does it hurt? It has to. How much did you hurt him?"

"Not nearly enough," Gabe answered her.

"What if he tells someone? I don't want you getting in trouble. He was only driving the car."

"Clara," he said sternly, "I made sure he won't tell anyone so I won't get in trouble. And he wasn't ONLY driving the car. He is a part of my team, since freshman year. He should have told me, some way, somehow. The fact that you picked up on his unusual behavior and figured out it was him, should NOT have been the way we found out. He deserved it."

Clara sighed. They had discussed it this morning briefly before school. Gabe wanted to know how Clara figured out Lucas was involved. She mentioned that out of the blue he texted her a strange message and then she remembered that when they were at the cabin, Connor had mentioned to Alex that Lucas had texted him asking a bunch of questions. When he saw him in science, he look relieved at first but then seemed tense. She went with her gut and thankfully she was right when confronting Jamie. She could sense Gabe's anger building as she told him. She knew he would confront Lucas today, she just didn't know that he would hit him. At least more than once. She ran her thumb over his knuckles. He hissed.

"I'm sorry," Clara went to pull her hand away but he held on.

"Baby, you have nothing to be sorry about, especially if you kiss it and make it all better when we get to my house." Gabe looked at her and grinned.

Her eyes softened. "Of course I will." She started the car. "But first, you are going to tell me what happened."

As they pulled out of the parking lot, Kristin was walking and she must have seen that it was Gabe's car. She lifted her hand to wave but stopped dead in her tracks when she noticed Clara was driving. Clara looked at her and smiled sweetly right as Gabe moved Clara's hair to the side and ran his hand down the length of it. Out of the corner of his eye, he noticed Kristin was there but ignored her.

"You got it." So he told her, leaving out the actual amount of times he punched Lucas. When they got back to house, she first cleaned his hand with warm water and then asked for a first aid kit. When he insisted he didn't need one, she crossed her arms and raised her eyebrow, and he reluctantly gave in. Each time she put her foot down, his eyes shined with pride. She felt respected and it made her like him even more.

"Will you tell me what is going on with Sarah?" Clara asked him as she was cleaning his hand.

"Don't worry about her." Gabe answered curtly.

Clara responded immediately, "Gabe, that isn't an answer." As she was finishing taking care of his hand she peered up at him and said softly, "This morning you promised me that you wouldn't keep me in the dark."

"Which I haven't. I told you about Lucas. Considering I want to lock you away and keep you safe while I reign chaos, I think that's progress for me." He paused a second and Clara could tell he was holding back but then looked resolved to speak. "Sarah isn't just about you. That family is messed up, Clara. I don't want you in their line of sight. When Sonia was almost raped last year," Gabe paused and Clara's eyes widened but he continued, "it was Sarah's cousin, who did it. Sarah's mom contributed to feeding lies to my aunt. The fact that she chose to believe her and not Sonia is a whole other story. If I get back at Sarah for what she did, their attention will be on me, not you. And Sarah's father will not go against my father. There's some messed up history there and I don't even know all of it." Clara was still reeling thinking about Sonia.

He lifted his hand to caress her jaw until he leaned his forehead to hers. "They already hurt you once, I can't let them do it again. Please let us take care of Sarah. I promise I will tell you everything afterwards."

Clara lifted her hand to cup his jaw. "You won't get hurt?"

He leaned in to her hand, "I won't get hurt."

"You won't get in trouble?" She asked him.

"I won't get in trouble," he confirmed. "I promise."

She nodded and held his gaze, "Please be careful. They aren't worth it, ok?"

"You're right. They aren't. But you are, Clara."

"You're such a sweet talker sometimes." She grabbed his hand and laid a kiss on the bandages. Clara then looked at him and smiled saying, "time to kiss it and make it all better." She then jumped up, wrapping her arms around his neck and her legs around his waist.

Surprised, Gabe braced for impact at the last minute and laughed. "Hell, yeah."

42

GABE

Gabe was adjusting his tie in the mirror of the hallway when Sonia walked down the steps. She looked fashionable and pristine as usual.

"Hey, can you help me with this?" he said to her.

"Sure," she murmured as she reached to adjust his tie.

"You ok?" he asked her sincerely.

Sonia sighed as she redid his tie with ease. "Yeah, just tired. Came to crash here last night. I just.." she paused, "dad told mom I was going to the event at the golf club with Sarah tonight. So the first few days, she was super excited and acted as though we were best friends. Then she proceeded to tell me to not ruin it, to not embarrass her, so I left, giving her some excuse and walked out the door."

"If they only knew," Gabe responded.

Sonia grinned, "Well, I never said I *wouldn't* embarrass her. But since she and Sarah's mom are friends, I think the right word will be horrified."

Gabe smirked and shrugged, "Serves her right for picking sides."

"She is going to be so pissed." Alex said as he walked in.

"Who's going to be pissed?" Gabe's father asked while walking down the stairs.

"You look really sharp uncle Ralph," Sonia complimented him.

Gabe's father responded, "Thank you Sonia. But don't try to change the subject."

Both Alex and Sonia glanced at Gabe who maintained a straight face. He hated lying to his father but he couldn't tell him the truth either. He sighed, "Don't worry about it, Dad. It's just something that we have to take care of."

Ralph raised his eyebrows, "Something or someone?" Gabe didn't answer. Ralph nodded his head. "You're not going to tell me what it is so I'm ready for it?"

Gabe grinned, "I can't."

"Does this have to do why all three of you all of a sudden are so interested in coming to the country club's event tonight?"

It was Sonia who answered, "Uncle Ralph, we come to events at the club now and again."

He looked at her pointedly, "Yes you do, a few times a year but we usually have to beg, bribe or demand to make it happen."

Gabe put his hands in his pockets. "Well tonight you don't have to. Don't worry. Seriously."

He stared at Gabe, "Ok, is everything all right with Clara? Why isn't she coming as well? You know she is welcome."

Again he didn't want to lie to his father so he responded, "She isn't coming tonight but everything is ok." Sonia looked away but Alex maintained a straight face. A face both of them practiced well.

Ralph's phone dinged with a message, "Ok, well I am picking up Liz and I will meet you all there. Be careful." He paused a second and studied all three of them prior to leaving.

"Is he going to be pissed?" Sonia asked.

"Nah, he'll be fine." Gabe said.

"If he knew what they did to Clara, he would probably pat you on the back." Alex commented. "And where is Clara, by the way?"

"She is going out with a few cousins. I asked Sal to watch over her tonight," Gabe answered.

"You mean keep her busy," Sonia replied, grabbing her shawl and heading outside.

"Same thing," Gabe said sternly. "Let's get this over with." He pulled out his phone and sent a text message. It was time.

Once they arrived at the country club, Gabe sat a moment in the car before getting out. Alex asked him, "You sure about this?"

"Yeah, I'm sure," Gabe said glancing at Sonia.

"Let's just hope you don't have to take it too far," Sonia responded.

Gabe smirked. "Don't underestimate my charm, Sonia. I've been at it for weeks." He had been texting with Sarah since she mentioned tonight, he wasn't going to back out now.

Sonia pressed her lips in a think line, "I sure hope so," as she stepped out of the car. He looked at Sonia quizzically. Connor had arrived as well and was waiting for them. They all walked into the ballroom capturing the attention of quite a few people. As they split up to go say hello to each of their parents, Sarah entered the ballroom, making a grand entrance with her family. Gabe wanted to roll his eyes but he maintained his composure. After a few minutes they all headed over to the table.

"Hi everyone! Sonia you look amazing!" Sarah went over to give her a hug.

"So do you of course," Sonia replied smiling.

Gabe made a point of smirking at Sarah, and his gaze travelled from her face all the way down and back up. Her eyes lit up and she bit her lip.

He was about to say something when Crystal, Sonia's mom and Samantha, Sarah's mom approached the table. "Just look at all of you, so handsome and beautiful. I'm glad you guys were able to connect with Sarah and make this happen," Crystal said.

"Indeed, look at all of you. Gabe, you look just like your father. Is he here as well?" Samantha asked.

"Yes, he is," Gabe answered.

"Wonderful, I will be sure to say hello. I'm so happy all of you are here together. You all need to spend time with each other. So glad we could put the past behind us!" Gabe glanced at Sonia and her clenched fists, Connor whispered something in her ear, and she relaxed and smiled murmuring her agreement.

"How about we get something to eat?" Connor suggested, and as soon as the two women left, he spoke quietly, "And something to drink."

"I'll take care of that," responded Alex. "Connor want to help me out?" They both headed towards the bar, asking for soda, while they also made sure to lift a bottle of some type of liquor, leaving the young bartender a hefty tip.

Gabe began walking towards the appetizer table, making sure to brush against Sarah. He leaned down and whispered, "You do look amazing Sarah." He then continued walking not waiting for her response. When he returned to the table, he sat down in the open spot next to Sarah and nodded to Alex to fill his drink. Connor started telling some crazy story to break the ice. Everyone began contributing stories and laughing. Gabe needed a break so he got up to go to the restroom and on his way out, Sarah was waiting for him.

"Hey."

"Hey, you usually wait outside of men's bathrooms?" he asked her grinning.

She giggled, "Gabe, you're so funny." They slowly began walking back to the ballroom.

"As you can see Kristin didn't come tonight."

"I noticed. Thanks for that. How were you able to make that happen?" Gabe asked her curiously.

She shrugged, "I just told her I couldn't bring anyone else. I blamed it on my parents. I also told her that Sonia told me you weren't actually coming."

"And she believed you?" Gabe persisted.

"I can be very convincing when I need to be. Can I ask why you didn't want her to come?"

"She doesn't seem to take the hint," he said softly. He took one of her perfectly styled curls and wrapped it around his finger. "She'd be in the way tonight."

Sarah let out a breath. "Is she why you distanced yourself and barely speak to me?"

He nodded. "I could never just talk to you without her jumping in. Remember the time in the hallway when you invited us to your party? That's why I didn't come that night. I knew she wouldn't leave me alone."

Sarah nodded. "I'll make sure it's not a problem any longer. What about Clara?"

"What about her?" Gabe questioned back.

"Well, you didn't bring her. What's going on with her?"

Gabe shrugged and stopped walking, "I guess I'm trying to distance myself. She's nice and all but I just don't want to deal with all the crap that surrounds her."

"You seemed pretty into her until most recently."

"I guess I was," he put his hands in his pockets and grimaced. "New girl at school and all. You know how it is, other guys wanted her, and I wanted to win. Kristin wouldn't leave me alone and she was friends with anyone else that would interest me so..." He blew out a breath. "Clara's a lot of drama so I'm slowly distancing myself."

She seemed as though she was thinking if she should say what came out next. "Claudia told me she walked away from you the other day in the parking lot and you didn't follow her."

"I didn't." He looked her straight in the eyes. At least this part was true.

Sarah smiled and whispered, "Sonia said she might change schools. Is that true?"

"So I hear," he responded.

"Why not just break up with her?" Sarah insisted.

"Why don't we head out to the patio to talk there, there's heating lamps." They headed outside. "Honestly? I feel bad, alright? There's just a lot going on with her. Plus if what Sonia says is true then..." Gabe didn't finish the sentence wanting her to arrive to a conclusion on her own. He hoped he sounded convincing. He could tell she still had some lingering doubt but that wouldn't stop her tonight.

"Then you don't have to and you can use that as an excuse." She nodded. "Well, then you can let loose tonight and have some fun."

"That's what I intended to do and exactly why I didn't bring her." Gabe smirked as he spoke, picking up one of her curls again. Her eyes lit up.

Alex walked up to them with Zoe on his arm. "Dinner's being served."

Gabe responded, "let's go do our due diligence so then we can cut out of here and have some fun. After you, Sarah." He made a motion with his hand for her to go first. When he got inside, his father approached him. Gabe hoped Sarah would continue to the table, but instead, she stuck to his side.

"Hey, son. Dinner is being served and they'll say a few words." Hi father glanced questionably at Sarah.

"Yeah we just went outside a few minutes." Gabe knew Sarah was waiting to see if he would involve her in the conversation with his father. If he didn't, the doubt towards him would linger, but he knew that if he did, then she would probably be a bit more trusting. He was cringing on the inside. He had hoped something like this wouldn't happen.

"Dad, this is my friend Sarah. I believe you already know her, she's Samantha's daughter, aunt Crystal's friend. I think you know her father."

Ralph nodded. "Of course I do. Hello Sarah. I believe I've seen you around the golf club now and again. So you're the one that got my son, niece and nephew to join us tonight."

"Hi, Mr. Caruso. Yes. I'm really glad they came tonight. Hopefully from now on, they will come more often." She turned to Gabe putting her hand on his arm and peering up at him through her eyelashes. "Right, Gabe?"

"Sure, why not?" He looked down at her and she batted her eyelashes before looping her arm through his. Sarah beamed.

Gabe's father remained quiet, looking at him but didn't voice any of the many questions that Gabe noticed in the depth of his gaze. "Enjoy your dinner, I'll see you both later."

As he walked to their table, he met Sonia's gaze who nodded. After he pulled out Sarah's chair for her to sit, Sonia went into action pulling Sarah close and he knew she would confirm what he said. He pushed his glass to Alex, needing something stronger to drink.

Alex held his gaze a moment, a silent conversation between the two of them. He made sure to lay on just enough charm that didn't seem like he was trying too hard and enough coldness to make him seem like a challenge. If the hour were any indication of where her head was at, he was pretty sure she was swallowing everything. Hook, line and sinker.

43

GABE

"How about we take the party to the golf course?" Sonia asked everyone. They all murmured their agreement and got up from the table, pulling on their coats or shawls. Everyone else was on the dance floor and barely noticed that they were leaving the ballroom. Alex with Zoe holding his hand, Connor who was sticking awfully close to Sonia, and Sarah with Gabe finally bringing up the rear, all headed towards the 15th hole. It was bit farther and much more private.

Alex looked at Gabe and nodded slightly. "To an amazing second half of the year!" Alex pulled out a bottle of vodka and passed it around. Gabe only pretended to take a shot. He wanted Sarah, on the other hand, to be a little bit tipsy. She was almost there. After she took a shot, he pretended to take another and passed it again to her, smirking. As he thought, she rose to the challenge.

Alex put his arm around Zoe. "See you in a bit, guys." Zoe giggled as he led her to the left where there was a lighted path in the trees.

The remaining four continued to walk forward. "You know, tonight was actually pretty fun. Why don't we usually come to these things?" Sonia asked laughing.

"Because they're usually stuffy and boring, but not tonight," responded Connor who stopped abruptly and grabbed Sonia lifting her over his shoulder. Both of them began laughing.

"Definitely, not boring tonight," Gabe murmured, his gaze on Sarah as he trailed his hand down her back towards her hip and pulled her to him. She relaxed.

"I gotta talk to Sonia right over here." Connor walked away.

Sarah looked at them curiously and turned to Gabe. "Are they...?"

"Nah, they're just giving us some privacy," Gabe grinned. He grabbed her hand. "This way." As he led her down a small hill, he pretended to take another sip of vodka before handing the bottle to her. "You know, you surprise me more and more."

"In a good way or a bad way?" Sarah asked him grinning.

"Oh, definitely good." He let his gaze trail down her body and back up. He took a step closer to her. "You know," he began to say softly, "it just dawned on me, that you're like me."

"What do you mean?" she questioned him.

He began trailing his fingers along her collar bone and circled around her, caressing her hair down her back. She began breathing heavily. He took a step forward and he nuzzled her neck. She shuddered as he gripped her waist lightly with his hand. He continued to finish the circle around her. "You're determined in a different way than most others. High school- it's all nonsense for you, isn't it? You want bigger. Better. All the other girls, they follow you. Even the seniors."

"Just like you," she whispered peering through her eyelashes up at him.

"Yeah, I guess. But you're resourceful. You fucking take charge and you demand respect." He tilted his head to look at her. "The other girls, that's why they don't last with me. They need me too much."

"They're weak, Gabe. We're not," Sarah responded. Her breathing hitched as Gabe ran his hand down her back to the curve of her ass. Gabe could tell she just wanted to get it all out. "Kristin, really, Gabe? She has no personality. She's weak, she does whatever I or anyone like us tells her to do. No backbone at all. But she got to you before I could, I saw her latch onto you like a leech. Initially I was livid but after I didn't care." This time she was circling Gabe. "I knew you would dump her. It was just a matter of time. People like us, we need someone strong next to us."

Gabe took a shot and handed her the bottle. After she took a sip she continued. "Clara? Now she kind of surprised me in a way. I guess now that I think about what you said, how you wanted to win, I get it. Being her hero would fulfill your need to feel dominant. To feel like the alpha male you are. But I knew her past would catch up to her." She stopped a second like she was thinking what to say next.

Gabe took the lead. "And it is. Someone helped with that though, didn't they? I guess I hoped that she would surprise me. Initially I was furious that someone would take her paper and show it to everyone or that they would pull a prank on her but then I realized something," as he looked at Sarah.

"What?" she whispered not seeming surprised about the prank part.

"That sooner or later, her past was going to come out and it was always going to be her crutch. Her weakness. She would use it as one, to play the victim. I don't want that. It totally turned me off."

Sarah exhaled and closed her eyes a moment. "She would hold you back. You and I. We're meant for better things, Gabe. I was patient and I can still be patient. But Kristin and Clara aren't right for you."

"Not like you are, right?" Gabe said softly. She shook her head. He grabbed her by the waist and as he nuzzled her neck, he carefully slid down the zipper to her dress. She was panting. "It doesn't bother you that I was with Kristin, one of your friends? Even though she just satisfied an itch I had? Or that she still wants to satisfy any itch I have?"

"You don't need her to satisfy you." Sara spoke, leaning her head to the side and Gabe finished pulling down her zipper.

"Why is that, Sarah?" Gabe asked her softly, taking a step back.

"Because I can do that." She took a step back and let go of her shawl.

"Show me." He goaded her. "Here. Now."

She looked around but barely hesitated as her dress fell to the floor. He shook his head. She smiled seductively, thinking he was shaking his head in awe. He took her hand and helped her to step out of it, pretending as he picked it up gently and put it to the side saying, "Wouldn't want it to get ruined." He traced his finger along her collar bone. He looked her straight in the eye as he began to take off his suit jacket. Her eyes flared triumphant, but suddenly he stopped.

"But, I'm still with Clara. For now. She's probably leaving anyway." Gabe said.

"It doesn't matter Gabe. Maybe if she were to find out, it would get her to leave sooner." Sarah said carefully.

"Would you do that for me?" Gabe asked her. "Like you helped prank her?"

"I.." She began.

"It's fine, Sarah." He laughed. "It opened my eyes, remember? I've known. Kristin told me that it was you."

Anger flared on her face, "She did?"

He nodded. "She thought it would help her. You know, put her in my good graces. She tried to act like she had nothing to do with it, but I know better. And I hate tattlers. I admit I was angry in the beginning, but the more I thought about it, the more you surprised me. You make things happen."

"I do." Sarah whispered, "and I will."

Sarah began to speak again but Gabe placed his finger on top of her lips. "But right now I don't fucking care. I mean look at you." Her eyes flared again. He finally took off his suit jacket and pulled off his tie and tilted his head smiling. Undoing the entire tie quickly, he approached her moving in on her lips. She immediately closed her eyes and leaned in for the kiss but Gabe stopped as he placed the tie over her eyes.

"Gabe, what are you doing?" she asked hesitantly. He came up behind her to finish tying it.

"What does it look like I'm doing?" She relaxed as he skimmed his fingertips along her arms. "Stay right there. I promise I'll make it worth your while." Gabe started taking a few steps back, looking behind him as Connor approached filming Sarah. Sonia took a few quick pics with Sarah's phone, sending it to all her contacts.

"And I'll make it worth yours, Gabe."

Gabe smirked. "I'm sure you will. Talk to me Sarah." Sarah was shuddering from the cold but it was like a dam broke and she began speaking about them and how they were on top. He caressed her hair and urged her to speak. Connor filmed about another minute until they quickly backed away and left her there talking to herself. Sonia erased everything from Sarah's phone and threw it in a bush nearby.

At a certain point, as they rushed up the path, Sonia asked, "where's her dress?"

Alex had reached them, "It wasn't there, I thought you had taken it."

"Don't worry, I've got it." All their heads turned to the right. There was Clara holding Sarah's dress in her hands, with her cousin Sal standing behind her grinning. *Shit.*

44

CLARA

Everyone decided to go to Gabe's house. On the way there, Clara asked Gabe to pull over, so she could put the dress in one of those big donation boxes. He briefly chuckled, when he saw her stuff it in there, but still didn't say a word. Clara could tell he was extremely tense yet nervous. He kept glancing at her as he drove home, opening his mouth to speak quite a few times, but nothing came out. She definitely was not ready to put him out of his misery just yet, so she just crossed her arms and looked out the window. His face when he saw her standing there holding Sarah's dress was priceless. She was thankful that she was able to convince Sal to bring her to the golf club. As she left with Gabe, Sal shook his head saying she was nuts. But he had smiled fondly and told her to make sure she wasn't late or it would be his ass on the line.

When they entered Gabe's house, Connor led them all to the basement and quickly went behind the bar to make them drinks. Clara went to the bar and poured herself a shot. Alex and Connor's eyes widened watching her doing so. Gabe observed Clara carefully. He was most likely trying to get a read on her as she just stared at him defiantly.

"How did you..." Alex began to ask but Sonia interrupted him.

"It was me." They all turned to her. "She couldn't stay on the outside anymore. It wasn't fair. You can yell at me later, but honestly," she looked at Clara, "I'd do it again. The only way Clara can move forward is by being some part of it. Doing what we did tonight made me realize that. Getting back at Sarah, helped me feel vindicated for what Sarah's cousin and her mom did to me. I wanted Clara to feel that way too." Clara's eyes softened. Sonia had confided in her when she told her the plan and Clara loved her friend even more.

Alex and Connor nodded. Gabe's jaw ticked. Clara didn't stop holding his gaze until she went and poured herself another drink and downed it and then she just continued staring at him.

"How about we go upstairs?" Alex spoke to Connor and Sonia. Sonia squeezed Clara's hand leaving them alone.

Gabe let out a breath and looked as though he was about to deal with a wild animal. In a way she felt like one. "Don't." Clara told him, "Whatever you're going to say don't."

"You don't even know what I'm going to say." Gabe told her. "Are you just going to stare at me and take another shot?" She smirked at him, as she took a bottle of vodka and poured some in her glass. "Then will you please say something?" He asked her but she stayed quiet. He groaned and sat down. He ran his hands through his hair until he left his hands hanging and lifted his gaze to look at her. He looked lost.

Clara exhaled. "I don't know what to say yet. I don't know if I'm supposed to kiss you for...for what you did. For doing whatever it takes to defend me or to slap you for touching her, for the things you said, and I didn't even hear it all, I'm sure."

"Clara...this is exactly why I didn't include you. I knew a part of you wouldn't want me to spew all those things from my mouth, and the other part would be hurt from them. It would leave you doubtful and I don't want you to doubt me. Ever."

"Did you kiss her?" Clara asked him.

"No." He answered quickly, straight in her eyes. No hesitation. She nodded.

"What if it had gotten to that?" She challenged him.

"It didn't." Gabe responded. They continued to stare at each other.

"But what if it did? What if..."

"It didn't! And if it would have gotten to that then I would have figured something out!" Gabe's voice was hard. He stood up from the couch and stalked towards her. Gabe stopped right in front of her but he didn't touch her. She ached for his touch, even if she didn't agree 100% with what he had done, she just wanted to be in his arms. Instead, she stood firm.

Watching him she asked, "Was there any truth to what you said to her?" He paused for a second but softened his voice.

"No, other than what I said about Kristin. But what I said about you? Of course not. I didn't mean any of that." Gabe tried to convince her. Clara let out a breath and broke her gaze looking at the floor. "Clara, don't doubt me now."

She lifted her gaze and looked in his eyes. They were so earnest and yet determined. "Sonia had warned me. But hearing you say those things, it was like hearing my biggest doubts and fears come to life. She was willing to have sex with you on a golf course! And here I am making you wait. I just. When I took her dress, it was like I was having an awful dream and you were there with her. I had to keep repeating to myself that it was all an act. I trust you Gabe. I do. But if it was me doing those things with another guy, would you feel great about it?" His jaw began ticking again. He shook his head. "How could you say those things? Was it easy?"

Gabe exhaled and ran his hands through his hair. "It was and it wasn't. There were moments that it wasn't because the shit coming out of my mouth about you, it bothered me. Complimenting her, left a sour taste in my mouth. Especially when my father saw me talking to her." He stopped a second. "I was embarrassed that he saw me with her even though I could tell he questioned it. But I'm going to be totally honest here and tell you that when I thought about why I was doing it, about all that she's done to you, then it wasn't hard. At all. I put on a show to get the result that she deserved. Period." Clara was quiet for a moment until Gabe reached out his hand to grab hers and goosebumps broke out across her skin. "Can I touch you now or are you going to throw that glass at my head?" She sighed.

Initially he hesitated but then pulled her closer, looking straight at her. "I don't lie especially to those I care about. I know that may sound hypocritical of me since I didn't tell you what was happening but if you didn't come tonight I had every intention of telling you what happened. I wouldn't have wanted you to hear it from someone else." Clara nodded.

"So you don't feel any twinge of remorse for what happened? For what we did?"

"No," he responded without breaking her gaze. "I don't care about Sarah, or that we humiliated her. I'd do it again. She hurt you. Her family hurt Sonia. We had taken care of the douche that dared touch Sonia. If he ever decides to come back we will finish him off." He paused looking at her intensely and continued, "But then they interfered with you. You're mine. And nobody fucks with what is mine. I love you Clara. Not Kristin, or Sarah. I love YOU." Clara gasped but he didn't break his stare. "Whatever it takes, I don't care who it is, I will always protect you."

Her eyes widened. "You love me?" she whispered in awe.

Gabe pulled her in his arms, towering over her and softly said, "Yeah, I do." Clara could feel her face flushing, as she was trying to contain her smile. He opened his mouth, "Clara..." but Clara stopped him with a kiss pulling away only slightly, with her lips still touching his she responded. "I love you too."

He let out a breath. "Thank God." He kissed her deeply before he pulled away to hold her tightly to him, with his head bent down near hers. "I'm sorry you had to see that. But I am not sorry for protecting you."

She pulled away and cupped his jaw. "It's done with her?"

"It's done. Sonia took a picture with her same phone and sent it to her friends, making sure to delete it so until someone texts her, she will have no idea, but Sonia changed her passcode and threw her phone in a bush with her purse. And Connor took a video as backup." She nodded. "And just for the record. You like that, with another guy, it's not happening. Ever. Did I mention, never?" She knew Gabe was trying to lighten the mood and lessen the sting of what she saw by getting her to laugh but what he didn't realize was that all of it went out the window the moment he told her he loved her.

"Should we call the others down here?" Gabe asked her, kissing her across her cheek to her ear and her special spot.

"I have to go soon," she answered breathlessly.

"Do you?" He pulled back and grinned, "I'm pretty sure there are rules to this."

"To what?"

"Well, I just told you I love you and you said the same. So I'm pretty sure we need to kiss for a while. Make out maybe. Be close. You know?" He pulled her closer, kissing the side of her mouth.

She smiled. "Oh yeah? I didn't realize there were rules to these things."

"Well, the great thing is, that we make our own rules so they sound like good rules to me." He slowly inched closer and began kissing her again until the door upstairs opened. She pulled back and he groaned. She grinned, he looked so handsome in his suit and his messy hair. He held her close with his hand on her hip, while his other hand ran through his hair and turned to the steps. "Hey, we were just going to call you guys."

"Were you?" Gabe's father stood there with Alex, Connor and Sonia behind him. Sonia grimaced. "So I guess now is a good time to explain?"

45

GABE

___

The following day Gabe sat at the kitchen table having a quick breakfast before going to get Clara. He thought back to last night's conversation with his father. Sonia and Connor had taken Clara home which he was not happy about, but his father insisted they speak then and not wait. Both Gabe and Alex had given his father the abbreviated version of the series of events that had led to embarrassing Sarah and leaving her in her bra and underwear in the cold on the golf course. That obviously involved what they did to Clara with her paper and their so called kidnapping prank. Since they hadn't gotten to Bruno yet, they didn't focus on him too much knowing that Gabe's father would try to interfere.

While he was sitting there, Gabe was waiting for his father to get back from playing golf with Sarah's father. When he walked through the door in the kitchen Gabe waited a few minutes until he couldn't take it anymore. "Well?" Gabe asked him as he put his hands in his pockets.

"Oh, he's mad. Really mad. Tried to come up with a series of ideas on how to punish you but I told him I would take care of that." He paused a second and leaned on the counter folding his arms. "He raised his voice, threatened revenge and then I told him that if one hair on your head was touched, or if anything came out that would ruin your or your cousin's and friend's reputation, then I would slap them with the biggest lawsuit that everyone would be talking about it for years. I told him that he should ask Sarah if she had done anything recently that could have provoked this behavior from you. Everyone knows that you don't cause trouble but they also know you don't put up with shit. I also told him that if his daughter lays a hand on Clara again, I would make sure she was charged with assault. She may not be sentenced but I would drag it out right until she had to leave for college and that would not look good on college applications. I also told him that there may or may not be a video."

Gabe tried to hide his grin. His father shook his head. "This doesn't get you off the hook, Gabe. I don't approve of what you did." He paused a second before adding, "but I understand it."

Gabe surprised said, "You do?"

"Yes, I do. At your age I probably would have done something similar. Probably worse actually. But next time, which I hope there won't be a next time, come to me first."

"Ok," Gabe responded hesitantly.

"I also expect all of you to volunteer at the Children's Advocate Center. So pick a weekend."

Gabe nodded. "Deal."

"Good and be home for dinner." Gabe was about to object when his father interrupted, "No excuses. And bring Clara. I feel like I should get to know her a bit better since you're ready to declare war for her." He had then winked and walked away leaving him a bit baffled.

Gabe went to pick up Clara from karate. He was waiting only a few minutes when she walked out and got in his car.

"Hey," Clara said.

"Hey," Gabe answered meeting her halfway for a kiss when she tried to pull away he grasped the back of her neck gently and pulled her in for another one.

"You ok?" she asked as she cupped his jaw. He kissed the inside of her palm.

"Yeah, I'm ok. Sorry I couldn't bring you home last night."

"It's ok. Are you sure your dad wasn't angry?"

"No, actually." He grasped her hand as he pulled away from the curb and glanced at her, "I think that he's not happy about what we did but he said he understands it." He glanced at her while she looked at him quizzically. "He wants you to come over for dinner tonight. Actually we can't say no."

"Why does he want to have dinner with me?"

"Honestly, he said that he thinks he needs to get to know you better since I'm ready to declare war for you. Don't worry. Seriously."

"Ok. Sure. He's probably like, I need to see what this girl is about that has my son doing crazy things over a stupid ass prank that they pulled on her," she stated anxiously.

"Or he could be thinking something else entirely."

"Yeah? Like what?" Clara challenged him.

"He could be thinking, I should get to know this amazing girl that my son wants to protect with all he's got. She's got to be something special for him to be as crazy as he is about her."

Clara looked at him and instantly relaxed. "How do you do that?"

"What?

"Just say something that totally calms me down. Although right now I'm definitely swooning."

Gabe grinned and shrugged. "I don't know, with you it comes easy."

"By the way, where are we going?" Clara asked him.

"Home. Your house or mine. I don't care. Listen, tomorrow we all have to talk about Bruno. And Monday we go back to school and I don't know who knows what and if Sarah will be there. But today I just want to be with you. I don't want to do anything. With you. All day." He squeezed her hand a tighter. Her eyes softened. "Until dinner time of course," he smiled. "What do you say? Want to do nothing with me?"

"I say that sounds wonderful," she responded. So they hung out at Clara's house for the entire day, under a blanket watching movies, dozing off and holding her in his arms. They went to his house for dinner. Clara had changed claiming she wanted to look nice but hell, she looked more than nice with a sweater and a skirt. She was glowing tonight and he couldn't stop looking at her. He was sure that both his father and Liz noticed.

Gabe thought his father would start with a lecture or a line of questioning but instead he did neither of those things. He told various stories of when Gabe was little, making Clara laugh. But for the most part, Gabe's father asked genuine questions trying to get to know Clara better and making her feel at ease. Liz contributed to the conversation in her usual warm way.

When they were done dinner Gabe stated, "Alex and Sonia will probably stay over tonight. Aunt Crystal went off on them."

His father answered, "I figured. I stopped by there this afternoon. Alex was there but Sonia had left and gone out. Uncle John and I tried to talk to her but she was livid. Not sure what good it did."

Gabe nodded, "Well, we'll go wait downstairs, they should be here in about an hour."

"Thank you for dinner." Clara said smiling at his father.

"You're welcome. I admit I didn't really give Gabe an option but I'm glad you came. We should do it more often." Gabe's father told her.

"Thanks, Dad. Liz, dinner was delicious." Liz thanked him and smiled a truly genuine smile and shared a warm look with his father.

Gabe followed Clara downstairs. She was on her phone. He waited until she was done and when she looked up at him, he arched an eyebrow. "Sorry, I texted Sonia again to make sure she was ok."

He smiled. "You don't have to apologize for checking on your friends, especially Sonia. It's one of the reasons why I love you."

She blushed and giggled nervously looking down at her feet. He took a step closer to her, and grabbed her cell and threw it gently on the couch. Gabe then tilted her chin up while he pulled her closer. "I meant what I said last night, Clara, I love you."

Just as his lips were on tops of hers, she whispered, "I love you too, Gabe."

46

CLARA

A week had gone by. Things were a bit unsettled but they were ok. So far, Sarah hadn't come back to school. Someone told her about the infamous text sent to most of her contacts of her in her bra and underwear so at this point, everyone in school had heard about it or seen the text.

Once Gabe and Clara arrived at school, they went to her locker first. While Gabe went to his locker, Clara spoke to Sonia a few steps away and she noticed Kristin from down the hall zero in on Gabe and begin walking towards him. Although she knew that she didn't have to worry about Kristin, it didn't mean that she was just going to stand there while Kristin tried to gain Gabe's attention. *Not happening.* Just as he shut his locker, Clara moved towards him. He looked at her, grinned and just as Kristin was about 5 feet away, he grabbed Clara and kissed her. Gabe pulled her closer as her hands wound around his neck. Catcalls rang out, until Leo and Alex approached. "Guys, get a room."

Gabe pulled away reluctantly. Clara could feel herself blush so she ducked her head in embarrassment, but Gabe smirked and just pulled her closer to shield her. Kristin huffed and turned away to head in the opposite direction.

Sonia who noticed Kristin's actions, shook her head and whispered, "Take the hint, jackass."

Gabe grinned and squeezed Clara's hand. He walked her to class and kissed her softly behind the ear. "I'll see you in English," and then joined Leo who smiled but hadn't really said anything. In fact, Clara noticed he was awfully quiet the past few days.

Later, when she got to English, Gabe and Connor were waiting outside for her. A look of relief briefly crossed his face when he saw her. *He's still worried, Clara thought to herself.* All three of them entered the classroom together. Kristin had her gaze fixed to the door and as she saw them, she smiled and said hello but no one answered. Clara caught a small smile on Kristin's face as she lowered her gaze. Kristin definitely had something in mind and in fact, at the end of class she approached them. "Can I talk to you guys a sec?"

Gabe sighed, but as Clara made a move to leave, Kristin said, "you too Clara, please." Curious, she nodded and they all walked outside. Connor questioned Gabe with his eyes as to whether to remain or not and after Gabe gave him a slight nod, Connor led them around the corner. Kristin looked at Connor and chuckled. "Ok, I guess I'll speak to all of you. I,..." She looked at all of them taking a deep breath and continued as she looked at Clara, "I just wanted to say I'm sorry. Once I figured out what they were doing, I should have stopped it. I should have come to one of you. It was awful and I should have never agreed to be involved."

Clara looked at Gabe and his eyes softened telling her it was her decision. She looked at Connor who at this point had leaned against the wall with his arms crossed and doubt written across his face. Initially Clara had intended to play along and accept her apology, but instead, she surprised herself and responded, "No."

"What?" Kristin said to her. Connor chuckled and Gabe smiled, pride in his gaze as he stepped behind Clara and pulled her back into his chest.

"You heard her she said no." Gabe responded.

"What does that mean? I apologized. I didn't say anything. I realize now that I made a mistake." Kristin continued to speak.

"It means I'm not buying it. It means I don't believe you're sorry. I think this is another tactic. It means that I think we've all underestimated you. Sarah and Jamie, they wear their attitude on their sleeve. Everyone says what they say about them but it's consistent. But you, no one really knows you. One minute you're nice, one minute you're not and I think it's because you change according to the situation. I think you are trying another angle. Not sure what that angle is but let it go, Kristin. Back off. So, my answer is no, I don't accept your apology."

Gabe's arms tightened around her before he spoke with a hard voice. "You heard her, Kristin. I don't know what is going on in your head. I'm not going to leave Clara and I'm not going to be with you. Move on and stay the hell away from me and my friends."

"Or we'll make sure to embarrass you just like we did Sarah, hell Sarah may do it herself," Connor added.

"Why would Sarah do anything to embarrass me? She is furious with all three of you and will come back swinging. Just watch, maybe I'll help her." Kristin retorted.

"She could try," Gabe said smiling, "or she could be really upset that her best friend betrayed her and told me all the information I needed to know."

Kristin's eyes widened. "But, you said you wouldn't say anything."

"Yeah, well, things change." Gabe stated.

"You...you.."

"I what? I didn't forget what part you played in all of this. You thought I did because I needed you to think that. I needed you to keep quiet, until we were ready." Clara held Kristin's gaze whose face had paled.

"Is this adding up in your head now?" Connor asked her.

"Fuck all of you." As she turned and rushed away. They watched her for a moment.

"She may come back, you know, at some point." Connor stated looking at the both of them.

"Let her come. I'll be ready." Clara responded.

"*We'll* be ready," Gabe emphasized.

Once school was over, the guys were busy with sports meetings so Clara and Sonia decided to study in the library. Before meeting her, Clara decided to unload a few things in the car. As she rounded a corner, a hand clamped over her mouth and she was pulled back into a hard chest. "Hello, Clara." *Bruno.* Clara tried to scream, but he laughed. He spun her around and pushed her against the wall. The way he positioned himself, made it seem as though they were embracing or making out. "Miss me?"

She glared at him but didn't answer. This time she wasn't scared, she was angry. She should have been more careful, knowing that he would try something else sooner or later. "I have to say you're smarter than I gave you credit for. Initially I thought we got away with what we did but then I started noticing things. Lucas had a black eye. Jamie looked miserable. And then finally Sarah. Someone from the football team showed me the text of her half naked. I figured you guys either knew about me or you would find out eventually. I couldn't wait for you to come after me so here I am coming after you. So you and I are going to come to an agreement." Clara didn't move.

"If you promise not to scream I'll take my hand off your mouth so we can talk." Clara nodded. "You promise?" he asked her softly, "if not, not only will you regret it but so will your loverboy."

Clara stilled and Bruno chuckled. She didn't trust Bruno and realized that if she stayed quiet and followed his instructions she may be able to figure out what he had in mind. He took his hand off her mouth slowly as Clara took a deep breath. Bruno stared at her. "Good." He said in a hard tone. "Try to scream and you'll regret it, understood?"

"I heard you the first time, asshole." Clara retorted. Bruno pushed himself closer to her and Clara grunted.

"Now, now, be nice. I'm being nice. I could be doing much worse to you right now but I'm not. Every day you've had someone with you. They all protect you. Gabe, Alex, your BFF. Even MY friend Leo protects you." His voice hardened as he spoke about Leo. "So I'm really happy that they finally left you alone."

"We didn't leave her alone." Leo was standing there with his hands fisted. Bruno closed his eyes a second and turned to face him, as he held Clara against the wall. "Let her go, Bruno."

"Are you really going to take sides, man? Her side? Their side?" Bruno challenged him.

"For God's sake Bruno! She's a girl and she's my friend. Do you think I would let anyone hurt my sisters or my girlfriend? So why would I let anyone, even you, hurt a friend? My friends would never hurt you intentionally."

"I'm your friend! Or at least I was!" Bruno yelled. Clara shifted slightly calculating.

"You can still be my friend. Just stop with the bullshit. You're dealing drugs, you're getting in trouble all over town and then you take Clara and threaten to hurt her? Dude, this Bruno is not my friend. What is happening to you?"

"You're forgetting where we came from. Our history. Man, we're like family," Bruno said furiously.

"Are we?" Leo said quietly. "Because my family wouldn't hurt my friends. Leave Clara alone. Let her go, Bruno. I won't be able to reel the guys in. They haven't done anything because of me and because of her. She asked them to drop it. But now, they're going to come after you with all they've got."

Bruno face turned hateful and he shook his head chuckling. "Your friends think they're untouchable. Always on top. Everyone listens to what they have to say. But that wasn't enough, was it?" He looked at Clara and then turned his angry gaze to Leo, "then they take you in their circle. They don't know you man, not like I do. Where were they when your father died? I was there. They won't be there in the future either. They'll dump you because you're not of their social status and then you'll come running back to me."

Leo shook his head. "Is that what this is about? About them being popular or that they accept me in their circle?"

"This is about people like them thinking they can do whatever they want and not face consequences." Bruno answered him.

"I don't think it's that at all." Clara whispered. Both of them turned their attention to her. During their conversation Bruno's attention was diverted so she was able to move. "Is it Bruno? Gabe and the others, they don't hurt people just to hurt them. They do it to fight back. I think it's more. I think you're jealous because they haven't accepted you. People respect them, but they don't respect you. Do they? They're considered Gods and you're considered a douche."

Bruno turned his hard gaze to Clara. "Oh, really?"

"Yes, Bruno, really," as she kneed him in the crotch with all she had. He crouched down grabbing his groin and she delivered two elbows to his face before pushing him away so he fell straight on his ass. Leo grabbed her wrist swiftly moving her behind him and took a few steps back.

Red with anger and probably pain, Bruno slowly tried to stand back up. Leo spoke, "Choose your next move wisely."

"You'd fight me? We're like brothers." Bruno wheezed out.

"If you think I would just stand here and let you attack her, then you don't know me at all, *brother*." He took a step closer to Bruno and his hands were fisted.

Bruno grunted in pain. "So, you're taking their side then?"

"I'm not taking sides, Bruno, you are. Just drop this. You keep bringing up our friendship, well what about you? Huh? Drop this for me. Just let it go, but if you don't, I can't help you anymore, and I won't." Leo countered.

Bruno looked at him, and glanced at Clara, his gaze hardening but he didn't respond.

Clara grabbed Leo's arm. "Come on, Leo. Let's go. It isn't worth it."

Leo stood rigid staring at his former friend for a few minutes. Slowly Bruno stood to his full height still wincing in pain but he didn't back down and neither did Leo.

"You're right, Clara, he isn't." He walked backward ensuring that Clara was behind him until he shook his head and turned the corner to head back to the library.

Minutes later, Gabe burst through the doors of the study room of the library where Clara, Leo and Sonia were waiting. She was slowly pacing along the back wall but she reached for him as he rushed towards her. He ran his hands over her hair, her shoulders, her arms checking her for any harm. Clara grabbed his hands and stopped him. "Hey, I'm ok, Gabe. I'm ok."

He looked at Leo. "Thanks, man."

Leo lifted his head and said, "I didn't really do anything, she's the one that gave it to him good. He's probably still in pain."

Gabe looked down at Clara who grinned a little and shrugged. "He had it coming. I should have delivered another punch or something."

Connor chuckled. "Why don't you guys tell us what happened?"

Together with Leo, Clara began to describe the episode with Bruno. With each passing moment Gabe grew more tense until of course when Clara fought back. Shaking his head he kissed her temple. "You were supposed to be at the team meeting. Is that why you weren't there? Did you know he would try this?" Gabe asked Leo.

"I've been keeping an eye on him. I just didn't have a great feeling and honestly, I was trying to see if I could talk to him and make sure he didn't do anything. I've known him since I was a kid. Yes he's always been wild and volatile but not like this."

"I'm sorry, Leo," Clara said looking down at the floor.

Leo shook his head. "Clara, it's not your fault. He's changed."

Connor was staring at Gabe, who suddenly let go of Clara. "Alex should be here soon, and he'll take you home. Leo?" Leo nodded.

"Wait, what? Where are you going?" Clara looked to Sonia for support, who shrugged.

"Don't worry," Gabe began to say.

"No. No way. Don't you start telling us not to worry."

"Clara...." Gabe started to say but Clara stepped up to him and stopped him from continuing.

"No, Gabe. Enough. This has to stop."

"This is the second time I wasn't there and he could've have seriously hurt you!" Clara's eyes widened with his outburst.

"What if he tries to hurt you again?" Connor asked her. Leo was quiet. So was Sonia but Gabe and Connor were looking at her expectantly for an answer.

"Then we take it to the principle or to his football coach." She turned to Leo. "You take it to your mom. I take it to my family. Gabe, you tell your father."

Gabe sighed and softened his tone. "Baby, I need to at least have a talk with him. I can't not do anything at all."

"Telling an adult may lead to him being expelled from the team and that would just make him angrier," Leo responded.

"Ok, I get it. But can't it wait until tomorrow? He isn't going to do something tonight." She looked at Sonia who nodded in accordance with Clara.

"That's what we did the first time. We waited."

Clara looked at everyone and asked, "Can you guys leave us alone a few minutes please?"

"Come on, both of you, let's get Alex up to speed." Sonia pushed them out the door.

Gabe exhaled and pulled her in his arms much more gently. He needed to hold her and Clara was hugging him back just as tight. "I don't have a good feeling about you leaving now. If you have to confront him, do it tomorrow on our turf." Her eyes pleaded with him. "Please, do it for me." Gabe groaned as he sat down and pulled her in his lap as he leaned his forehead to hers. "Gabe, please," she repeated.

"I am doing this for you. If something were to happen to you because of him, I'll lose it Clara, I don't know what I'll do."

She nodded, "I get it. But he deals drugs and you don't know who he's with. They could be dangerous. Confront him, just do it somewhere safe and with backup."

Gabe closed his eyes a moment. "I should have taken care of him first. I shouldn't have waited until now."

"You did the right thing by waiting."

"How could you say that? Bruno tried to hurt you today. I know you downplayed it, Clara. You're my girlfriend so I should have taken care of this sooner." His eyes radiated anger.

"But, instead, you took care of me. I needed you then to help me get through it," she stopped speaking and cupped his face, "just like I need you now."

Gabe's eyes flared and he crashed his lips to hers. Clara kissed him back just as fervently. God, she wanted him. Thank goodness for privacy in this room. Clara pulled away just a tad but Gabe was quick to yank her back to him. She whispered, "Promise me, not now."

He sighed, "Fine, I promise," sealing it with another deep kiss. She moved even closer and he moaned. After several moments his lips slowly made their way down her neck, to her collarbone when there was a knock on the door.

"Why are we always fucking interrupted?" Gabe groaned, his breathing uneven, his forehead on her shoulder.

Clara ran her hands at the nape of his neck. "Well, we are in the library." She straightened herself out and smoothed his hair, before answering, "Come in!" Gabe tickled her side causing her to squirm and let out a slight shriek when Alex walked in with an arched eyebrow and shaking his head. But just like that, he turned serious quickly. "You ok, Clara?"

Her facial expression softened, "Yeah, I'm ok."

Nodding but still searching her face for a moment until he turned his question to Gabe. "So, what are we doing?" All of them looking expectantly at Gabe.

Gabe's gaze was intently on her. "Nothing for now. Let's go home. But tomorrow he is fucking mine." Clara breathed a sigh of relief and kissed him hard on the mouth as Gabe stood up and carried her out of there.

47

CLARA

Gabe: *Connor and Sonia r coming to pick u up. I'll see u at school.*

Clara was reading the message when she heard a car honk their horn. Worried about Gabe, she kissed Julia on the temple and hurried outside.

She quickly typed a response. *Y?*

Gabe: *Just car trouble, baby. If I don't see you before do not leave Connor's side.*

Both messages beeped through as she was walking to the car. She was relieved it was just car trouble even though it seemed a bit coincidental because she also knew he would take care of Bruno without her being there. But she hoped that she would be able to at least talk to him beforehand.

Clara: *Ok, be safe.* And then added. *I love u.*

Gabe: *And I love u.*

As she hopped in the car, Connor was the first to say, "Good morning, C"

"Good morning."

"Morning." Sonia reached back and squeezed her hand.

"I'm stopping at Wawa to get some coffee and something to eat." He looked in the mirror at her and smiled ruefully. "I had to leave earlier to come get you guys so I'm starving."

"Sure, you are." Sonia smirked. "But, I could definitely use a coffee, so fine."

Clara responded, "A coffee sounds perfect. Sorry you had to wake up earlier today, Connor."

"I'm not. I get to drive the two hottest chicks to school. I'm not complaining. I just really need to eat something. Plus, I take my job of keeping both of you out of harm's way seriously, whether Gabe asked me or not." He looked in the mirror again, "so for today, both of you will be blessed with my company all day." Clara was quiet for a few minutes. She understood what they were doing. Hell, she accepted their protective behavior, she would do the same for all of them.

But last night after receiving a text message, Gabe seemed strange and left shortly thereafter. He obviously had been super tense after what happened so she didn't blame him when he didn't stay for dinner. But when she texted him before bed, he hadn't responded until 2 am when she found the message after waking up this morning.

"Were you with Gabe last night?" Clara asked Connor.

Connor whipped his gaze to Clara in the mirror obviously surprised at her question. Sonia was staring at him and then furrowed her brow as if thinking of something. Connor looked at Sonia and blew out a breath. He was silent for a little while. "Yes."

Clara knew that Connor would not tell her what or where they had gone. But that didn't stop Sonia from asking. "So, you're not going to tell us where you went? Alex was with you too."

"No, I'm not."

"Luckily they're ok so means it couldn't have been too dangerous," Clara started to say,

"and we know it doesn't involve other girls," Sonia continued.

"What? No, it didn't at all." Connor stated, "Gabe wouldn't do that. We wouldn't do that." He looked at both Clara in the backseat and at Sonia briefly when he said that.

"But the fact you won't tell us where you went, which I didn't expect you to, means that we wouldn't be happy about it," Clara finished.

"There's a good reason, that's all I'm going to say." He parked the car and got out. "Come on, let's grab some breakfast." He quickly started to joke around and change the subject shutting down any more questions at least while they were in the Wawa.

When they got in the car Clara did have another question, "Will Gabe be at school today?"

Connor answered quickly, "Yeah, why wouldn't he be?" But something was off in his tone. "But we both know he has to take care of something so, Clara, please, Gabe listened to you last night so today, just please listen to us. Do not leave my side."

"What are you going to walk me to every class?" Clara snorted.

He chuckled. "Pretty much, yeah."

"Aren't you taking this to an extreme? I'm in school, remember?"

"You were in school when Bruno got to you yesterday. Gabe can't be distracted."

"What are you all going to do?" Clara asked quietly.

"For starters, we're going to beat the shit out of him. Then after that," Connor hesitated but then added, "it depends if he gets the message."

"Let's hope he gets the freaking message," Sonia said quietly as she shook her head. "He's obsessed, and I'm not sure with what." She looked at Clara behind her.

They finally pulled into the school parking lot and Clara looked around for Gabe or his car but didn't see it. Connor turned around to look at Clara in the eyes. "Please, Clara, don't go anywhere by yourself."

"I'm with him on this Clara."

"Alright," but Connor continued to look at her expectantly until she said, "I won't go anywhere without you or the others."

He breathed a sigh of relief as he stepped out of his SUV. As they started walking, Connor put both his arms around them. "Come on girls." Both Sonia and Clara shook their heads, Connor was going to milk the attention their entrance would bring. As they were walking, she had a feeling of someone watching her so she turned her head to the right and stopped. Connor and Sonia stopped as well.

"You, ok?"

She shook her head. "Yeah, I'm fine. You just got me feeling all paranoid, now."

Connor looked around and frowned. "Just stay close, C."

They all headed inside, everyone parting to let them by, inquisitive looks from some of them since Connor had an arm around the both of them.

"What's up, man?" Bobby called out shaking his head.

"Hey, Bobby." Connor grinned, enjoying the attention. They stopped at Clara's locker first and then headed to Connor's. Clara kept looking around for Gabe but to no avail.

"Hey!" Clara jumped slightly. It was Alex, his hair wet from having taken a shower.

"Lacrosse practice this morning?" Clara asked him.

Alex grunted. "Yeah, got to get into kickass shape. You guys good?" Connor nodded, a silent conversation happening between them. All four of them, were about to go straight to Sonia's locker when down the hallway to the right, there was a bunch of commotion. Cops were there asking everyone to clear the hallway. The principle was there as well when the custodian handed him a set of keys.

"This one," one of the officers said as he pointed to the locker.

All four of them got closer, pushing through the crowd that had formed but when anyone of them tried to object, one look from Connor or Alex and they quickly moved out of the way. Henry, was also there watching the scene unfold, when Giuseppe, approached them.

Alex asked him, "What's going on?"

"I don't know man. But my locker is right there and they made me move. Not sure what they're looking for."

"Who's locker is that?" asked Sonia. Giuseppe looked at the locker, as if he was remembering everyone that was near him when his eyes widened.

"Shit, it's Bruno's. I can imagine what they're looking for."

"Yeah, I think we all know what they're looking for." Henry commented and Connor nodded.

Right at that moment, Bruno approached, a moment of panic across his face but he hid it immediately. "What's going on?"

"Is this your locker?" One of the cops asked him. Bruno looked at the principle.

"Bruno, is this your locker? Remember, it will take me two minutes to go look it up, it's best you cooperate," the principle reminded him.

He nodded. Connor had already stepped in front of Clara and Sonia, with Alex right next to him. Henry also moved slightly to shield her from the other side. Clara tried to peek through Connor and Giuseppe to see what was going on. Giuseppe glanced at her and the others when realization hit him and he also took a step back shielding her but allowing her to look. He nodded slightly. There was literally a wall surrounding her.

All of a sudden, Clara saw Sonia looking behind them, Leo was pushing through when he came to halt, his eyes widened. The principle opened the locker and one of the officers stepped forward rummaging through it. The cop searching through the locker, pulled out the jacket and a few other things located there, he then reached his hand to the back and to the top. He froze glancing at Bruno and at his colleague who stepped closer to Bruno. The cop pulled a grey cloth pouch stuck to the top of the locker and opened it. He looked inside, pulling a small plastic baggie filled with pills. He quickly stuck it back in and then raised his gaze to Bruno.

"Let's take him down to the station." The other cop grabbed Bruno, and pulled his hands behind his back, calling for backup from the device on his shoulder. The first officer continued searching coming up with another gray pouch stuck to the top section of the locker.

"That isn't mine. I have no idea where that came from." Bruno struggled.

"Yeah, yeah that's what they all say." The cop cuffing him said.

The principle was shaking his head. "Anything you need officers, we will fully cooperate. I'm sure there is a reasonable explanation to this."

Leo stepped forward torn between worry for his friend but anger as well. The students in the hallway parted, the guys pushing

Clara and Sonia to the side so the cop holding Bruno could walk through and he was met by another cop at the entrance. Bruno kept repeating that it wasn't his.

"That stuff isn't mine. I don't." But then stopped as realization hit him that he was probably going to say something stupid. The cops read him his rights and Bruno kept his head down until he lifted it and noticed Alex standing there with his arms crossed over his chest. Bruno's gaze was fixated on him until he moved to Connor and kept looking around him.

"Someone set me up. I don't sell drugs." A few students snickered and he glared at them. Right at that moment, Gabe walked into the hallway with his father right next to him. Both of them looking at the scene in front of them. Gabe quickly glanced around until he saw Alex and Connor with a question mark on his face. Connor shifted to show him Clara was right there. Gabe looked relieved.

"It was you, wasn't it?" Bruno started yelling at Gabe.

"Be quiet," the officer stated.

"It was him. I'm sure it was him, he must have planted it earlier." Bruno was grasping at straws, not knowing obviously that Gabe had just gotten there.

Gabe's father smirked. "I'd be careful about your accusations, seeing as though he just got here with me. I was actually here to speak to the principle about something important, maybe something you know?" Ralph indicated that he was in the know about Bruno who stilled and quieted down immediately. Clara was extremely confused. Did Gabe's father know about Bruno and what he'd done? Was that why Gabe came late? The cops led Bruno out and put him in the cop car.

"Everyone get in class, let's go." The principle yelled out. Gabe stepped forward towards the others looking at Alex who shook his head slightly. Clara frowned, until Gabe's fingers came up to her face, smoothing over her forehead and pulling her close. She looked up at him.

"Did that really just happen?" Clara asked in disbelief.

"Sure the hell seems like it." Sonia answered as she looked cautiously at all of them. "Perfect timing, isn't it?" she asked suspiciously.

"Yeah it is." Connor spoke. Henry looked at Gabe who was looking around until his gaze landed on Lucas. Lucas glanced at him and shook his head ever so slightly as if answering the person next to him but Clara could tell he was answering Gabe's silent question. Gabe relaxed.

Gabe's father approached after having been outside speaking to the cops. "Well, it seems as though, everyone's late to class so you don't need me to let you in. I also told the principle I needed to speak to him but we'll do it later this week." His gaze travelled across each one of them, stopping at Clara, "Clara."

"Hi Mr. Caruso." He smiled and looked at Gabe, becoming serious again.

"That was Bruno?" Gabe nodded. "Ok, I'll see what I can find out, but the cops will be here to check his other lockers so you guys might get out early. Keep me posted if you do. And if they want to question any of you or any of your other friends, call me."

"Thanks, Uncle Ralph." Alex answered.

"Thanks, Dad." Gabe responded at the same time.

As Ralph left, Leo drew closer to the group. In a hard tone he says, "Did you guys have anything to do with this?"

"No." Gabe answered knowing it was he the one that Leo was truly questioning. Leo looked at him a second searching for the truth "You sure? It's rather convenient, don't you think?"

"It is. But I had nothing to do with it." Leo stared at him a few seconds and then nodded seeming content with the answer. "Sorry but then who was it?"

"Did you ever think it could be Bruno himself?" Sonia had the courage to ask.

"He wouldn't be careless and hide two pouches with drugs in his locker," Leo retorted.

"Yeah, he's volatile but he's not totally stupid." Alex answered.

Henry kept looking at Gabe and the others. "Well, the cops will figure it out. I've got to get to class." Everyone murmured their agreement, but Giuseppe was the only one who left with him.

"Leo, since you're his friend the cops may want to talk to you. Call me so my dad can be there with you." Gabe said.

Leo sighed and nodded. "Yeah they probably will. Thanks."

He walked away when Connor said, "I'm going after him. You're good with Clara, right?"

"Yeah, I'll walk her and Sonia to class." Gabe answered.

"I can take it from here, Bruno isn't here, remember? But you guys need to go after Leo. He needs you." Sonia replied, squeezing Clara's arm.

"You coming too?" Connor asked Alex.

"Yeah." Alex followed right after him towards Leo, waving to Gabe and Clara.

Clara looked up at Gabe who leaned down to peck her softly on the lips and they started walking.

"Ask, Clara."

She whipped her head towards him. "How do you know I was going to ask you something?"

"Clara, it's me. I notice everything about you."

"Are you sure you didn't have anything to do with what happened to Bruno?"

"I didn't."

"But you would have done something like that if you needed to, right?" Clara asked but already knew the answer, stating it rather matter of fact.

Gabe pulled her over into an alcove and held her close and said quietly, "I would do whatever I needed to do to make sure you were safe. Except maybe kill the guy." Gabe smirked at her and she rolled her eyes until he turned serious again. "I won't lose sleep over what may happen to him. He chose his path. Even if it was planted, the truth is that he does deal drugs. But I had nothing to do with this."

"I know. But then if it wasn't Bruno who was it?"

"I don't know baby, all I know is that if I ever find out, I'd thank them. Come on, let's go to class."

48

GABE

He dropped Clara off to class and headed to his own class where Henry was sitting. He lifted his chin to Gabe who sat down right next to him.

"You have anything to do with what just happened?" Henry asked him quietly. Everyone in class was talking about the scene with Bruno. The teacher was trying to get everyone's attention but failed repeatedly.

"No, I didn't, but I'm glad someone did."

"Yeah so am I."

Henry hesitated, "you asked me for help. If he comes back, you still have it."

"Thanks, man."

After class, Alex texted him and they met in their usual quiet hallway with Connor.

"Thanks for taking Clara to school today, Connor."

"Anytime." Connor hesitated a second.

"No I didn't have time to do anything."

"I know you didn't." They both looked at Alex and raised their eyebrows in question.

"It wasn't me either. I got here early and scoped everything out but the custodian was actually cleaning the classrooms in that hallway at that time. I know we said we were going to do it this week but if it wasn't you or me, who was it?"

"I don't know. Lucas was supposed to get the weed but I'm pretty sure he didn't," Gabe stated.

"That definitely wasn't weed in there." Connor smirked.

"Exactly, whoever did it, went all out. Two pouches filled with pills?" Alex said incredulously.

"The cops were searching his gym locker too and they're still here now. Word is that we get out at 11." Connor told them.

"Ok, just keep your heads down. We have nothing to be afraid of since we didn't do anything." Gabe stated.

"I know but it's kind of freaky that this was one of our ideas." Alex said.

"Agreed, but again, it was either Bruno himself thinking he could get away with anything. Or someone beat us to it."

"But who?"

"I don't know Connor but I sure would like to." Gabe contemplated. "They may bring us all in for questioning. Some of the football players too."

Alex nodded, "Well, let's see how this plays out. Clara should be safe now."

"Yeah, but I'm still not letting her out of my sight." Gabe smirked.

"I think you're enjoying this protecting shit a bit too much," Alex laughed. Connor chuckled right along with him.

"Oh I am."

49

EPILOGUE

Months later

Bruno was waiting sentencing for possession of narcotics. A lot of narcotics. They found marijuana and ecstasy at his house, and of course all the drugs at school in both lockers.

The cops eventually did question some of Bruno's friends especially Leo, being he had known him a long time. But Gabe's father, true to his word, was right there with him. Leo's mother was so thankful, crying and hugging Gabe's father saying she would repay him. But he told her that he didn't want anything in return, and to just continue doing what she is doing because she raised a great guy.

They also questioned Gabe and the others, seeing as they didn't get along. But the cops realized that none of them had anything to do with planting evidence as Bruno had suggested. They all had alibis plus the drugs they found had a specific stamp on them according to the police.

Although Clara knew they didn't have anything to do with what happened to Bruno, she did question where they went the night before the incident, but Gabe either evaded the question or distracted her, so she decided to let it go. Leo went to see Bruno, and after repeatedly telling him that Gabe and the others weren't behind it, Bruno started to think it could have been one of the guys from a rival drug gang. Hopefully he continued to think that.

Everything was pretty much back to normal or maybe not normal but in a pretty good place. Sarah returned to school eventually and although she was no longer friends with Kristin, she was still friends with Jamie. However they both steered clear of Clara and the others.

Sonia had planned an amazing prom. Clara was deep in soccer training as were Connor and Gabe. Alex was busy with lacrosse and already being scouted by colleges. School was almost over and then on to their senior year.

Clara closed the door to her car. Gabe was speaking to Bobby on the sidewalk, he noticed her and smiled. She began to walk towards him realizing that she forgot her water bottle. As she turned back, she stilled and slowly turned her head to the right. Clara felt as though someone was staring at her so she looked around carefully trying to figure it out. There were a ton of students walking into school. She shook her head. They stared at her all the time, not sure why she felt today was any different.

"Hey, what's wrong?"

Gabe had approached and he looked at her in concern. As she looked at him she sighed. It was cliché for sure, but the effect he had on her hadn't changed and he always seemed to notice when something with her wasn't right. Gabe pulled her close and pecked her lips. "You ok?" Another peck.

"Yeah, I'm fine. Just paranoid." This time she kissed him.

With his arm around her waist, he cupped her jaw with his other hand. "It's over, baby."

She nodded, "I know. I guess I just need more time to remember that."

He narrowed his eyes slightly at her but then relaxed, kissing her on the temple and pulling her close. He took a deep breath. With

Bruno awaiting trial Gabe had considerably been more at ease, but he still worried about her especially since she slowly began opening up a bit more with him. "Let's go. I'm glad it's half a day today. Then I get you all to myself this weekend down the shore," as he waggled his eyebrows.

She chuckled. Today was a half a day and there was the annual Spring Festival at school and right after they were all leaving for Sonia and Alex's beach house for the weekend. Clara was excited. Vince was coming down with his girlfriend too. Gabe didn't seem to mind that her aunt and uncle seemed a bit strict wanting Vince there, he respected it. Plus he knew that Vince trusted them and wouldn't be hovering.

As she began walking with Gabe, however, she couldn't shake this feeling of being watched. She took a deep breath. *Breath, Clara.*

The day went by quickly, they only had three classes and then most of the students were finishing setting up before the actual event started. Everyone in school pretty much helped, as they raised funds for various clubs and teams for next year.

At the end of the day, as soon as it turned dark, one of the parents who lived in a mansion close by, would set off fireworks to kick off the holiday weekend.

The weather had been beautiful all day. Gabe and the soccer team had organized valet parking so more people came, making the event successful for pretty much everyone.

It was the end of the night and everyone was waiting for the fireworks to start. Gabe and the others had placed their cars strategically so they could have a great view. All their families had been there to support, but had left, since by the time they cleaned everything up it would be a while. Gabe was leaning up against his car with Clara in front of him. He kissed her behind her ear and she shivered. Gabe grinned as he nuzzled her neck.

The fireworks started and they all looked at the sky. Clara sighed. "What was that sigh about baby?" Gabe whispered. She turned her head to look at him and he smiled that special smile of his meant only for her. God she loved him.

"I was just thinking that I can't wait to sleep in your arms this weekend. I want to stay up and watch the sun rise with you. Would you do that with me?"

Gabe groaned and turned her around, holding her tightly against him. He buried his face in her neck. "Don't you know that I would do anything for you?"

"You guys are missing the fireworks," Connor said ruefully. Sonia swatted his arm. Clara laughed as she looked at them. Something was going on between them, Clara saw it but hadn't said anything. Not even to Sonia. When Sonia was ready, she would talk to her about it, just like she had about her family issues.

She kissed Gabe on his neck this time and glanced at sky taking in the fireworks. "Happy now, Connor?" Everyone chuckled. Bobby was there holding Giada's hand. Leo and Claudia. Giuseppe, Henry and a few others. Alex was standing next to Rosie and seemed awfully tense.

Clara looked at Gabe who was eyeing Alex curiously when all of a sudden Alex bent down to tie his shoe which wasn't untied. He stood up and turned around smiling as if he was going to crack a joke. "Clara?"

She smiled at him, "Yeah, Alex?"

He lowered his voice, "Keep smiling, and don't look right away but who's the douche staring at you with the hoodie near the black Charger."

Clara continued to smile and carefully looked over, thinking it could probably be someone from her old school or one of her cousins' friends. But when those eyes met hers, her heart started racing and her smile dropped. She instantly stiffened.

"Clara?" It was Gabe, he looked at her in concern and noticed the panic in her face. He quickly looked up and noticed the guy staring at her.

"Clara?" It was Alex this time and he stepped in front of her. "Who is that?" she gasped and pushed him out of the way. It couldn't be. The guy with the hoodie wasn't there anymore. Sonia and the others approached her in concern. She frantically looked around the parking lot.

Gabe grabbed her by her arms gently. "Clara, look at me. Who was that guy?"

She looked up at him, eyes wide and swallowed. "It was. I'm pretty sure it was," she shook her head. *It couldn't be him, could it?* She looked up at Gabe, then at Alex and back to Gabe. "It was Cain."

ACKNOWLEDGMENTS

I truly have quite a few people to thank.

I started writing this book when my father became ill with Kidney disease and Dementia and through it all, with the support of quite a few people, I was able to put this book on paper.

Thank you to Federica, whether is was watching over my kids as an au pair, telling me I could do it as a friend, or as my beta reader. Thank you.

Thank you to Rosanna, the first time I told you about this book your first words were, "I'm so proud of you." You don't know what that meant me to me. Thank you for your support and motivation as well as being one of my beta readers.

Thank you to my third Beta reader, Barb, your encouraging words really mean a lot. I am so glad that when I pushed submit, you were there with me. Thank you.

Thank you to Manuela Biase and Jennette Fischer for my beautiful cover.

Thank you to Loreta, you told me you weren't surprised that I wrote a book, since I always was telling stories when I was younger. Thanks for talking me through scenes when you had no idea what the book was about.

And thank you to all of those friends, family, acquaintances and strangers, that have offered a kind word of support, there are really too many of you to name and I'm afraid I'll forget someone but thank you! To my mom who always had a delicious meal ready for me or to watch her grandchildren while I wrote. To my husband, who doubted that I could write a book in the beginning, as it seemed such a hefty thing to do with a full time job, 3 kids, a household and all the others things I seem to get involved in here or there. Don't doubt me again, baby, but thank you for all the promo you do and the fish dinners you cook.

And finally and most importantly to my 3 G's. I'm determined to get on that cool mom list sooner or later. All I can say is that behind it all, you are the drive and determination that I seem to find through this and almost anything I put in my head to do. I want you to know, that it doesn't matter how old you or how late you think you are, if you have a dream or a passion, go for it. If it's something that lights your soul on fire, that brings you pride, you can do anything you put your mind to, anything your put heart into and anything that lights your soul and I will ALWAYS be in the corner cheering you on. (I am the loud soccer mom after all.)

I would also like to thank Connor, Colin and anyone else that helped get answers to my many high school and soccer questions.

And a special thanks to anyone reading this book! Your support means a lot!